The Ringer

Edgar Wallace

DODO PRESS

The Ringer

Edgar Wallace

1925

DEDICATION:

TO Sir Gerald Du Maurier

My dear Gerald, This book is "The Gaunt Stranger" practically in the form that you and I shaped it for the stage. Herein you will find all the improvements you suggested for "The Ringer"—which means that this is a better story than "The Gaunt Stranger."

Yours, EDGAR WALLACE.

The Ringer

CHAPTER 1

The Assistant Commissioner of Police pressed a bell on his table, and, to the messenger who entered the room a few seconds after: "Ask Inspector Wembury if he will be good enough to see me," he said.

The Commissioner put away into a folder the document he had been reading. Alan Wembury's record both as a police officer and as a soldier was magnificent. He had won a commission in the war, risen to the rank of Major and had earned the Distinguished Service Order for his fine work in the field. And now a new distinction had come to him.

The door opened and a man strode in. He was above the average height. The Commissioner looked up and saw a pair of good—humoured grey eyes looking down at him from a lean, tanned face.

"Good morning, Wembury."

"Good morning, sir."

Alan Wembury was on the sunny side of thirty, an athlete, a cricketer, a man who belonged to the out—of—doors. He had the easy poise and the refinement of speech which comes from long association with gentlemen.

"I have asked you to come and see me because I have some good news for you," said the Commissioner.

He had a real affection for this straight—backed subordinate of his. In all his years of police service he had never felt quite as confident of any man as he had of this soldierly detective.

"All news is good news to me, sir," laughed Alan.

He was standing stiffly to attention now and the Commissioner motioned him to a chair.

"You are promoted divisional inspector and you take over 'R' Division as from Monday week," said the chief, and in spite of his self—control, Alan was taken aback. A divisional inspectorship was one of the prizes of the C. I.D. Inevitably it must lead in a man of his years to a central inspectorship; eventually inclusion in the Big Four, and one knows not what beyond that.

"This is very surprising, sir, '" he said at last. "I am terribly grateful. I think there must be a lot of men entitled to this step before me—"

Colonel Walford shook his head.

"I'm glad for your sake, but I don't agree, " he said. And then, briskly: "We're making considerable changes at the Yard. Bliss is coming back from America; he has been attached to the Embassy at Washington—do you know him? "

Alan Wembury shook his head. He had heard of the redoubtable Bliss, but knew little more about him than that he was a capable police officer and was cordially disliked by almost every man at the Yard.

"'R' Division will not be quite as exciting as it was a few years ago, " said the Commissioner with a twinkle in his eye; "and you at any rate should be grateful. "

"Was it an exciting division, sir? " asked Alan, to whom Deptford was a new territory.

Colonel Walford nodded. The laughter had gone out of his eyes; he was very grave indeed when he spoke again.

"I was thinking about The Ringer—I wonder what truth there is in the report of his death? The Australian police are almost certain that the man taken out of Sydney Harbour was this extraordinary scoundrel. "

Alan Wembury nodded slowly.

The Ringer!

The very name produced a little thrill that was unpleasantly like a shiver. Yet Alan Wembury was without fear; his courage, both as a soldier and a detective, was inscribed in golden letters. But there was something very sinister and deadly in the very name of The Ringer,

The Ringer

something that conjured up a repellent spectacle... the cold, passionless eyes of a cobra.

Who had not heard of The Ringer? His exploits had terrified London. He had killed ruthlessly, purposelessly, if his motive were one of personal vengeance. Men who had good reason to hate and fear him, had gone to bed, hale and hearty, snapping their fingers at the menace, safe in the consciousness that their houses were surrounded by watchful policemen. In the morning they had been found stark and dead. The Ringer, like the dark angel of death, had passed and withered them in their prime.

"Though The Ringer no longer haunts your division, there is one man in Deptford I would like to warn you against, " said Colonel Walford, "and he—"

"Is Maurice Meister, " said Alan, and the Commissioner raised his eyebrows in surprise.

"Do you know him? " he asked, astonished. "I didn't know Meister's reputation as a lawyer was so widespread. "

Alan Wembury hesitated, fingering his little moustache.

"I only know him because he happens to be the Lenley's family lawyer, " he said.

The Commissioner shook his head with a laugh. "Now you've got me out of my depth: I don't even know the Lenleys. And yet you speak their name with a certain amount of awe. Unless, " he said suddenly, "you are referring to old George Lenley of Hertford, the man who died a few months ago? "

Alan nodded.

"I used to hunt with him, " mused the Commissioner. "A hard—riding, hard-drinking type of old English squire. He died broke, somebody told me. Had he any children? "

"Two, sir, " said Alan quietly.

The Ringer

"And Meister is their lawyer, eh? " The Commissioner laughed shortly. "They weren't well advised to put their fortune in the hands of Maurice Meister. "

He stared through the window on to the Thames Embankment. The clang of tram bells came faintly through the double windows. There was a touch of spring in the air; the bare branches along the Embankment were budding greenly, and soon would be displayed all their delicate leafy splendour. A curious and ominous place, this Scotland Yard, and yet human and kindly hearts beat behind its grim exterior.

Walford was thinking, not of Meister, but of the children who were left in Meister's care.

"Meister knew The Ringer, " he said unexpectedly, and Wembury's eyes opened.

"Knew The Ringer, sir? " he repeated.

Walford nodded.

"I don't know how well; I suspect too well—too well for the comfort of The Ringer if he's alive. He left his sister in Meister's charge—Gwenda Milton. Six months ago, the body of Gwenda Milton was taken from the Thames. " Alan nodded as he recalled the tragedy. "She was Meister's secretary. One of these days when you've nothing better to do, go up to the Record Office—there was a great deal that didn't come out at the inquest. "

"About Meister? "

Colonel Walford nodded.

"If The Ringer is dead, nothing matters, but if he is alive"—he shrugged his broad shoulders and looked oddly under the shaggy eyebrows at the young detective—"if he is alive, I know something that would bring him back to Deptford—and to Meister. "

"What is that, sir? " asked Wembury.

Again Walford gave his cryptic smile.

The Ringer

"Examine the record and you will read the oldest drama in the world—the story of a trusting woman and a vile man."

And then, dismissing The Ringer with a wave of his hand as though he were a tangible vision awaiting such a dismissal, he became suddenly the practical administrator.

"You are taking up your duties on Monday week. You might like to go down and have a look round, and get acquainted with your new division?"

Alan hesitated.

"If it is possible, sir, I should like a week's holiday," he said, and in spite of himself, his tanned face assumed a deeper red.

"A holiday? Certainly. Do you want to break the good news to the girl?" There was a good—humoured twinkle in Walford's eyes.

"No, sir." His very embarrassment seemed to deny his statement. "There is a lady I should like to tell of my promotion," he went on awkwardly. "She is, in fact—Miss Mary Lenley."

The Commissioner laughed softly.

"Oh, you know the Lenleys that much, do you?" he said, and Alan's embarrassment was not decreased.

"No, sir; she has always been a very good friend of mine," he said, almost gently, as though the subject of the discussion were one of whom he could not speak in more strident tones. "You see, I started life in a cottage on the Lenley estate. My father was head gardener to Squire Lenley, and I've known the family ever since I can remember. There is nobody else in Lenley village"—he shook his head sadly—"who would expect me—I—" He hesitated, and Walford jumped in.

"Take your holiday, my boy. Go where you jolly well please! And if Miss Mary Lenley is as wise as she is beautiful—I remember her as a child—she will forget that she is a Lenley of Lenley Court and you are a Wembury of the gardener's cottage! For in these democratic days, Wembury,"—there was a quiet earnestness in his voice—"a man is what he is, not what his father was. I hope you will never be obsessed by a sense of your own unworthiness. Because, if you are"—he paused, and again his eyes twinkled—"you will be a darned fool!"

Alan Wembury left the room with the uneasy conviction that the Assistant Commissioner knew a great deal more about the Lenleys than he had admitted.

The Ringer

CHAPTER 2

IT seemed that the spring had come earlier to Lenley village than to grim old London, which seems to regret and resist the tenderness of the season, until, overwhelmed by the rush of crocuses and daffodils and yellow—hearted narcissi, it capitulates blandly in a blaze of yellow sunshine.

As he walked into the village from the railway station, Alan saw over the hedge the famous Lenley Path of Daffodils, blazing with a golden glory. Beyond the tall poplars was the roof of grey old Lenley Court.

News of his good fortune had come ahead of him. The bald—headed landlord of the Red Lion Inn came running out to intercept him, a grin of delight on his rubicund face.

"Glad to see you back, Alan, " he said. "We've heard of your promotion and we're all very proud of you. You'll be Chief of the Police one of these days. "

Alan smiled at the spontaneous enthusiasm. He liked this old village; it was a home of dreams. Would the great, the supreme dream, which he had never dared bring to its logical conclusion, be fulfilled?

"Are you going up to the Court to see Miss Mary? " and when he answered yes, the landlord shook his head and pursed his lips. He was regret personified. "Things are very bad up there, Alan. They say there's nothing left out of the estate either for Mr. John or Miss Mary. I don't mind about Mr. John: he's a man who can make his way in the world—I wish he'd get a better way than he's found. "

"What do you mean? " asked Alan quickly. The landlord seemed suddenly to remember that if he was speaking to an old friend he was also speaking to a police officer, and he became instantly discreet.

"They say he's gone to the devil. You know how people talk, but there's something in it. Johnny never was a happy sort of fellow; he's forgotten to do anything but scowl in these days. Poverty doesn't come easy to that young man. "

The Ringer

"Why are they at the Court if they're in such a bad way? It must be an expensive place to keep up. I wonder John Lenley doesn't sell it?"

"Sell it!" scoffed the landlord. "It's mortgaged up to the last leaf on the last twig! They're staying there whilst this London lawyer settles the estate, and they're going to London next week, from what I hear."

This London lawyer! Alan frowned. That must be Maurice Meister, and he was curious to meet the man about whom so many strange rumours ran. They whispered things of Maurice Meister at Scotland Yard which it would have been libel to write, slander to say. They pointed to certain associations of his which were unjustifiable even in a criminal lawyer, whose work brought him into touch with the denizens of the underworld.

"I wish you'd book me a room, Mr. Griggs. The carrier is bringing my bag from the station. I'll go to up the Court and see if I can see John Lenley."

He said "John," but his heart said "Mary." He might deceive the world, but he could not deceive his own heart.

As he walked up the broad oak—shaded drive, the evidence of poverty came out to meet him. Grass grew in the gravelled surface of the road; those fine yew hedges of the Tudor garden before which as a child he had stood in awe had been clipped by an amateur hand; the lawn before the house was ragged and unkempt. When he came in sight of the Court his heart sank as he saw the signs of general neglect. The windows of the east wing were grimy—not even the closed shutters could disguise their state; two windows had been broken and the panes not replaced.

As he came nearer to the house, a figure emerged from the shadowy portico, walked quickly towards him, and then, recognising, broke into a run.

"Oh, Alan!"

In another second he had both her hands in his and was looking down into the upturned face. He had not seen her for twelve months. He looked at her now, holding his breath. The sweet, pale

The Ringer

beauty of her caught at his heart. He had known a child, a lovely child; he was looking into the crystal—clear eyes of radiant womanhood. The slim, shapeless figure he had known had undergone some subtle change; the lovely face had been moulded to a new loveliness.

He had a sense of dismay. The very fringe of despair obscured for the moment the joy which had filled his heart at the sight of her. If she had been beyond his reach before, the gulf, in some incomprehensible manner, had widened now.

With a sinking heart he realised the gulf between this daughter of the Lenleys and Inspector Wembury.

"Why, Alan, what a pleasant sight! " Her sad eyes were brightened with laughter. "And you're bursting with news! Poor Alan! We read it in the morning newspaper. "

He laughed ruefully.

"I didn't know that my promotion was a matter of world interest, " he said.

"But you're going to tell me all about it. " She slipped her arm in his naturally, as she had in the days of her childhood, when the gardener's son was Mary Lenley's playmate, the shy boy who flew her kite and bowled and fielded for her when she wielded a cricket bat almost as tall as herself.

"There is little to tell but the bare news, " said Alan. "I'm promoted over the heads of better men, and I don't know whether to be glad or sorry! "

He felt curiously self—conscious and gauche as they paced the untidy lawn together.

"I've had a little luck in one or two cases I've handled, but I can't help feeling that I'm a favourite with the Commissioner and that I owe my promotion more to that cause than to any other. "

"Rubbish! " she scoffed. "Of course you've had your promotion on merit! "

The Ringer

She caught his eyes looking at the house, and instantly her expression changed.

"Poor old Lenley Court! " she said softly. "You've heard our news, Alan? We're leaving next week. " She breathed a long sigh. "It doesn't bear thinking about, does it? Johnny is taking a flat in town, and Maurice has promised me some work. "

Alan stared at her.

"Work? " he gasped. "You don't mean you've got to work for your living? "

She laughed at this.

"Why, of course, my dear—my dear Alan. I'm initiating myself into the mysteries of shorthand and typewriting. I'm going to be Maurice's secretary. "

Meister's secretary!

The words had a familiar sound. And then in a flash he remembered another secretary, whose body had been taken from the river one foggy morning, and he recalled Colonel Walford's ominous words.

"Why, you're quite glum, Alan. Doesn't the prospect of my earning a living appeal to you? " she asked, her lips twitching.

"No, " he said slowly, and it was like Alan that he could not disguise his repugnance to the scheme. "Surely there is something saved from the wreck? "

She shook her head.

"Nothing—absolutely nothing! I have a very tiny income from my mother's estate, and that will keep me from starvation. And Johnny's really clever, Alan. He has made quite a lot of money lately—that's queer, isn't it? One never suspected Johnny of being a good business man, and yet he is. In a few years we shall be buying back Lenley Court. "

Brave words, but they did not deceive Alan!

The Ringer

CHAPTER 3

HE saw her look over his shoulder, and turned. Two men were walking towards them, Though it was a warm day in early summer, and the Royal Courts of Justice forty miles away, Mr. Meister wore the conventional garb of a successful lawyer. The long—tailed morning coat fitted his slim figure faultlessly, his black cravat with its opal pin was perfectly arranged. On his head was the glossiest of silk hats, and the yellow gloves which covered his hands were spotless. A sallow, thin—faced man with dark, fathomless eyes, there was something of the aristocrat in his manner and speech. "He looks like a duke, talks like a don and thinks like a devil, " was not the most unflattering thing that had been said about Maurice Meister.

His companion was a tall youth, hardly out of his teens, whose black brows met at the sight of the visitor. He came slowly across the lawn, his hands thrust into his trousers pockets, his dark eyes regarding Alan with an unfriendly scowl.

"Hallo! " he said grudgingly, and then, to his companion: "You know Wembury, don't you, Maurice—he's a sergeant or something in the police. "

Maurice Meister smiled slowly.

"Divisional Detective Inspector, I think, " and offered his long, thin hand. "I understand you are coming into my neighbourhood to add a new terror to the lives of my unfortunate clients! "

"I hope we shall be able to reform them, " said Alan good—humouredly. "That is really what we are for! "

Johnny Lenley was glowering at him. He had never liked Alan, even as a boy and now for some reason, his resentment at the presence of the detective was suddenly inflamed.

"What brings you to Lenley? " he asked gruffly. "I didn't know you had any relations here? "

"I have a few friends, " said Alan steadily.

The Ringer

"Of course he has! " It was Mary who spoke. "He came to see me, for one, didn't you, Alan? I'm sorry we can't ask you to stay with us, but there's practically no furniture left in the house. "

John Lenley's eyes snapped at this.

"It isn't necessary to advertise our poverty all over the kingdom, my dear, " he said sharply. "I don't suppose Wembury is particularly interested in our misfortunes, and he'd be damned impertinent if he was! "

He saw the hurt look on his sister's face, and his unreasonable annoyance with the visitor was increased. It was Maurice Meister who poured oil upon the troubled water.

"The misfortunes of Lenley Court are public property, my dear Johnny, " he said blandly. "Don't be so stupidly touchy! I, for one, am very glad to have the opportunity of meeting a police officer of such fame as Inspector Alan Wembury. You will find your division rather a dull spot just now, Mr. Wembury. We have none of the excitement which prevailed when I first moved to Deptford from Lincoln's Inn Fields. "

Alan nodded.

"You mean, you're not bothered with The Ringer? " he said.

It was a perfectly innocent remark, and he was quite unprepared for the change which came to Meister's face. He blinked quickly as though he had been confronted with a brilliant light. The loose mouth became in an instant a straight, hard line. If there was not fear in those inscrutable eyes of his, Alan Wembury was very wide of the mark.

"The Ringer! " His voice was husky. "Ancient history, eh? Poor beggar, he's dead! "

He said this with almost startling emphasis. It seemed to Alan that the man was trying to persuade himself that this notorious criminal had passed beyond the sphere of human activity.

"Dead... drowned in Australia. "

The Ringer

The girl was looking at him wonderingly.

"Who is The Ringer? " she asked.

"Nobody you would know anything about, or ought to know, " he said, almost brusquely. And then, with a little laugh: "We're all talking 'shop, ' and criminal justice is the worst kind of 'shop' for a young lady's ears. "

"I wish to heaven you'd find something else to talk about, " growled John Lenley fretfully, and was turning away when Maurice Meister asked: "You are at present in a West End division, aren't you, Wembury? What was your last case? I don't seem to remember seeing your name in the newspapers. "

Alan made a little grimace.

"We never advertise our failures, " he said. "My last job was to inquire into some pearls that were stolen from Lady Darnleigh's house in Park Lane on the night of her big Ambassadors' party. "

He was looking at Mary as he spoke. Her face was a magnet which lured and held his gaze. He did not see John Lenley's hand go to his mouth to check the involuntary exclamation, or the quick warning glance which Meister shot at the young man. There was a little pause.

"Lady Darnleigh? " drawled Maurice. "Oh, yes, I seem to remember... as a matter of fact, weren't you at her dance that night, Johnny? "

He looked at the other and Johnny shook his shoulder impatiently.

"Of course I was... I didn't know anything about the robbery till afterwards. Haven't you anything else to discuss, you people, than crimes and robberies and murders? "

And, turning on his heel, he slouched across the lawn.

Mary looked after him with trouble in her face.

"I wonder what makes Johnny so cross in these days—do you know, Maurice? "

The Ringer

Maurice Meister examined the cigarette that burnt in the amber tube between his fingers. "Johnny is young; and, my dear, you mustn't forget that he has had a very trying time."

"So have I," she said quietly. "You don't imagine that it is nothing to me that I am leaving Lenley Court?" Her voice quivered for a moment, but with a resolution that Alan could both understand and appreciate, she was instantly smiling. "I'm being very pathetic; I shall be weeping on Alan's shoulder if I am not careful. Come along, Alan, and see what is left of the rosery—perhaps when you have seen its present condition, we will weep together!"

CHAPTER 4

JOHNNY LENLEY looked alter them until they had disappeared from view. His face was pale with anger, his lips trembled.

"What brings that swine here? " he demanded.

Maurice Meister, who had followed across the lawn, looked at him oddly.

"My dear Johnny, you're very young and very crude. You have the education of a gentleman and yet you behave like a boor! "

Johnny turned on him in a fury.

"What do you expect me to do—shake him cordially by the hand and bid him welcome to Lenley Court? The fellow's risen from the gutter. His father was our gardener—"

Maurice Meister interrupted him with a chuckle of malicious enjoyment.

"What a snob you are, Johnny! The snobbery wouldn't matter, " he went on in a more serious tone, "if you would learn to conceal your feelings. "

"I say what I think, " said Johnny shortly.

"So does a dog when you tread on his tail, " replied Maurice. "You fool! " he snarled with unexpected malignity. "You half—wit! At the mention of the Darnleigh pearls you almost betrayed yourself. Did you realise to whom you were talking, who was probably watching you? The shrewdest detective in the C. I.D.! The man who caught Hersey, who hanged Gostein, who broke up the Flack Gang. "

"He didn't notice anything, " said the other sulkily, and then, to turn the conversation to his advantage: "You had a letter this morning, was there anything about the pearls in it—are they sold? "

The anger faded from the lawyer's face; again he was his suave self.

The Ringer

"Do you imagine, my dear lad, that one can sell fifteen thousand pounds' worth of pearls in a week? What do you suppose is the procedure—that one puts them up at Christie's?"

Johnny Lenley's lips tightened. For a while he was silent. When he spoke his voice had lost some of its querulous quality.

"It was queer that Wembury was on the case—apparently they've given up hope. Of course, old Lady Darnleigh has no suspicion—"

"Don't be too sure of that," warned Meister. "Every guest at No. 304, Park Lane, on that night is suspect. You, more than any, because everybody knows you're broke. Moreover, one of the footmen saw you going up the main stairs just before you left."

"I told him I was going to get my coat," said Johnny Lenley quickly, and a troubled look came to his face. "Why did you mention that I was there to Wembury?"

Maurice laughed.

"Because he knew; I was watching him as I spoke. There was the faintest glint in his eyes that told me. I'll set your mind at ease; the person at present under suspicion is her unfortunate butler. Don't imagine that the case has blown over—it hasn't. Anyway, the police are too active for the moment for us to dream of disposing of the pearls, and we shall have to wait a favourable opportunity when they can be placed in Antwerp."

He threw away the end of the thin cigarette, took a gold cigarette-case from his waistcoat pocket, selected another with infinite care and lit it, Johnny watching him enviously.

"You're a cool devil. Do you realise that if the truth came out about those pearls it would mean penal servitude for you, Maurice?"

Maurice sent a ring of smoke into the air.

"I certainly realise it would mean penal servitude for you, my young friend. I fancy that it would be rather difficult to implicate me. If you choose for your amusement to be a robber baron, or was it a Duke of Padua?—I forget the historical precedent—and engage yourself in these Rafflesish adventures, that is your funeral entirely. Because I

The Ringer

knew your father and I've known you since you were a child, I take a little risk. Perhaps the adventure of it appeals to me—"

"Rot! " said Johnny Lenley brutally. "You've been a crook ever since you were able to walk. You know every thief in London and you've 'fenced'—"

"Don't use that word! " Maurice Meister's deep voice grew suddenly sharp. "As I told you just now, you are crude. Did I instigate this robbery of Lady Darnleigh's pearls? Did I put it into your head that thieving was more profitable than working, and that with your education and entry to the best houses you had opportunities which were denied to a meaner—thief? "

This word was as irritating to Johnny Lenley as "fence" had been to the lawyer.

"Anyway, we are in, the same boat, " he said. "You couldn't give me away without ruining yourself. I don't say you instigated anything, but you've been jolly helpful, Maurice. Some day I'll make you a rich man. "

The dark, sloe—like eyes turned slowly in his direction. At any other time this patronage of the younger man would have infuriated Meister; now he was only piqued.

"My young friend, " he said precisely, "you are a little over—confident. Robbery with or without violence is not so simple a matter as you imagine. You think you're clever—"

"I'm a little bit smarter than Wembury, " said Johnny complacently.

Maurice Meister concealed a smile.

It was not to the rosery that Mary led her visitor but to the sunken garden, with its crazy paving and battered statuary. There was a cracked marble bench overlooking a still pool where water—lilies grew, and she allowed him to dust a place for her before she sat down.

"Alan, I'm going to tell you something. I'm talking to Alan Wembury, not to Inspector Wembury, " she warned him, and he showed his astonishment.

The Ringer

"Why, of course... " He stopped; he had been on the point of calling her by name. "I've never had the courage to call you Mary, but I feel—old enough! "

This claim of age was a cowardly expedient, he told himself, but at least it was successful. There was real pleasure in her voice when she replied: "I'm glad you do. 'Miss Mary' would sound horribly unreal. In you it would sound almost unfriendly. "

"What is the trouble? " he asked, as he sat down by her side.

She hesitated only a second.

"Johnny, " she said. "He talks so oddly about things. It's a terrible thing to say, Alan, but it almost seems as though he's forgotten the distinction between—right and wrong. Sometimes I think he only says these things in a spirit of perversity. At other times I feel that he means them. He talks harshly about poor, dear father, too. I find that difficult to forgive. Poor daddy was very careless and extravagant, but he was a good father to Johnny—and to me, " she said, her voice breaking.

"What do you mean when you say Johnny talks oddly? "

She shook her head.

"It isn't only that: he has such strange friends. We had a man here last week—I only saw him, I did not speak to him—named Hackitt. Do you know him? "

"Hackitt? Sam Hackitt? " said Wembury in surprise. "Good Lord, yes! Sam and I are old acquaintances! "

"What is he? " she asked.

"He's a burglar, " was the calm reply. "Probably Johnny was interested in the man and had him down—"

She shook her head.

"No, it wasn't for that. " She bit her lip. "Johnny told me a lie; he said that this man was an artisan who was going to Australia. You're sure this is your Sam Hackitt? "

The Ringer

Alan gave a very vivid, if brief, description of the little thief.

"That is he, " she nodded. "And, of course, I know he was—an unpleasant sort of man. Alan, you don't think that Johnny is—bad, do you? "

He had never thought of Johnny as a possible subject for police observation. "Of course not! "

"But these peculiar friends of his—? "

It was an opportunity not to be passed.

"I'm afraid, Mary, you're going to meet a lot of people like Hackitt, and worse than Hackitt, who isn't a bad soul if he could keep his fingers to himself. "

"Why? " she asked in amazement.

"You think of becoming Meister's secretary—Mary, I wish you wouldn't. "

She drew away a little, the better to observe him.

"Why on earth, Alan...? Of course, I understand what you mean. Maurice has a large number of clients, and I'm pretty sure to see them, but they won't corrupt my young mind! "

"I'm not afraid of his clients, " said Alan quietly. "I'm afraid of— Maurice Meister. "

She stared at him as though he were suddenly bereft of his senses.

"Afraid of Maurice? " She could hardly believe her ears. "Why, Maurice is the dearest thing! He has been kindness itself to Johnny and me, and we've known him all our lives. "

"I've known you all your life, too, Mary, " said Alan gently, but she interrupted him.

"But, tell me why? " she persisted. "What do you know against Maurice? "

The Ringer

Here, confronted with the concrete question, he lost ground.

"I know nothing about turn, " he admitted frankly. "I only know that Scotland Yard doesn't like him. "

She laughed a low, amused laugh.

"Because he manages to keep these poor, wretched criminals out of prison! It's professional jealousy! Oh, Alan, " she bantered him, "I didn't believe it of you! "

No good purpose could be served by repeating his warning. There was one gleam of comfort in the situation; if she was to work for Meister she would be living in his division. He told her this.

"It will be rather dreadful, won't it, after Lenley Court? " She made a little face at the thought. "It will mean that for a year or two I shall have no parties, no dances—Alan, I shall die an old maid! "

"I doubt that, " he smiled, "but the chances of meeting eligible young men in Deptford are slightly remote, " and they laughed together.

CHAPTER 5

MAURICE MEISTER stood at the ragged end of a yew hedge and watched them. Strange, he mused, that never before had he realised the beauty of Mary Lenley. It needed, he told himself, the visible worship of this policeman to stimulate his interest in the girl, whom in a moment of impulse, which later he regretted, he had promised to employ. A bud, opening into glorious flower. Unobserved, he watched her; the contour of her cheek, the poise of her dark head, the supple line of her figure as she turned to rally Alan Wembury. Mr. Meister licked his dry lips. Queer that he had never thought that way about Mary Lenley. And yet...

He liked fair women. Gwenda Milton was fair, with a shingled, golden head. A stupid girl, who had become rather a bore. And from a bore she had developed into a sordid tragedy. Maurice shuddered as he remembered that grey day in the coroner's court when he had stood on the witness stand and had lied and lied and lied.

Turning her head, Mary saw him and beckoned him, and he went slowly towards them.

"Where is Johnny? " she asked.

"Johnny at this moment is sulking. Don't ask me why, because I don't know. "

What a wonderful skin she had—flawless, unblemished! And the dark grey eyes, with their long lashes, how adorable! And he had known her all her life and been living under the same roof for a week, and had not observed her values before!

"Am I interrupting a confidential talk? " he asked.

She shook her head, but she did not wholly convince him. He wondered what these two had been speaking about, head to head. Had she told Alan Wembury that she was coming to Deptford? She would sooner or later, and it might be profitable to get in first with the information.

"You know, Miss Lenley is honouring me by becoming my secretary? "

"So I've heard, " said Alan, and met the lawyer's eyes. "I have told Miss Lenley"—he spoke deliberately; every word had its significance—"that she will be living in my division... under my paternal eye, as it were."

There was a warning and a threat there. Meister was too shrewd a man to overlook either. Alan Wembury had constituted himself the girl's guardian. That would have been rather amusing in other circumstances. Even as recently as an hour ago he would have regarded Alan Wembury's chaperonage as a great joke. But now...

He looked at Mary and his pulse was racing.

"How interesting! " his voice was a little harsh and he cleared his throat. "How terribly interesting! And is that duty part of the police code? "

There was the faintest sneer in his voice which Alan did not miss.

"The duty of a policeman, " he said quietly, "is pretty well covered by the inscription over the door of the Old Bailey. "

"And what is that? " asked Meister. "I have not troubled to read it. "

"'Protect the children of the poor and punish the wrongdoer, '" said Alan Wembury sternly.

"A noble sentiment! " said Maurice. And then: "I think that is for me. "

He walked quickly towards a telegraph messenger who had appeared at the end of the garden.

"Is Maurice annoyed with you? " asked Mary.

Alan laughed.

"Everybody gets annoyed with me sooner or later. I'm afraid my society manners are deplorable. "

She patted the hand that lay beside hers on the stone bench.

The Ringer

"Alan," she said, half whimsically, half seriously, "I don't think I shall ever be annoyed with you. You are the nicest man I know."

For a second their hands met in a long, warm clasp, and then she saw Maurice walking back with the unopened telegram in his hand.

"For you," he said jovially. "What a thing it is to be so important that you can't leave the office for five minutes before they wire for you—what terrible deed has been committed in London in your absence?"

Alan took the wire with a frown. "For me?" He was expecting no telegram. He had very few personal friends, and it was unlikely that his holiday would be curtailed from headquarters.

He tore open the envelope and took out the telegram. It was closely written on two pages. He read: "Very urgent stop return at once and report to Scotland Yard stop be prepared to take over your division tomorrow morning stop Australian police report Ringer left Sydney four months ago and is believed to be in London at this moment message ends."

The wire was signed "Walford."

Alan looked from the telegram to the smiling old garden, from the garden to the girl, her anxious face upturned to his.

"Is anything wrong?" she asked.

He shook his head slowly.

The Ringer was in England!

His nerves grew taut at the realisation. Henry Arthur Milton, ruthless slayer of his enemies—cunning, desperate, fearless.

Alan Wembury's mind went back to Scotland Yard and the Commissioner's office. Gwenda Milton—dead, drowned, a suicide!

Had Maurice Meister played a part in the creation of that despair which had sent her young soul unbidden to the judgment of God? Woe to Maurice Meister if this were true!

The Ringer

CHAPTER 6

The Ringer was in London!

Alan Wembury felt a cold thrill each time the thought recurred on his journey to London.

It was the thrill that comes to the hunter, at the first hint of the man-slaying tiger he will presently glimpse.

Well named was The Ringer, who rang the changes on himself so frequently that police headquarters had never been able to circulate a description of the man. A master of disguise, a ruthless enemy who had slain without mercy the men who had earned his hatred.

For himself, Wembury had neither fear nor hatred of the man he was to bring down; only a cold emotionless understanding of the danger of his task. One thing was certain—the Ringer would go to the place where a hundred bolts and hiding places were ready to receive him.

To Deptford...?

Alan Wembury gave a little gasp of dismay. Mary Lenley was also going to Deptford—to Meister's house, and The Ringer could only have returned to England with one object, the destruction of Maurice Meister. Danger to Meister would inevitably mean danger to Mary Lenley. This knowledge took some of the sunlight of the spring sky and made the grim facade of Scotland Yard just a little more sinister.

Though all the murderers in the world were at large, Scotland Yard preserved its equanimity. He came to Colonel Walford's room to find the Assistant Commissioner immersed in the particulars of a minor robbery.

"You got my wire?" said Walford, looking up as Alan came in. "I'm awfully sorry to interrupt your holiday. I want you to go down to Deptford to take charge immediately und get acquainted with your new division."

"The Ringer is back, sir?"

The Ringer

Watford nodded. "Why he came back, where he is, I don't know—in fact, there is no direct information about him and we are merely surmising that he has returned."

"But I thought—"

Walford took a long cablegram from the basket on his table. "The Ringer has a wife. Few people know that," he said. "He married her a year or two ago in Canada. After his disappearance, she left this country and was traced to Australia. That could only mean one thing. The Ringer was in Australia. She has now left Australia just as quickly as she left this country; she arrives in England tomorrow morning."

Alan nodded slowly.

"I see. That means that The Ringer is either in England or is making for this country."

"You have not told anybody?" the Commissioner asked. "I'd forgotten to warn you about that. Meister was at Lenley Court, you say? You didn't tell him?"

"No, sir," said Alan, his lips twitching. "I thought, coming up in the train, that it was rather a pity I couldn't—I would like to have seen the effect upon him!"

Alan could understand how the news of The Ringer's return would flutter the Whitehall dovecotes, but he was unprepared for the extraordinarily serious view which Colonel Walford took of the position.

"I'll tell you frankly, Wembury, that I would much rather be occupying a place on the pension list than this chair at Scotland Yard when that news is published."

Alan looked at him in astonishment; the Commissioner was in deadly earnest.

"The Ringer is London's favourite bogy," Colonel Walford said, "and the very suggestion that he has returned to England will be quite sufficient to send all the newspaper hounds of Fleet Street on my track. Never forget, Wembury, he is a killer, and he has neither fear nor appreciation of danger. He has caused more bolts to be shot than any other criminal on our list! The news that this man is at large and in London will arouse such a breeze that even I would not weather it! "

"You think he'll be beyond me? " smiled Alan.

"No, " said Walford surprisingly, "I have great hopes of you—and great hopes of Dr. Lomond. By the way, have you met Dr. Lomond? "

Alan looked at him in surprise. "No, sir, who is he? "

Colonel Walford reached for a book that lay on his table, "He is one of the few amateur detectives who have impressed me, " he said. "Fourteen years ago he wrote the only book on the subject of the criminal that is worth studying. He has been in India and Tibet for years and I think the Under—Secretary was fortunate to persuade him to fill the appointment. "

"What appointment, sir? "

"Police surgeon of 'R' Division—in fact, your new division, " said Walford. "You are both making acquaintance with Deptford at the same time. "

Alan Wembury turned the closely—set pages of the book. "He is a pretty big man to take a fiddling job like this, " he said and Walford laughed.

"He has spent his life doing fiddling jobs—would you like to meet him? He is with the Chief Constable at the moment. "

He pressed a bell and gave instructions to the messenger who came. "Lomond is rather a character—terribly Scottish, a little cynical and more than a little pawky. "

"Will he help us to catch The Ringer? " smiled Alan and he was astonished to see the Commissioner nod.

"I have that feeling, " he said.

The Ringer

The door opened at that moment and a tall bent figure shuffled in. Alan put his age at something over fifty. His hair was grey, a little moustache drooped over his mouth and the pair of twinkling blue eyes that met Alan's were dancing with good—humour. His homespun suit was badly cut, his high—crowned felt hat belonged to the seventies.

"I want you to meet Inspector Wembury who will be in charge of your division, " said Walford and Wembury's hand was crushed in a powerful grip.

"Have ye any interesting specimens in Deptford, inspector? I'd like fine to measure a few heids. "

Alan's smile broadened.

"I'm as ignorant of Deptford as you—I haven't been there since before the war, " he said.

The doctor scratched his chin, his keen eyes fixed on the younger man, "I'm thinkin' they'll no' be as interesting as the Lolos. Man, there's a wonderful race, wi' braci—cephalic heads, an' a que—er development of the right parietal... "

He spoke quickly, enthusiastically when he was on his favourite subject.

Alan seized an opportunity when the doctor was expounding a view on the origin of some mysterious Tibetan tribe to steal quietly from the room. He was not in the mood for anthropology.

An hour later as he was leaving Scotland Yard he met Walford as he was coming out of his room and walked with him to the Embankment, "Yes—I got rid of the doctor, " chuckled the colonel, "he's too clever to be a bore, but he made my head ache! " Then suddenly: "You're handing over that pearl case to Burton—the Darnleigh pearls I mean. You have no further clue? "

"No, sir, " said Alan. He had almost forgotten that there was such a case in his hands.

The Commissioner was frowning. "I was thinking, after you left, what a queer coincidence it was that you were going to Lenley

The Ringer

Court. Young Lenley was apparently at Lady Darnleigh's house on the night of the robbery, " and then, seeing the look that came to his subordinate's face, he went on quickly: "I'm not suggesting that he knew anything about it, of course, but it was a coincidence. I wish we could clear up that little mystery. Lady Darnleigh has too many friends in Whitehall for my liking and I get a letter from the Home Secretary every other day asking for the latest news. "

Alan Wembury went on his way with an uneasy mind. He had known that Johnny was at the house on the night of the robbery but he had never associated "the Squire's son" with the mysterious disappearance of Lady Darnleigh's pearls. There was no reason why he should, he told himself stoutly. As he walked across Westminster Bridge he went over again and again that all too brief interview he had had with Mary.

How beautiful she was! And how unapproachable! He tried to think of her only, but against his will a dark shadow crept across the rosy splendour of dreams: Johnny Lenley.

Why on earth should he, and yet—the Lenleys were ruined.... Mary was worried about the kind of company that Johnny was keeping. There was something else she had said which belonged to the category of unpleasant things. Oh, yes, Johnny had been "making money" Mary told him a little proudly. How?

"Rot! " said Alan to himself as an ugly thought obtruded upon his mind. "Rubbish! "

The idea was too absurd for a sane man to entertain. The next morning he handed over all the documents in the case to Inspector Burton and walked out of Scotland Yard with almost a feeling of relief. It was as though he had shaken himself clear of the grisly shadow which was obscuring the brightness of the day.

The week which followed was a very busy one for Alan Wembury. He had only a slight acquaintance with Deptford and its notables. The grey—haired Scots surgeon he saw for a minute or two, a shrewd old man with laughing eyes and a fund of dry Scottish humour, but both men were too busy in their new jobs to discuss The Ringer.

The Ringer

Mary did not write, as he had expected she would, and he was not aware that she was in his district until one day, walking down the Lewisham High Road, somebody waved to him from an open taxicab and turning, he saw it was the girl. He asked one of his subordinates to find out where she and Johnny were staying and with no difficulty located them at a modern block of flats near Malpas Road, a building occupied by the superior artisan class. What a tragic contrast to the spacious glories of Lenley Court! Only his innate sense of delicacy prevented his calling upon her, and for this abstention at least one person was glad.

The Ringer

CHAPTER 7

"I SAW your copper this morning, " said Johnny flippantly. He had gone back to lunch and was in a more amiable mood than Mary remembered having seen him recently.

She looked at him open—eyed.

"My 'copper'? " she repeated.

"Wembury, " translated Johnny. "We call these fellows 'busies' and I've never seen a busier man, " he chuckled. "I see you're going to ask what' busy' means. It is a thieves' word for detective. "

He saw a change come to her face.

"'We' call them? " she repeated. "You mean 'they' call them, Johnny. "

He was amused as he sat down at the table.

"What a little purist you're becoming, Mary, " he said. "We, or they, does it matter? We're all thieves at heart, the merchant in his Rolls and the workman on the tram, thieves every one of them! "

Very wisely she did not contest the extravagant generalisation.

"Where did you see Alan? "

"Why the devil do you call him by his Christian name? " snapped Johnny. "The man is a policeman, you go on as though he were a social equal. "

Mary smiled at this as she cut a round of bread into four parts and put them on the bread plate.

"The man who lives on the other side of the landing is a plumber, and the people above us live on the earnings of a railway guard. Six of them, Johnny—four of them girls. "

He twisted irritably in his chair. "That's begging the question. We're only here as a temporary expedient. You don't suppose I'm going to be content to live in this poky hole all my life? One of these days I'll buy back Lenley Court."

"On what, Johnny?" she asked quietly.

"On the money I make," he said and went back to his bete noire. "Anyway, Wembury isn't the sort of fellow I want you to know," he said. "I was talking to Maurice about him this morning, and Maurice agrees that it is an acquaintance we ought to drop."

"Really?" Mary's voice was cold. "And Maurice thinks so too—how funny!"

He glanced at her suspiciously.

"I don't see anything amusing about it," he grumbled. "Obviously, we can't know—"

She was standing facing him on the other side of the table, her hands resting on its polished surface.

"I have decided to go on knowing Alan Wembury," she said steadily. "I'm sorry if Maurice doesn't approve, or if you think I'm being very common. But I like Alan—"

"I used to like my valet, but I got rid of him," broke in Johnny irritably.

She shook her head.

"Alan Wembury isn't your valet. You may think my taste is degraded, but Alan is my idea of a gentleman," she said quietly, "and one cannot know too many gentlemen."

He was about to say something sharp, but checked himself, and the matter had dropped for the moment.

The next day Mary Lenley was to start her new life. The thought left her a little breathless. When Maurice had first made the suggestion that she should act as his secretary the idea had thrilled her, but as the time approached she had grown more and more apprehensive. The project was one filled with vague unpleasant possibilities and

The Ringer

she could not understand why this once pleasing prospect should now have such an effect upon her.

Johnny was not up when she was ready to depart in the morning, and only came yawning out of his bedroom when she called him.

"So you're going to be one of the working classes, " he said almost jovially. "It will be rather amusing. I wouldn't let you go at all, only—"

"Only? " she waited.

Johnny's willingness that she should accept employment in Maurice's office had been a source of wonder to her, knowing his curious nature.

"I shall be about, keeping an eye on you, " he said good—humouredly.

A few minutes later she was hurrying down crooked Tanners Hill toward a neighbourhood the squalor of which appalled her. Flanders Lane has few exact parallels in point of grime and ugliness, but Mr. Meister's house was most unexpectedly different from all the rest.

It stood back from the street, surrounded by a high wall which was pierced with one black door which gave access to a small courtyard, behind which was the miniature Georgian mansion where the lawyer not only lived but had his office.

An old woman led her up the worn stairs, opened a heavy ornamental door and ushered her into an apartment which she was to know very well indeed. A big panelled room with Adam decorations, it had been once the drawing-room of a prosperous City merchant in those days when great gentlemen lived in the houses where now the poor and the criminal herded like rats.

There was an air of shabbiness about the place and yet it was cheerful enough. The walls were hung about with pictures which she had no difficulty in recognising as the work of great masters. But the article of furniture which interested her most was a big grand piano which stood in an alcove. She looked in wonder at this and then turned to the old woman.

The Ringer

"Does Mr. Meister play this?"

"Him?" said the old lady with a cackle of laughter. "I should say he does!"

From this chamber led a little doorless ante—room which evidently was used as an office, for there were deed boxes piled up against one wall and a small desk on which stood a covered typewriter.

She had hardly taken her survey when the door opened and Maurice Meister came quickly in, alert and smiling. He strode toward her and took both her hands in his.

"My dear Mary," he said, "this is delightful!"

His enthusiasm amused her.

"This isn't a social call, Maurice," she said. "I have come to work!"

She drew her hands free of his. Had they always been on these affectionate terms, she wondered. She was puzzled and uneasy. She tried to reconstruct from her memory the exact relationship that Maurice Meister had stood to the family. He had known her since she was a child. It was stupid of her to resent this subtle tenderness of his.

"My dear Mary, there's work enough to do—title deeds, evidence," he looked vaguely round as though seeking some stimulant to his imagination.

And all the time he looked he was wondering what on earth he could find to keep her occupied.

"Can you type?" he asked.

He expected a negative and was amazed when she nodded.

"I had a typewriter when I was twelve," she smiled. "Daddy gave it to me to amuse myself with."

Here was relief from a momentary embarrassment. Maurice had never wished or expected that his offer to employ the girl should be taken seriously—never until he had seen her at Lenley Court and realised that the gawky child he had known had developed so wonderfully.

"I will give you an affidavit to copy, " he said, searching feverishly amongst the papers on his desk. It was a long time before he came upon a document sufficiently innocuous for her to read. For Maurice Meister's clientele was a peculiar one, and he, who through his life had made it a practice not to let his right hand know what his left hand did, found a difficulty in bringing himself to the task of handing over so much of his dubious correspondence for her inspection. Not until he had read the paper through word by word did he give it to her.

"Well, Mary, what do you think of it all? " he demanded, "and do, please, sit down, my dear! "

"Think of it all? This place? " she asked, and then, "You live in a dreadful neighbourhood, Maurice. "

"I didn't make the neighbourhood. I found it as it is, " he answered with a laugh. "Are you going to be very happy here, Mary? "

She nodded. "I think so. It is so nice working for somebody one has known for so long—and Johnny will be about. He told me I should see a lot of him. "

Only for a second did the heavy eyelids droop. "Oh, " said Maurice Meister, looking past her. "He said you'd see a lot of him, eh? In business hours, by any chance? "

She did not detect the sarcasm in his tone.

"I don't know what are your business hours, but it is rather nice, isn't it, having Johnny? " she asked. "It really doesn't matter working for you because you're so kind, and you've known me such a long time, but it would be rather horrid if a girl was working for somebody she didn't know, and had no brother waiting on the doorstep to see her home. "

He had not taken his eyes from her. She was more beautiful even than he had thought. Hers was the type of dainty loveliness which so completely appealed to him. Darker than Gwenda Milton, but finer. There was a soul and a mind behind those eyes others; a latent

The Ringer

passion as yet unmoved; a dormant fire yet to be kindled. He felt her grow uncomfortable under the intensity of his gaze, and quick to sense this, he was quicker to dispel the mist of suspicion which might soon gather into a cloud.

"I had better show you the house, " he said briskly, and led her through the ancient building.

Before one door on the upper floor he hesitated and finally, with an effort, slipped the key in the lock and threw open the door.

Looking past him, Mary saw a room such as she had not imagined would be found in this rather shabby old house. In spite of the dust which covered everything it was a beautiful apartment, furnished with a luxury that amazed her. It seemed to be a bed and sitting—room, divided by heavy velvet curtains which were now drawn. A thick carpet covered the floor, the few pictures that the room contained had evidently been carefully chosen. Old French furniture, silver light brackets on the walls, every fuse and every fitting spoke of lavish expenditure.

"What a lovely room! " she exclaimed when she had I recovered her breath.

"Yes... lovely. " He stared gloomily into the nest which had once known Gwenda Milton, in the days before tragedy had come to her. "Better than Malpas Mansions, Mary, eh? " The frown had vanished from his face; he was his old smiling self. "A little cleaning, a little dusting, and there is a room for a princess—in fact, my dear, I shall put it entirely at your disposal. "

"My disposal! " she stared at him. "How absurd, Maurice! I am living with Johnny and I couldn't possibly stay here, ever. "

He shrugged.

"Johnny? Yes. But you may be detained one night—or Johnny may be away. I shouldn't like to think you were alone in that wretched flat. "

He closed and locked the door and followed her down the stairs.

"However, that is a matter for you entirely, " he said lightly. "There is the room if you ever need it. "

She made no answer to this, for her mind was busy with speculation. The room had been lived in, she was sure of that. A woman had lived there— it was no man's room. Mary felt a little uneasy. Of Maurice Meister and his private life she knew nothing. She remembered vaguely that Johnny had hinted of some affair that Meister had had, but she was not curious.

Gwenda Milton!

She remembered the name with a start. Gwenda Milton, the sister of a criminal. She shivered as her mind strayed back to that gorgeous little suite, peopled with the ghost of a dead love, and she had the illusion that a white face, tense with agony, was peering at her as she sat at the typewriter. She looked round with a shudder, but the room was empty and from somewhere near at hand she heard the sound of a man humming a popular tune.

Maurice Meister did not believe in ghosts.

The Ringer

CHAPTER 8

ON the afternoon of the day that Mary Lenley went to Meister's house the Olympic was warped into dock at Southampton. The two Scotland Yard men who had accompanied the ship from Cherbourg, and who had made a very careful scrutiny of the passengers, were the first to land and took up their station at the foot of the gangway. They had a long time to wait whilst the passport examinations were taking place, but soon the passengers began to straggle down to the quay.

Presently one of the detectives saw a face which he had not seen on the ship. A man of middle height, rather slight, with a tiny pointed beard and a black moustache appeared at the ship's side and came slowly down.

The two detectives exchanged glances and as the passenger reached the quay one of them stepped to his side and said: "Excuse me, sir, I did not see you on the ship. " For a second the bearded man surveyed the other coldly. "Are you making me responsible for your blindness? " he asked.

They were looking for a bank robber who had crossed from New York, and they were taking no chances. "May I see your passport? "

The bearded passenger hesitated, then slipping his hand into his inside pocket pulled out, not a passport but a leather note—case. From this he extracted a card. The detective took it and read: CENTRAL INSPECTOR BLISS. C.I. D. Scotland Yard. Attached Washington Embassy.

"I beg your pardon, sir. "

The detective pushed the card back into the other's hand and his attitude changed.

"I didn't recognise you, Mr. Bliss. You hadn't grown a beard when you left the Yard. "

"Who are you looking for? " he asked harshly.

The second detective gave a brief explanation.

The Ringer

"He's not on the ship, I can tell you that, " said Bliss, and with a nod turned away.

He did not carry his bag into the Customs, but depositing it at his feet, he stood with his back to the wall of the Custom House and watched the passengers disembark. Presently he saw the girl for whom he had been looking.

Slim, svelte, immensely capable, entirely and utterly fearless—this was the first impression Inspector Bliss had received. He never had reason to revise his verdict. Her olive skin was faultless, the dark eyes under delicately pencilled eyebrows were insolent, knowledgeable. Here was a girl not to be tampered with, not to be fooled; an exquisite product of modernity. Expensively and a little over—dressed, perhaps. One white hand glittered with diamonds. Two large stones flashed on the lobes of her pink ears. As she brushed past him there came to the sensitive nostrils of Mr. Bliss the elusive fragrance of a perfume that was strange to him.

She had come on board at Cherbourg, and it was, he thought, a remarkable coincidence that they should have travelled to England on the same boat, and that she had not recognised him. Following her into the Custom House, he watched her thread her way through piles of luggage under the indicator M. His own customs examination was quickly finished. He handed his bag to a porter and told him to find a seat in the waiting train, and then he strolled toward where the girl, now hidden in the little crowd of passengers, was pointing out her baggage to the customs officer.

As though she were aware of his scrutiny she looked over her shoulder twice, and on the second occasion their eyes met, and he saw a look of wonder—or was it apprehension? —come into her face.

When her head was turned again, he approached nearer, so near that looking round, she almost stared into his face, and gasped.

"Mrs. Milton, I believe? " said Bliss.

Again that look. It was fear, beyond doubt.

The Ringer

"Sure! That's my name, " she drawled. She had the soft cultured accent of one who had been raised in the Southern States. "But you certainly have the advantage of me. "

"My name is Bliss. Central Inspector Bliss of Scotland Yard, " he said.

Apparently the name had no significance, but as he revealed his calling, he saw the colour leave her cheeks, to flow back again instantly.

"Isn't that interesting? " she said, "and what can I do for—Central Inspector Bliss of Scotland Yard? "

Every word was like a pistol shot. There was no doubt about her antagonism.

"I should like to see your passport. "

Without a word she took it from a little hand—bag and handed it to him. He turned the leaves deftly and examined the embarkation stamps.

"You've been in England quite recently? "

"Sure! I have, " she said with a smile. "I was here last week. I had to go to Paris for something. From there I made the trip from Cherbourg—I was just homesick to hear Americans talking. "

She was looking hard at him, puzzled rather than frightened.

"Bliss? " she said thoughtfully, "I can't place you. Yet, I've got an idea I've met you somewhere. "

He was still examining the embarkation marks.

"Sydney, Genoa, Domodossola—you're a bit of a traveller, Mrs. Milton, but you don't move quite so fast as your husband. "

A slow smile dawned on the beautiful face.

The Ringer

"I'm too busy to tell you the story of my life, or give you a travelogue, " she said, "but maybe you want to see me about something more important? "

Bliss shook his head. In his sour way he was rather amused.

"No, " he said, "I have no business with you, but I hope one day to meet your husband. "

Her eyes narrowed.

"Do you reckon on getting to heaven too? " she asked sardonically. "I thought you knew Arthur was dead? "

His white teeth appeared under his bearded lips for a second.

"Heaven is not the place I should go to meet him, " he said.

He handed back her passport and turning on his heel walked away.

She followed him with her eyes until he was out of sight, and then with a quick little sigh turned to speak to the customs officer. Bliss! The ports were being watched.

Had The Ringer reached England? She went cold at the thought. For Cora Ann Milton loved this desperate man who killed for the love of the killing, and who was now an Ishmael and a wanderer on the face of the earth with the hands of all men against him and a hundred police packs hot on his trail.

As she walked along the platform she examined each carriage with a careless eye. After a while she found the man she sought. Bliss sat in the corner of the carriage, apparently immersed in a morning newspaper.

"Bliss! " she said to herself. "Bliss! "

Where had she seen his face before? Why did the sight of this dour-looking man fill her soul with terror? Cora Ann Milton's journey to London was a troubled one.

CHAPTER 9

WHEN Johnny Lenley called at Meister's house that afternoon, the sight of his sister hard at work with her typewriter was something of a shock to him. It was as if he recognised for the first time the state of poverty into which the Lenleys had fallen.

She was alone in the room when he came and smiled up at him from a mass of correspondence.

"Where's Maurice?" he asked, and she indicated the little room where Meister had his more important and confidential interviews which the peculiar nature of his clientele demanded.

"That's a rotten job, isn't it?"

He hoped she would say "no" and was relieved when she laughed at the question.

"It is really very interesting," she said, "and please don't scowl, Johnny, this is less boring than anything I have done for years!"

He looked at her for a moment in silence; he hated to see her thus—a servant. Setting his teeth he crossed the room and knocked at the door of Meister's private bureau.

"Who is there?" asked a voice.

Johnny tried to turn the handle but the door was locked. Then he heard the sound of a safe closing, the bolt slipped back and the lawyer appeared.

"What is the secret?" grumbled Johnny as he entered the private apartment.

Meister closed the door behind him and motioned him to a chair.

"I have been examining some rather interesting pearls," he said meaningly, "and naturally one does not invite the attention of all the world to stolen property."

"Have you had an offer for them?" asked Johnny eagerly.

The Ringer

Maurice said he had. "I want to get them off to Antwerp tonight," he said.

He unlocked the little safe in the corner of the room, took out a flat cardboard box, and removing the lid he displayed a magnificent row of pearls embedded in cotton wool.

"There are at least twenty thousand pounds worth," said Johnny, his eyes brightening.

"There is at least five years' penal servitude," said Maurice brutally, "and I tell you frankly, Johnny, I'm rather scared."

"Of what?" sneered the other. "Nobody is going to imagine that Mr. Meister, the eminent lawyer, is 'fencing' Lady Darnleigh's pearls." Johnny chuckled as the thought occurred to him. "By gad! You'd cut a queer figure in the dock at the Old Bailey, Maurice, Can't you imagine the evening newspapers running riot over the sensational arrest and conviction of Mr. Maurice Meister, late of Lincoln's Inn Fields, and now of Flanders Lane, Deptford."

Not a muscle of Maurice's face moved, only the dark eyes glowed with a sudden baleful power.

"Very amusing," he said evenly. "I never credited you before with an imagination." He carried the pearls to the light and examined them, before he replaced the cardboard lid.

"You have seen Mary?" he asked in a conversational tone.

Johnny nodded.

"It is beastly to see her working, but I suppose it is all right. Maurice—"

The lawyer turned his head.

"Well?"

"I've been thinking things over. You had a girl in your service named Gwenda Milton?"

"Well?" said Maurice again.

The Ringer

"She drowned herself, didn't she? Have you any idea why?"

Maurice Meister was facing him squarely now. Not so much as a flicker of an eyelid betrayed the rising fury within him.

"The jury said—" he began.

"I know what the jury said," interrupted Johnny roughly, "but I have my own theory."

He walked slowly to the lawyer and touched him lightly on the shoulder as he emphasised every word.

"Mary Lenley is not Gwenda Milton," he said. "She is not the sister of a fugitive murderer, and I am expecting a little better treatment for her than Gwenda Milton received at your hands."

"I don't understand you," said Meister. His voice was very low and distinct.

"I think you do." Johnny nodded slowly. "I want you to understand that there will be very serious trouble if Mary is hurt! They say that you live in everlasting fear of The Ringer—you would have greater cause to fear me if any harm came to Mary!"

Only for a second did Maurice drop his eyes.

"You're a little hysterical, Johnny," he said, "and you're certainly not in your politest mood this morning. I think I called you crude a week ago, and I have no reason to revise that description. Who is going to harm Mary? As for The Ringer and his sister, they are dead!"

He picked up the pearls from the table, again removed the lid and apparently his eyes were absorbed in the contemplation of the pearls again.

"As a jewel thief—"

He got so far when there came a gentle tap at the door.

"Who's there?" he asked quickly.

"Divisional Inspector Wembury!"

The Ringer

CHAPTER 10

MAURICE MEISTER had time hastily to cover the pearls, toss them back into the safe and lock it before he opened the door. In spite of his iron nerve, the sallow face of the lawyer was drawn and white, and even his companion showed signs of mental strain as Alan appeared. It was Johnny who made the quicker recovery.

"Hallo, Wembury! " he said with a forced laugh. "I don't seem to be able to get away from you! "

There was evidence of panic, of deadly fear, something of breathless terror in the attitude of these men. What secret did they hold in common? Alan was staggered by an attitude which shouted "guilt" with a tongue of brass.

"I heard Lenley was here, " he said, "and as I wanted to see him—"

"You wanted to see me? " said Johnny, his face twitching. "Why on earth should you want to see me? "

Wembury was well aware that Meister was watching him intently. No movement, no gesture, no expression was lost on the shrewd lawyer. What were they afraid of? Alan wondered, and his heart sank when, looking past them, he saw Mary at her typewriter, all unconscious of evil. "You know Lady Darnleigh, don't you? " he asked.

John Lenley nodded dumbly.

"A few weeks ago she lost a valuable string of pearls, " Alan went on, "and I was put in charge of the case. "

"You? " Maurice Meister's exclamation was involuntary.

Alan nodded. "I thought you knew that. My name appeared in the newspapers in connection with the investigations. I have handed the case over to Inspector Burton, and he wrote me this morning asking me if I would clear up one little matter that puzzled him. "

The Ringer

Mary had left her typewriter and had joined the little group. "One little matter that was puzzling him? " repeated John Lenley mechanically. "And what was that? "

Wembury hesitated to put the question in the presence of the girl. "He wanted to know what induced you to go up to Lady Darnleigh's room. "

"And I have already given what I think is the natural explanation, " snapped Johnny.

"That you were under the impression you had left your hat and coat on the first floor? His information is that one of the footmen told you, as you were going upstairs, that the coats and hats were on the ground floor. "

John Lenley avoided his eyes. "I don't remember, " he said. "I was rather rattled that night. I came downstairs immediately I recognised my mistake. Is it suggested that I know anything about the robbery? " His voice shook a little.

"Of course no such suggestion is put forward, " said Wembury with a smile, "but we have to get information wherever we can. "

"I knew nothing of the robbery until I read about it in the newspapers and—"

"Oh, Johnny, " Mary gasped the words, "you told me when you came home there had been a—"

Her brother stared her into silence. "It was two days after, you remember, my dear, " he said slowly and deliberately. "I brought the newspaper in to you and told you there had been a robbery. I could not have spoken to you that night because I did not see you. "

For a moment Alan wondered what the girl was going to say, but with a tremendous effort of will she controlled herself. Her face was colourless, and there was such pain in her eyes that he dared not look at her.

"Of course, Johnny, I remember... I remember, " she said dully. "How stupid of me! "

The Ringer

A painful silence followed.

Alan was looking down at the worn carpet; his hand was thrust into his jacket pocket. "All right, " he said at last. "That, I think, will satisfy Burton. I am sorry to have bothered you. " He did not look at the girl: his stern eyes were fixed upon Johnny Lenley. "Why don't you take a trip abroad, Lenley? " He spoke with difficulty. "You are not looking quite as well as you might. "

Johnny shifted uneasily under his gaze. "England is good enough for me, " he said sulkily. "What are you, Wembury, the family doctor? "

Alan paused. "Yes, " he said at last, "I think that describes me, " and with a curt nod he was gone.

Mary had gone back to her typewriter but not to work. With a gesture Maurice led the young man back to his room and closed the door quietly.

"I suppose you understand what Wembury meant? " he said.

"Not being a thought reader, I didn't, " replied Johnny. He was hovering between rage and amusement. "He has got a cheek, that fellow! When you think that he was a gardener's boy... "

"I should forget all that, " said Mr. Meister savagely. "Remember only that you have given yourself away, and that the chances are from today onward you will be under police observation—which doesn't very much matter, Johnny, but I shall be under observation, too, and that is very unpleasant. The only doubt I have is as to whether Wembury is going to do his duty and communicate with Scotland Yard. If he does you will be in serious trouble. "

"So will you, " replied Johnny gruffly. "We stand or fall together over this matter, Maurice. If they find the pearls where will they be? In your safe! Has that occurred to you? "

Maurice Meister was unruffled, could even smile.

"I think we are exaggerating the danger to you, " he said lightly. "Perhaps you are right and the real danger is to me. They certainly have a down on me, and they'd go far to bring me to my knees. " He looked across at the safe. "I wish those beastly things were a

The Ringer

thousand miles away. I shouldn't be surprised if Mr. Wembury returned armed with a search warrant, and if that happened the fat would be in the fire! "

"Why not post them to Antwerp? " asked the other.

Meister smiled contemptuously.

"If I am being watched, as is very likely, " he said, "you don't suppose for one moment that they would fail to keep an eye on the post office? No, the only thing to do with those wretched pearls is to plant them somewhere for a day or two. "

Johnny was biting his nails, a worried look on his face.

"I'll take them back to the flat, " he said suddenly. "There are a dozen places I could hide them. "

If he had been looking at Maurice he would have seen a satisfied gleam in his eyes.

"That is not a bad idea, " said the lawyer slowly. "Wembury would never dream of searching your flat—he likes Mary too much. "

He did not wait for his companion to make up his mind, but, unlocking the safe, took out a box and handed it to the other. The young man looked at the package dubiously and then slipped it into his inside pocket.

"I'll put it into the box under my bed, " he said, "and let you have it back at the end of the week. "

He did not stop to speak to Mary as he made his way quickly through the outer room. There was a sense of satisfaction in the very proximity of those pearls, for which he had risked so much, that gave him a sense of possession, removed some of the irritable suspicion which had grown up in his mind since Meister had the handling of them.

As he passed through crowded Flanders Lane a man turned out of a narrow alley and followed him. As Johnny Lenley walked up Tanners Hill, the man was strolling behind him, and the policeman on point duty hardly noticed him as he passed, never dreaming that

The Ringer

within reach of his gloved hand was the man for whom the police of three continents were searching—Henry Arthur Milton, otherwise known as The Ringer.

The Ringer

CHAPTER 11

LONG after Lenley had taken his departure Maurice Meister strode up and down his tiny sanctum, his hands clasped behind him.

A thought was taking shape in his mind—two thoughts indeed, which converged, intermingled, separated and came together again—Johnny Lenley and his sister.

There had been no mistaking the manner in Lenley's voice. Meister had been threatened before and now, so far from moving him from his half-formed purpose, it needed only the youthful and unbalanced violence of Johnny Lenley to stimulate him in the other direction. He had seen too much of Johnny lately. Once there was a time when the young man was amusing—then he had been useful. Now he was becoming not only a bore but a meddlesome bore. He opened the door gently and peeped through the crack. Mary was sitting at her typewriter intent upon her work.

The morning sun flooded the little room, and made a nimbus about her hair. Once she turned her face in his direction without realising that she was being watched. It was difficult to find a fault in the perfect contour of her face and the transparent loveliness of her skin. Maurice fondled his chin thoughtfully. A new interest had come into his life, a new chase had begun. And then his mind came uneasily back to Johnny.

There was a safe and effective way of getting rid of Johnny, with his pomposity, his threats and his stupid confidence.

That last quality was the gravest danger to Maurice. And when Johnny was out of the way many difficulties would be smoothed over. Mary could not be any more adamantine than Gwenda had been in the earliest stages of their friendship.

Inspector Wembury!

Maurice frowned at the thought. Here was a troublemaker on a different plane from Lenley. A man of the world, shrewd, knowledgeable, not lightly to be antagonised. Maurice shrugged his shoulders. It was absurd to consider the policeman, he thought. After all, Mary was not so much his friend as his patroness. She was

The Ringer

wholly absorbed in her work when he crossed the room and went softly up the stairs to the little suite above.

As he opened the door he shivered. The memory of Gwenda Milton and that foggy coroner's court was an ugly one. A little decoration was needed to make this room again as beautiful as it had been. The place must be cleaned out, decorated and made not only habitable but attractive. Would it attract Mary—supposing Johnny were out of the way? That was to be discovered. His first task was to settle with John Lenley and send him to a place where his power for mischief was curtailed. Maurice was a wise man. He did not approach or speak to the girl after the interview with her brother, but allowed some time to elapse before he came to where she was working.

The little lunch which had been served to her was uneaten.

She stood by the window, staring down into Flanders Lane, and at the sound of his voice she started.

"What is the matter, my dear? " Maurice could be very fatherly and tender. It was his favourite approach.

She shook her head wearily. "I don't know, Maurice. I'm worried—about Johnny and the pearls. "

"The pearls? " he repeated, in affected surprise. "Do you mean Lady Darnleigh's pearls? "

She nodded. "Why did Johnny lie? " she asked. "It was the first thing he told me when he came home, that there had been a robbery in Park Lane and that Lady Darnleigh had lost her jewels. "

"Johnny was not quite normal, " he said soothingly. "I shouldn't take too much notice of what he said. His memory seems to have gone to pieces lately. "

"It isn't that. " She was not convinced. "He knew that he had told me, Maurice: there was no question of his having forgotten. " She looked up anxiously into his face. "You don't think—" She did not complete the sentence.

"That Johnny knew anything about the robbery? Rubbish, my dear! The boy is a little worried—and naturally! It isn't a pleasant

The Ringer

sensation to find yourself thrown on to the world penniless as Johnny has. He has neither your character nor your courage, my dear."

She sighed heavily and went back to her desk, where there was a neat little pile of correspondence which she had put aside. She turned the pages listlessly and suddenly withdrew a sheet.

"Maurice, who is The Ringer?" she asked.

He glared back at the word.

"The Ringer?"

"It's a cablegram. You hadn't opened it. I found it amongst a lot of your old correspondence."

He snatched the paper from her. The message was dated three months before, and was from Sydney. By the signature he saw it was from a lawyer who acted as his agent in Australia, and the message was brief: "Man taken from Sydney Harbour identified, not Ringer, who is believed to have left Australia."

Mary was staring at the lawyer. His face had gone suddenly haggard and drawn; what vestige of colour there had been in his cheeks had disappeared.

"The Ringer!" he muttered... "Alive!"

The hand that held the paper was shaking, and, as though he realised that some reason for his agitation must be found, he went on with a laugh: "An old client of mine, a fellow I was rather keen on— but a scoundrel, and more than a scoundrel."

As he spoke he tore the form into little pieces and dropped the litter into the wastepaper basket. Then unexpectedly he put his arm about her shoulder.

"Mary, I would not worry too much about Johnny if I were you. He is at a difficult age and in a difficult mood. I am not pleased with him just now."

She stared at him wonderingly.

… The Ringer

"Not pleased with him, Maurice? Why not?"

Maurice shrugged his shoulders.

"He has got himself mixed up with a lot of unpleasant people—men I would not have in this office, and certainly would not allow to associate with you."

His arm was still about her shoulder, and she moved slightly to release herself from this parental embrace. She was not frightened, only a little uncomfortable and uneasy, but he allowed his arm to drop as though his gesture had been born in a momentary mood of protection, and apparently did not notice the movement by which she had freed herself.

"Can't you do something for him? He would listen to you," she pleaded.

But he was not thinking of Johnny. All his thoughts and eyes were for the girl. She was holding his arms now, looking up into his face, and he felt his pulses beating a little faster. Suppose Johnny took the detective's advice and went off to the Continent with the pearls—and Mary! He would find no difficulty in disposing of the necklace and would secure a sum sufficient to keep him for years. This was the thought that ran through Meister's mind as he patted the girl's cheek softly.

"I will see what can be done about Johnny," he said. "Don't worry your pretty head any more."

In his private office Meister had a small portable typewriter. Throughout the afternoon she heard the click—click of it as he laboriously wrote his message of betrayal.

That evening, when Inspector Wembury came back to Flanders Lane Police Station, he found a letter awaiting him. It was typewritten and unsigned and had been delivered by a district messenger from a West Central office. The message ran:

'The Countess of Darnleigh's pearl necklace was stolen by John Lenley of 37, Malpas Mansions. It is at present in a cardboard carton in a box under his bed.'

The Ringer

Alan Wembury read the message and his heart sank within, him, for only one course was open to him, the course of duty.

CHAPTER 12

WEMBURY knew that he would be well within his rights if he ignored this typewritten message, for anonymous letters are a daily feature of police life. Yet he realised that it was the practice that, if the information which came thus surreptitiously to a police station coincided with news already in the possession of the police, or if it supported a definite suspicion, inquiries must be set afoot.

He went to his little room to work out the problem alone. It would be a simple matter to hand over the inquiry to another police officer, or even to refer it to... But that would be an act of moral cowardice.

There was a small sliding window in the door of his office which gave him a view of the charge room, and as he pondered his problem a bent figure came into his line of vision and, acting on an impulse, he jumped up from the table, and, opening the door beckoned Dr. Lomond. Why he should make a confidant of this old man who was ignorant of police routine he could not for the life of him explain. But between the two men in the very short period of their acquaintance there had grown a queer understanding.

Lomond looked round the little room from under his shaggy brows.

"I have a feeling that you're in trouble, Mr. Wembury, " he said, his eyes twinkling.

"If that's a guess, it's a good one, " said Alan.

He closed the door behind the police surgeon and pushed forward a chair for him. In a few words he revealed the problem which was exercising his mind, and Lomond listened attentively.

"It's verra awkward. " He shook his head. "Man, that's almost like a drama! It seems to me there's only one thing for you to do, Mr. Wembury— you'll have to treat John Lenley as though he were John Smith or Thomas Brown. Forget he's the brother of Miss Lenley, and I think, " he said shrewdly, "that is what is worrying you most—and deal with this case as though it were somebody you had never heard of. "

Alan nodded slowly.

The Ringer

"That, I'm afraid, is the counsel I should give myself, if I were entirely unprejudiced in the matter."

The old man took a silver tobacco box from his pocket and began slowly to roll a cigarette.

"John Lenley, eh?" he mused. "A friend of Meister's!"

Alan stared at him. The doctor laid significant emphasis on the lawyer's name.

"Do you know him?"

Lomond shook his head.

"Through my career," he said, "I have followed one practice when I come to a strange land—I acquire the local legends. Meister is a legend. To me he is the most interesting man in Deptford, and I'm looking forward to meeting him."

"But why should Johnny Lenley's friendship with Meister—" began Alan, and stopped. He knew full well the sinister importance of that friendship.

Maurice Meister was something more than a legend: he was a sinister fact. His acquaintance with the criminal law was complete. The loopholes which exist in the best drawn statutes were so familiar to him that not once, but half a dozen times, he had cleared his clients of serious charges. There were suspicious people who wondered how the poor thieves who employed him raised the money to pay his fees. There were ill—natured persons who suggested that Meister paid himself out of the proceeds of the robbery and utilised the opportunities he had as a lawyer to obtain from his clients the exact location of the property they had stolen. Many a jewel thief on the run had paused in his flight to visit the house in Flanders Lane, and had gone on his way, leaving in the lawyer's hands the evidence which would have incriminated him. He acted as a sort of banker to the larger fry, and exacted his tribute from the smaller.

"Let me see your anonymous letter," said the doctor.

The Ringer

He carried the paper to the light and examined the typewritten characters carefully.

"Written by an amateur, " he said. "You can always tell amateur typists, they forget to put the spaces between the words; but, more important, they vary the spaces between the lines. "

He pursed his lips as though he were about to whistle.

"Hum! " he said at last. "Do you rule out the possibility that this letter was written by Meister himself? "

"By Meister? " That idea had not occurred to Alan Wembury. "But why? He's a good friend of Johnny's. Suppose he were in this robbery, do you imagine he would trust John Lenley with the pearls and draw attention to the fact that a friend of his was a thief? "

The doctor was still frowning down at the paper.

"Is there any reason why Meister should want John Lenley out of the way? " he asked.

Alan shook his head.

"I can't imagine any, " he said, and then, with a laugh: "You're taking rather a melodramatic view, doctor. Probably this note was written by some enemy of Lenley's—he makes enemies quicker than any man I know. "

"Meister, " murmured the doctor, and held the paper up to the light to examine the watermark. "Maybe one day you'll have an opportunity, inspector, of getting a little of Mr. Meister's typewriting paper and a specimen of lettering. "

"But why on earth should he want Johnny Lenley out of the way? " insisted Alan. "There's no reason why he should. He's an old friend of the family, and although it's possible that Johnny has insulted him, that's one of Johnny's unpleasant little habits. That's no excuse for a civilised man wanting to send another to penal servitude—"

"He wishes Mr. John Lenley out of the way"—Lomond nodded emphatically. "That is my eccentric view. Inspector Wembury, and if I am an eccentric, I am also a fairly accurate man! "

The Ringer

After the doctor left, Alan puzzled the matter over without getting nearer to the solution. Yet he had already discovered that Dr. Lomond's conclusions were not lightly to be dismissed. The old man was as shrewd as he was brilliant. Alan had read a portion of his book, and although twenty years old, this treatise on the criminal might have been written a few weeks before.

He was in a state of indecision when the telephone bell in his room shrilled. He took up the instrument and heard the voice of Colonel Walford.

"Is that you, Wembury? Do you think you can come up to the Yard? I have further information about the gentleman we discussed last week."

For the moment Alan had forgotten the existence of The Ringer. He saw now only an opportunity of taking counsel with a man who had not only proved a sympathetic superior, but a very real friend.

Half an hour later he knocked at the door of Colonel Walford's room, and that moment was one of tragic significance for Mary Lenley.

The Ringer

CHAPTER 13

JOHN LENLEY, after a brief visit to his house, where, behind a locked door, he packed away carefully a small cardboard box, had gone to town to see a friend of the family.

Mary came home to an empty flat. Her head was aching, but that was as nothing to the little nagging pain at her heart. The little supper was a weariness to prepare—almost impossible to dispose of.

She had eaten nothing since breakfast, she remembered, and if she had failed to recall the fact, the queer and sickly sensation of faintness which had come over her as she was mounting the stone steps of Malpas Mansions was an unpleasant reminder of her abstinence.

She forced herself to eat, and was brewing her second cup of tea when she heard a key turn in the lock and John Lenley came in. His face was as black as thunder, but she had ceased to wonder what drove Johnny into those all too frequent tempers of his. Nor was there need to ask, for he volunteered the cause of his anger.

"I went out to the Hamptons' to tea, " he said, as he sat down at the table with a disparaging glance at its meagre contents. "They treated me as though I were a leper—and those swine have been entertained at Lenley Court times without number! "

She was shocked at the news, for she had always regarded the Hamptons as the greatest friends of her father.

"But surely, Johnny, they didn't—they weren't horrible because of our— I mean because we have no money? "

He growled something at this.

"That was at the back of it, " he said at last. "But I suspect another cause. "

And then the reason flashed on her, and her heart thumped painfully.

"It was not because of the Darnleigh pearls, Johnny? " she faltered.

The Ringer

He looked round at her quickly.

"Why do you ask that? —Yes, it was something about that old fool's jewellery. They didn't say so directly, but they hinted as much."

She felt her lower lip trembling and bit on it to gain control.

"There is nothing in that suggestion, is there, Johnny?" It did not sound like her voice—it was a sound that was coming from far away—a strange voice suggesting stranger things.

"I don't know what you mean!" he answered gruffly, but he did not look at her.

The room spun round before her eyes, and she had to grasp the table for support.

"My God! You don't think I am a thief, do you?" she heard him say.

Mary Lenley steadied herself.

"Look at me, Johnny!" Their eyes met. "You know nothing about those pearls?"

Again his eyes wandered. "I only know they're lost! What in hell do you expect me to say?" He almost shouted in a sudden excess of weak anger. "How dare you, Mary... cross—examine me as though I were a thief! This comes from knowing cads like Wembury...!"

"Did you steal Lady Darnleigh's pearls?"

The tablecloth was no whiter than her face. Her lips were bloodless. He made one effort to meet her eyes again, and failed.

"I—" he began.

Then came a knock at the door. Brother and sister looked at one another.

"Who is that?" asked Johnny huskily.

She shook her head.

The Ringer

"I don't know; I will see."

Her limbs were like lead as she dragged them to the door; she thought she was going to faint. Alan Wembury stood in the doorway, and there was on his face a look which she had never seen before.

"Do you want me, Alan?" she asked breathlessly.

"I want to see Johnny."

His voice was as low as hers and scarcely intelligible. She opened the door wider and he walked past her into the dining—room. Johnny was standing where she had left him, by the little round table covered with the remains of the supper, and the clang of the door as Mary closed it came to his ears like the knell of doom.

"What do you want, Wembury?" John Lenley spoke with difficulty. His heart was beating so thunderously that he felt this man must hear the roar and thud of it.

"I've just come from Scotland Yard." Alan's voice was changed and unnatural. "I've seen Colonel Walford, and told him of a communication I received this afternoon. I have explained the"—he sought for words— "the relationship I have with your family and the regard in which I hold it, and just why I should hesitate to do my job."

"What is your job?" asked Lenley after a moment of silence.

"Immediately, I have no business."—Wembury chose his words deliberately and carefully. "Tomorrow I shall come with a warrant to search this house for the Darnleigh pearls."

He heard the smothered sob of the girl, but did not turn his head.

John Lenley stood rigid, his face as white as death. He was ignorant of police procedure, or he would have realised how significant was Alan's statement that he did not possess a search warrant. Wembury sensed this ignorance, and made one last desperate effort to save the girl he loved from the tragic consequences of her brother's folly.

The Ringer

"I have no search warrant and no right to examine your flat," he said. "The warrant will be procured by tomorrow morning."

If John Lenley had a glimmering of intelligence, and the pearls were hidden in the flat, here was a chance to dispose of them, but the opportunity which Alan offered was not taken.

It was sheer mad arrogance on Lenley's part to reject the chance that was given to him. He would not be under any obligation to the gardener's son!

"They are in a box under the bed," he said. "You knew that or you wouldn't have come. I am not taking any favours from you, Wembury, and I don't suppose I should get any if I did. If you feel any satisfaction in arresting a man whose father provided the cottage in which you were born, I suppose you are entitled to feel it."

He turned on his heel, walked into his room, and a few seconds later came back with a small cardboard box which he laid on the table. Alan Wembury was momentarily numbed by the tragedy which had overwhelmed this little household. He dared not look at Mary, who stood stiffly by the side of the table. Her pallid face was turned with an agonised expression of entreaty to her brother, and it was only now that she could find speech.

"Johnny! How could you!"

He wriggled his shoulders impatiently.

"It is no use making a fuss, Mary," he said bluntly. "I was mad!"

Turning suddenly, he caught her in his arms, and his whole frame shook as he kissed her pale lips.

"Well, I'll go," he said brokenly, and in another instant had wrenched himself free of her kiss and her clinging hands, and had walked out of the room a prisoner.

The Ringer

CHAPTER 14

NEITHER Alan Wembury nor his prisoner spoke until they were approaching Flanders Lane Police Station, and then Johnny asked, without turning his head.

"Who gave me away?"

It was only the rigid discipline of twelve years' police work that prevented Alan from betraying the betrayer.

"Information received," he answered conventionally, and the young man laughed.

"I suppose you've been watching me since the robbery," he said. "Well, you'll get promotion out of this, Wembury, and I wish you joy of it."

When he faced the desk sergeant his mood became a little more amiable, and he asked if Maurice Meister could be intimated. Just before he went to the cell he asked, "What do I get for this, Wembury?"

Alan shook his head. He was certain in his mind that, though it was a first offence, nothing could save Johnny Lenley from penal servitude.

It was eleven o'clock at night, and rain was falling heavily, when Alan came walking quickly down the deserted stretch of Flanders Lane, towards Meister's house. From the opposite side of the road he could see above the wall the upper windows; one window showed a light. The lawyer was still up, possibly was interviewing one of his queer clients, who had come by a secret way into the house to display his ill—gotten wares or to pour a tale of woe into Meister's unsympathetic ear. These old houses near the river were honeycombed with cellar passages, and only a few weeks before, there had been discovered in the course of demolition a secret room which the owner, who had lived in the place for twenty years, had never suspected.

As he crossed the road, Alan saw a figure emerge from the dark shadow of the wall which surrounded the lawyer's house. There was

The Ringer

something very stealthy in the movements of the man, and all that was police officer in Wembury's composition, was aroused by this furtiveness. He challenged him sharply, and to his surprise, instead of turning and running, as the Flanders Laner might be expected to do in the circumstances, the man turned and came slowly towards him and stood revealed in the beam of Inspector Wembury's pocket lamp, a slight man with a dark, bearded face. He was a stranger to the detective, but that was not remarkable. Most of the undesirables of Deptford were as yet unknown to Alan.

"Hallo! Who are you, and what are you doing here? " he asked, and immediately came the cool answer:

"I might ask you the same question! "

"I am a police officer, " said Alan Wembury sternly, and he heard a low chuckle.

"Then we are brothers in misfortune, " replied the stranger, "for I am a police officer, too. Inspector Wembury, I presume? "

"That is my name, " said Alan, and waited.

"I cannot bother to give you my card, but my name is Bliss—Central Detective Inspector Bliss—of Scotland Yard. "

Bliss? Alan remembered now that this unpopular police officer had been due to arrive in England on that or on the previous day. One fact was certain: if this were Bliss, he was Alan's superior officer.

"Are you looking for something? " he asked.

For a while Bliss made no reply.

"I don't know what I'm looking for exactly. Deptford is an old division of mine, and I was just renewing acquaintance with the place. Are you going to see Meister? "

How did he know it was Meister's house, Alan wondered. The lawyer had only gone to live there since Bliss had left for America. And what was his especial interest in the crook solicitor? As though he were reading the other's thoughts, Bliss went on quickly: "Somebody told me that Meister was living in Deptford. Rather a

The Ringer

'come down' for him. When I knew him first, he had a wonderful practice in Lincoln's Inn."

And then with an abrupt nod he passed on the way he had been going when Wembury had called him back. Alan stood by the door of Meister's house and watched the stranger till he was out of sight, and only then did he ring the bell. He had some time to wait, time for thought, though his thoughts were not pleasant. He dared not think of Mary, alone in that desolate little flat, with her breaking heart and her despair. Nor of the boy he had known, sitting on his plank bed, his head between his hands, ruin before him.

Presently he heard a patter of slippered feet coming across the courtyard, and Meister's voice asked: "Who is that?"

"Wembury."

A rattle of chains and a shooting of bolts, and the door opened. Though he wore his dressing—gown, Wembury saw, when they reached the dimly lit passage, that Meister was fully dressed; even his spats had not been removed.

"What is the trouble, Mr. Wembury?"

Alan did not know how many people slept in the house or what could be overheard. Without invitation he walked up the stairs ahead of the lawyer into the big room. The piano was open, sheets of music lay on the floor. Evidently Meister had been spending a musical evening. The lawyer closed the door behind him.

"Is it Johnny?" he asked.

Was it imagination on Alan's part, or was the lawyer's voice strained and husky.

"Why should it be Johnny?" he demanded. "It is, as a matter of fact. I arrested him an hour ago for the Darnleigh pearl robbery. He has asked me to get into communication with you."

Maurice did not reply: he was looking down at the floor, apparently deep in thought.

The Ringer

"How did you come to get the information on which he was arrested, or did you know all the time that Johnny was in this? " he asked at last.

Alan was looking at him keenly, and under his scrutiny the lawyer shuffled uneasily.

"I am not prepared to tell you that—if you do not know! " he said. "But I have promised Lenley that I will carry his message to you, and that ends my duty so far as he is concerned. "

The lawyer's eyes were roving from one object in the room to another. Not once did he look at Wembury.

"It is curious, " he said, shaking his head sorrowfully, "but I had a premonition that Johnny had been mixed up in this Darnleigh affair. What a fool! Thank God his father is dead—"

"I don't think we need bother our heads with pious wishes, " said Alan bluntly. "The damnable fact is that Lenley is under arrest for a jewel robbery. "

"You have the pearls? "

Alan nodded.

"They were in a cardboard box—there was also a bracelet stolen, but that is not in the box, " he said slowly. "Also I have seen a sign of an old label, and I think I shall be able to trace the original owner of the box. "

And then, to his astonishment, Meister said: "Perhaps I can help you. I have an idea the box was mine. Johnny asked me for one a week ago. Of course, I had no notion of why he wanted it, but I gave it to him. It may be another box altogether, but I should imagine the carton is mine. "

Momentarily Alan Wembury was staggered. He had had a faint hope that he might be able to connect Meister with the robbery, the more so since he had discovered more than he had told. The half—obliterated label had obviously been addressed to Meister himself, yet the lawyer could not have been aware of this fact. It was one of the slips that the cleverest criminals make. But so quick and glib was he that he had virtually destroyed all hope of proving his complicity in the robbery—unless Johnny told. And Johnny was not the man who would betray a confederate.

"What do you think he will get? " asked Maurice.

"The sentence? You seem pretty certain that he is guilty. "

Maurice shrugged. "What else can I think—obviously you would not have arrested him without the strongest possible evidence. It is a tragedy! Poor lad! "

And then all the dark places in this inexplicable betrayal were lit in one blinding flash of understanding. Mary! Wembury had scoffed at the idea that Meister wished to get her brother out of the way. He could see no motive for such an act of treachery. But now all the hideous possibilities presented themselves to him, and he glared down at the lawyer. He knew Meister's reputation; knew the story of Gwenda Milton; knew other even less savoury details of Meister's past life. Was Mary the innocent cause of this wicked deed? Was it to gain domination over her that Johnny was being sent into a living grave? This time Meister met his eyes and did not flinch.

CHAPTER 15

"I DON'T think you need trouble about Miss Lenley. " Alan's voice was deadly cold. "Fortunately she lives in my division, and she trusts me well enough to come to me if she's in any trouble. "

He saw the slow smile dawn upon the lawyer's face.

"Do you think that is likely. Inspector Wembury? " Meister asked. His voice had a quality of softness which was almost feline. "As I understand, you had the unhappy task of arresting her brother: is she likely to bring her troubles to you? "

Alan's heart sank. The thought of Mary's attitude towards him had tortured him since the arrest. How could she continue to be friendly with the man who was immediately responsible for the ruin and disgrace of her brother?

"The Lenleys are an old family, " Meister went on. "They have their modicum of pride. I doubt if poor Mary will ever forgive you for arresting her brother. It will be terribly unjust, of course, but women are illogical. I will do what I can for Miss Lenley, just as I shall do what I can for Johnny. And I think my opportunities are more obvious than yours. Can I see Johnny to—night? "

Alan nodded.

"Yes, he asked me if you would see him at once, though I'm afraid you can do very little for him. No bail will be granted, of course. This is a felony charge. "

Maurice Meister hurried to the door that led to his room, slipping off his dressing—gown as he went.

"I will not keep you waiting very long, " he said. Left alone in the big room, Alan paced up and down the worn carpet, his hands behind him, his chin on his breast. There was something subtly repulsive in this atmosphere. The great piano, the faded panelling, the shabby richness of the furnishing and decoration. The room seemed to be over—supplied with doors: he counted four, in addition to the curtain which hid the alcove. Where did all these lead to? And what stories could they tell, he wondered.

The Ringer

Particularly interested was he in one door which was heavily bolted and barred, and he was staring at this when, to his amazement, above the frame glowed suddenly a long red light. A signal of some kind—from whom? Even as he looked, the light died away and Meister came in, struggling into his overcoat.

"What does that light mean, Mr. Meister?"

The lawyer spun round. "Light? Which light?" he asked quickly, and following the direction of the detective's finger, he gasped. "A light?" incredulously. "You mean that red lamp? How did you come to notice it?"

"It lit up a few minutes ago and went out again." It was not imagination on his part: the lawyer's face had gone a sickly yellow.

"Are you sure?" And then, quickly: "It is a substitute for a bell—I mean, if you press the bell on the outer door the lamp lights up; bells annoy me."

He was lying, and he was frightened too. The red lamp had another significance. What was it?

In those few seconds Meister had become ill at ease, nervous; the hand that strayed constantly to his mouth trembled. Glancing at him out of the corner of his eye, when he thought he was free from observation, Alan saw him take a small golden box from his pocket, pinch something from its contents and sniff at his thumb and finger. "Cocaine," guessed Wembury, and knew that his theory was right when almost immediately the lawyer became his old buoyant self.

"You must have imagined it—probably a reflection from the lamp on the table," he said.

"But why shouldn't there be somebody at the front door?" asked Alan coolly, and Meister made an effort to correct his error.

"Very probably there is," He hesitated. "I wonder if you would mind, inspector—would it be asking you too much to go down to the front gate and see? Here is the key!"

Alan took the key from the lawyer's hand, went downstairs across the courtyard and opened the outer gate. There was nobody there.

The Ringer

He suspected, indeed he was sure, that the lawyer had asked him to perform this service because he wished to be alone in the room for a few minutes, possibly to investigate the cause of and reason for that signal.

As he went up the stairs he heard a sharp click as though a drawer had closed, and when he came into the room he found Meister pulling on his gloves with an air of nonchalance.

"Nobody? " he asked. "It must have been your imagination, inspector, or one of these dreadful people of Flanders Lane playing a trick. "

"The lamp hasn't lit since I left the room? " asked Alan, and when Meister shook his head, "You are sure? "

"Absolutely, " said the lawyer, and too late saw he was trapped.

"That is very curious. " Wembury looked hard at him. "Because I pressed the front door bell, and if the lamp was what you said it was, it should have lit up again, shouldn't it? "

Meister murmured something about the connections being out of order, and almost hustled him from the room.

Alan was not present at the interview at the police station. He left Meister in the charge of the station sergeant, and went home to his lodgings in Blackheath Road with a heavy heart. He could do nothing for the girl; not so much as suggest a woman who would keep her company. He could not guess that at that moment, when his heart ached for her, Mary had a companion, and that companion a woman.

CHAPTER 16

LONG after Johnny Lenley had been taken away Mary Lenley sat numbed, paralysed to inaction by the overwhelming misfortune which had come to her. She sat at the table, her hands clasped before her, staring down at the white cloth until her eyes ached. She wished she could weep, but no tears had come. The only reminder she had of the drama that had been played out under that roof was the empty feeling in her breast, it was as though her heart had been taken from her.

Johnny a thief! It wasn't possible, she was dreaming. Presently she would wake up from this horrible nightmare, hearing his voice calling her from the lawn... But she was not at Lenley Court: she was in a block of industrial flats, sitting on a cheap chair, and Johnny was in a prison cell. The horror of it made her blood run cold. And Alan—what vicious trick of fate had made him Johnny's captor? She had a vivid memory of that scene which had preceded Johnny's arrest. Every word Alan had spoken had been burnt into her brain. Too well she realised that Wembury had risked everything to save her brother. He had given him a chance. Johnny had only to keep silence and spend the night in getting rid of those pearls, and he would have been with her now. But his fatal hauteur had been his undoing. She had no bitterness in her soul against Alan Wembury, only a great sorrow for him, and the memory of his drawn face hurt her almost as much as Johnny's mad folly.

She heard the bell tinkle faintly. It rang three times before she understood that somebody was at the front door. Alan perhaps, she thought, and, getting up stiffly, went out into the hall and opened the door. A woman stood there dressed in a long black mackintosh; a black hat enhanced the fairness of her hair and skin. She was beautiful, Mary saw, and apparently a lady.

"You've made some mistake—" she began.

"You're Mary Lenley, aren't you? " An American, noted Mary, and looked her astonishment. "Can I see you? "

The girl stood aside, and Cora Ann Milton walked into the room and looked round. There was a faint hint of disparagement in her glance, which Mary was too miserable to resent.

The Ringer

"You're in trouble, aren't you?"

Uninvited, she sat down by the half—opened drawer of the table, took a jewelled case from her bag and lit a cigarette.

"Yes, I'm in trouble—great trouble," said Mary, wondering how this woman knew, and what had brought her here at such an hour.

"I guessed that. I hear Wembury pulled your brother for a jewel theft— he caught him with the goods, I guess?"

Mary nodded slowly. "Yes, the pearls were in this house. I had no knowledge that they were here."

She wondered in a dim way whether this American was Lady Darnleigh; so many members of the aristocracy have been recruited from the United States that it was possible.

"My name's Milton—Cora Ann Milton," said the woman, but the name meant nothing to Mary Lenley. "Never heard of me, kid?"

Mary shook her head. She was weary in body and soul, impatient that this intruder into her sorrow should leave her.

"Never heard of The Ringer?"

Mary looked up quickly.

"The Ringer? You mean the criminal who is wanted by the police?"

"Wanted by everybody, honey." Despite the flippancy of her tone, Cora Ann's voice shook a little. "By me more than anybody else— I'm his wife!"

Mary got up quickly from her chair. It was incredible! This beautiful creature the wife of a man who walked everlastingly in the shadow of the gallows!

"I'm his wife," nodded Cora Ann. "You don't think it's a thing to boast about? That's where you're wrong." And then, abruptly: "You're working for Meister, aren't you?"

"I am working for Mr. Meister, " said Mary quietly; "but really, Mrs. —"

"Mrs. Milton, " prompted Cora.

"Mrs. Milton, I don't quite understand the object of your visit at this time of night. "

Cora Ann Milton was regarding the room with shrewd, appraising eyes.

"It's not much of an apartment you've got, but it's better than that cute little suite of Meister's. "

She saw the colour—come into the girl's face and her eyes narrowed.

"He's shown it to you eh? Gosh, that fellow's a quick worker! "

"I don't understand what you mean. " Mary was slow to anger, but now she felt her resentment merging into anger. At the back of her mind was a confused idea that, but for Johnny's misfortune, this woman would never have dared to see her. It was as though his arrest had qualified her tor admission to the confidence of the underworld.

"If you don't know what I mean, I won't say much more about it, " said the woman coolly. "Does Meister know I'm back? "

Mary shook her head. Mrs. Milton was sitting by the table, and was taking a handkerchief from the little bag on her lap: she was very deliberate and self—possessed. "I don't think he's very much interested in your movements, Mrs. Milton, " said Mary wearily. "Do you mind if I ask you not to stay? I've had a great shock this evening and I'm not in a mood to discuss Mr. Meister or your husband or anybody. "

But Cora Ann Milton was not easily abashed. "I guess when all this trouble is over you'll be working late at Meister's house, " she said, "and I'm wondering whether you'd like to have my address? "

"Why on earth—" began Mary.

The Ringer

"Why on earth! " mimicked the other. "I guess this is an age of freedom when the only place you see a chaperon is a museum. But I should like you to get in touch with me if... anything happens. There was another girl once... but I guess you don't want any awful example. And, say, I'd be much obliged to you if you'd not mention the fact to dear Maurice that The Ringer's wife is in town. "

Mary hardly listened to the latter part of the speech. She walked to the door and opened it suggestively. "That means I've got to go, " said Cora Ann with a good—natured smile. "I'm not blaming you, kid. I guess I'd feel that way myself if some dame came floating in on me with all that guardian angel stuff. "

"I don't require guardianship, thank you. I have a number of friends—"

She stopped. A number of friends! Not in all London, in all the country, was there any to whom she could turn in her trouble, except to—Alan Wembury. And Maurice?

Why did she hesitate at Maurice? In the last day or two a subtle change had come over their relationship. He was no longer the natural refuge and adviser to whom she would go in her distress.

Cora Ann was watching her from the doorway; keen, shrewd eyes seemed to be reading her every thought. "That man Wembury's a decent fellow. I hope you're not going to be sore at him for pinching your brother? "

Mary made a weary gesture: she had reached almost the end of her tether.

Long after the girl had gone, she sat by the table, trying to understand just what this visit of Cora Ann Milton's meant. Had she followed the woman down the stairs, she might have discovered.

Cora turned into the dark, deserted street, walked a few paces, and then, as if by magic from some mysterious underground trap, a man appeared by her side, so unexpectedly and silently that she started and took a step away from him.

"Oh!... you scared me! " she breathed.

The Ringer

"Did you see the girl?"

"Yes, I saw her. Arthur"—her voice was broken and agitated—"why do you stay here? Don't you realise, you fool, what danger..."

She heard his low chuckle.

"Cora Ann, you talk too much," he said lightly. "By the way, I saw you this afternoon."

"You saw me?" she gasped. "Where were you?" Suddenly: "Arthur, how am I to know you when I see you? I've got that spookish feeling that you're round me all the time, and I'm for ever peering into people's faces as I pass them—I'll be pinched for being too fresh one of these days!"

Again he chuckled.

"Surely my own loving wife would know me?" he said ironically. "The eyes of love could penetrate any disguise."

He heard her teeth snap in anger. Arthur Milton had the trick of infuriating this beautiful wife of his.

"I'll know what you look like now," she said.

Suddenly there was a click and a white beam of light flashed in his face.

"You're a fool!" he said roughly, as he knocked the lamp down. "When you can see, others can see."

"I wish 'em joy!" she whispered. For she had looked into a face that was covered from forehead to chin by a square of black silk, through which a pair of wide—set eyes stared down at her.

"Did you get my letter?" he demanded.

"Yes—the code, you mean. I thought the newspapers did not publish code messages?"

He did not answer and mechanically she felt in her bag. The envelope she had put there was gone.

The Ringer

"What is it?" he asked quickly and when she told him: "Cora, you're a goop! You must have dropped it in this girl Lenley's flat! Go and get it!"

Cora Ann hurried up the stairs and knocked at the door. It was immediately answered by Mary.

"Yes, I've come back," said the woman breathlessly. "I dropped a letter here somewhere: I've only just missed it."

Mary turned back and together they searched the flat, turning up carpets and shaking out curtains, but there was no sign of the letter.

"You must have lost it elsewhere." The woman was so agitated that she was sorry for her. "Did it have any money—"

"Money? No," said Cora Ann impatiently. "I wish it had."

She looked round the room in bewilderment. "I know I had it before I came in."

"Perhaps you left it at your own home?" suggested Mary, but Cora Ann shook her head, and after another thorough search she began to doubt whether she had brought it out with her.

Mary Lenley closed the door upon her finally with heartfelt thanksgiving, walked listlessly back to the table and sat down. Her tea was cold and bitter. She pulled open a little drawer in the table where the spoons were kept, and looked down in amazement. The letter for which they had sought lay on top of a miscellaneous collection of spoons and forks. It was simply inscribed on the envelope "Cora Ann", and had no address. Perhaps the address was inside, she thought, and after some hesitation pulled out its contents, a square white card covered with groups of letters and figures, written in an almost microscopic hand. It did not need any very great acumen on her part to know that she was looking at a code: if she had been more experienced in such matters, she would have realised how ingenious a code it was.

She replaced the card, put it again in the drawer and waited for the woman to return. What had happened was obvious: when she had taken her handkerchief from the bag, the letter bad slipped into the

The Ringer

drawer, which had been slightly open, and in moving she must have closed the drawer, which ran very easily, without noticing the fact.

That night, before she went to bed, Mary took the letter into her room and locked it away in one of the drawers of her dressing—table where she kept her few trinkets, and, having locked it away, forgot all about it.

The Ringer

CHAPTER 17

IT was a month later that Mary Lenley sat in the marble hall of the Central Criminal Court and waited with folded hands and a set, tragic face for the jury's finding. She had gone into court and had heard the preliminaries of the evidence, but the sight of that neat figure in the dock was more than she could bear, and she had gone out to wait with fatalistic resignation for the final curtain of the drama.

The door leading to the court opened and Alan Wembury came out and walked over to her.

"Is it—ended?" she asked huskily.

Wembury shook his head. "Very soon now, I think," he said quietly.

He looked as if he had not slept, he was hollow—eyed, haggard, a man distracted.

"I'm sorry, Alan." She put out her hand and gently touched his. The touch of her hand almost brought the tears to his eyes.

"You don't know how I feel about this, Mary; and the horrible thing is that I am getting the credit for the arrest—I had a letter from the Commissioner yesterday congratulating me!"

She smiled faintly.

In every tragedy there is a touch of grotesque comedy, and it seemed to be supplied in this case by the unsought honour that had come to this reluctant police officer.

He sat by her side and tried to comfort her, and if his efforts were a little awkward, a little gauche, she understood. And then Maurice came into the hall, his old, immaculate self. His silk hat was more shiny than ever, his spats were like the virgin snow. He might have come straight from a wedding party but for his lugubrious countenance.

"The judge is summing up," he said. "I wish you'd go into court, Wembury, so that you can bring news of what happens."

The Ringer

It was a crude request, which Alan diagnosed as a wish on the part of the lawyer to be alone with Mary.

"There goes a very clever young man," said Meister, as he watched the broad—shouldered figure of the detective disappear through the swing doors. "Unscrupulous, but then all police officers are unscrupulous. A climber, but all police officers are ambitious."

"I've never found Alan unscrupulous," said Mary.

Maurice Meister smiled. "That is perhaps a strong word to employ," he agreed carelessly. "After all, the man had to do his duty, and he was very ingenious in the method he employed to trap poor Johnny."

"Ingenious? Trap?" She frowned at him.

"That did not come out in the evidence. Nothing that is detrimental to the police force ever comes out in police court evidence, my dear," said Maurice with a meaning smile. "But I am on the inside of things, and I happen to know that Wembury has been on Johnny's trail ever since the robbery was committed. That was why he came down to Lenley Court."

She stared at him. "Are you sure? I thought—"

"You thought he came down to see you, to get your congratulations on his promotion?" said Maurice. "That is a natural error. My dear, if you think the matter over, you will realise that a detective officer must always pretend to be doing something other than he actually is doing. If you were to tax Wembury with his little act of duplicity, he would of course be indignant and deny it."

She thought a while. "I don't believe it," she said. "Alan told me that he had not associated Johnny with the crime until he received an anonymous letter."

"S—sh!" said Meister warningly.

Alan had come out of the court and was walking towards them.

The Ringer

"The judge will be another ten minutes, " he said, and then, before Meister could warn her, the girl asked: "Alan, is it true that you have been watching Johnny for a long time? "

"You mean in connection with this offence? No, I knew nothing about it. I did not suspect Johnny until I had a letter, written by somebody who was in a very favourable position to know all about the robbery. "

His eyes were on Maurice Meister.

"But when you came down to Lenley Court—"

"My dear, "—it was Maurice who interrupted hastily—"why ask the inspector these embarrassing questions? "

"It doesn't embarrass me, " said Alan curtly. "I went to Lenley Court to see Miss Lenley and to tell her of my promotion. You're not suggesting that my visit had anything to do with the robbery, are you? "

Maurice shrugged his shoulders.

"I was probably giving you credit that you did not deserve, " he said, with an attempt to pass the matter off humorously. "As a solicitor I am not unacquainted with these mysterious letters which the police are supposed to receive, and which cover the operations of their—noses, I think is the word for police informer. "

"You know it's the word for police informer, Mr. Meister, " said Alan. "And there was nothing mysterious about the letter which betrayed Lenley, except the writer. It was written on typewriting paper, Swinley Bond No. 14. "

He saw Meister start.

"I have made a few inquiries amongst the stationers of Deptford, and I have discovered that that particular paper is not supplied locally. It comes from a law stationer's in Chancery Lane and is their own especial property. I tell you that in case you would like to take the inquiry any further. "

The Ringer

With a nod he left them together. "What does he mean?" asked the girl, a little worried.

"Does anyone know what any police officer means?" asked Maurice, with a forced laugh.

She was thoughtful for a while, and sat for a long time without speaking.

"He suggested that Johnny had been betrayed by—by somebody—"

"Somebody who did not live in Deptford, obviously," said Maurice quickly. "Really, my dear, I shouldn't take too much notice of that cock-and-bull story. And it would be well if you did not see too much of Wembury in the future."

"Why?" she asked, looking at him steadily.

"There are many reasons," replied Maurice slowly. "In the first place, I have a clientele which would look a little askance at me if my secretary were a friend of a police officer. Of course," he went on hurriedly, as he saw the look in the girl's face, "I have no wish to dictate to you as to your friends. But I want to be of help to you, Mary. There are one or two matters which I would like to discuss after this unpleasant business is over. You can't live alone in Malpas Mansions."

"Johnny will be sent to prison, of course?" she nodded.

It was not the moment for delicacy.

"Johnny will be sent to penal servitude," said Meister: "you've got to get that fast in your mind. This may mean seven years for him, and you must reconcile yourself to that possibility. As I say, you can't live alone—"

"I can't live anywhere else but Malpas Mansions," she said. The note of determination in her voice was unmistakable. "I know you mean to be kind, Maurice, but there are some things which I cannot do. If you care to employ me, I'll be pleased to work for you. I don't think I'm sufficiently competent to work for anybody else, and I'm sure no other employer would give me the wages you have offered. But I'm living at Malpas Mansions until Johnny returns."

The Ringer

There came a dramatic interruption. The swing door opened and Alan Wembury walked out. He stood stock still for a moment, looking at her, and then slowly paced across the tiled floor.

"Well? " she asked breathlessly.

"Three years penal servitude, " said Alan. "The judge asked if anything was known of him and I went into the box and told the Bench all I knew. "

"And what did you know? " asked Meister. He was on his feet now, facing the detective.

"I know that he was a decent boy who has been ruined by associating with criminals, " said Wembury between his teeth; "and some day I am going to take the man who ruined Johnny Lenley, and put him in that court. " He pointed back to the swing door. "And when I go into the box it will not be to plead for the prisoner but to tell the judge a story that will send the man who betrayed John Lenley to a prison from which he will never come out! "

The Ringer

CHAPTER 18

To Maurice Meister, The Ringer was dead. He treated as a jest, or as one of those stupid legends which to the criminal mind is gospel, all the stories of Henry Arthur Milton's presence in England. The three months which followed Johnny's sentence were too full to allow him time even to consider with any seriousness the whispered hints which came to him from his unsavoury clients.

Scotland Yard, which acts only on definite knowledge, had taken no step to warn him, and that was the most comforting aspect of the situation. Mary came regularly to work, and from being an ornament to the establishment, developed into a most capable typist. She often wondered whether it would not be fair to Maurice to tell him of the interview she had had with Cora Ann Milton; but since The Ringer's name was never again mentioned, she thought it wisest to let the matter drop. If she had not severed all association with Alan Wembury, she saw very little of him. Twice she had almost met him in the street, but he had obviously avoided her. At first she was hurt, but then she realised that it was Alan's innate delicacy which was responsible. One day in the High Street she saw him and before he could escape intercepted him.

"Alan, you're being very unkind, " she said, and added mischievously: "People think that you will not know me because of my dubious relations! "

He went red and white at this, and she was instantly sorry. There was something childlike about Alan.

"Of course I meant nothing of the sort. But you're being I rather a pig, aren't you? You've avoided me like the plague. "

"I thought I was being rather delicate, " he said ruefully, and, grasping the nettle firmly: "Have you heard from Johnny? "

She nodded. "He is quite cheerful, and already making plans for the future, " she said, and added: "Won't you take me to tea somewhere on Wednesday—that is my early day? "

It was a very happy, man who went back to the station house. Indeed, he was so cheerful that old Dr. Lomond, busy at the

The Ringer

sergeant's desk writing a report upon a drunken motorist, looked over his glasses and rallied him in his dour way.

"Have ye had money left ye?"

"Something better than that," smiled Alan. "I've rid myself of a dull ghost."

Lomond clucked his lips derisively as he signed his name with a flourish and blotted the report.

"That means that you've had a quarrel with a girl, and she's suddenly decided to make it up," he said. He had an uncanny habit of getting into the mind of his audience. "I'm no' saying that matrimony is no' a good thing for any man. But it must be terribly risky for a police officer."

"I'm not contemplating matrimony," laughed Alan.

"Then I wonder ye're not ashamed of yourself," said the doctor as he shuffled down to the fire and shook off the ash of his cigarette into the grate.

"You ought to be a happy man," said Alan. "Colonel Walford told me he had written you a letter of thanks for the work you did in the Prideaux case."

The old man shook his head.

"Man, I'm no' proud of my work. But poisoners I abominate, and Prideaux was the most cold—blooded poisoner I have ever known. A strange man with a queer occiput. Have you ever noticed the occiput of poisoners? It juts oot from the back of the heid."

As he was talking a stocky, poorly dressed man had come into the charge room. There was a grin on his unshaven face as he made his way to the sergeant at the desk. He had all the aplomb of a man in familiar surroundings, and as he laid his ticket of leave on the desk he favoured the sergeant with a friendly nod.

"Why, Hackitt!" said Wembury. "I didn't know you were out."

The Ringer

He shook hands with the ex—convict and Sam Hackitt's grin broadened.

"I got my brief last Monday, " he said. "Old Meister's giving me a job. "

"What, Sam, are you going into the law? "

The idea tickled Hackitt.

"No, I'm going to clean his boots! It's a low job for a man of my ability, Mr. Wembury, but what can you do when the police are 'ounding you down all the time? "

"Hounding grandmothers! " said Alan, with a smile "You fellows hound yourselves down. So you're going to valet Meister, are you? I wish you luck. "

Sam Hackitt scratched his unshaven chin thoughtfully.

"They tell me Johnny Lenley's been put away, Mr. Wembury? That's bad luck. "

"Did you know him? " asked Alan.

Sam Hackitt hesitated.

"Well, I can't say that I know him. I went down to the country to see him once, when he was a swell. I knew he was on the crook then, and somebody put up a joke for him and me. "

Alan knew what "a joke" meant in the argot of the criminal classes: it meant a robbery, big or small.

"But I didn't take it on, " said Sam. "It was a bit too dangerous for me, and I don't like working with amachoors. They're bound to give you away if they're a bit too impetuous. Especially as this gentlemen who was putting up the money for the joke wanted us to carry a shooter—not for me, thank you! "

Alan was acquainted with the professional burglar's horror of firearms. But surely the man who had planned the robbery was as

The Ringer

well aware of the dangers of a burglar being captured with firearms in his possession?

"Who is the Big Fellow, Sam? " he asked, never for one moment expecting a truthful reply; for only in a moment of direst necessity would a thief betray his "big fellow" or employer.

"Him? Oh, he's a chap who lives in Sheffield, " said Sam vaguely. "I didn't like the job, so I didn't take it on. He's a nice boy—that young Lenley, I mean. It's a pity he went crook, a gentleman of his education. "

And then he changed the subject abruptly.

"Mr. Wembury, what's this yarn about The Ringer being in London? I heard about it when I was in Maidstone, and I sent a letter to your boss. "

Alan was surprised. The Ringer belonged to another plane, and although the little criminals were greatly intrigued by the operations of this super—criminal, he had not connected any of them with the man for whom the police were searching.

"He's drowned, as a matter of fact, " said Sam comfortably. "I read about it when I was in 'stir'. " [Stir = Prison. E.W.]

"Did you know him, Sam? "

Again the ex—convict scratched his chin.

"I'm one of the few people who've seen him without his make—up, " he grinned. "The Ringer, eh? What a lad! There never was a bloke who could disguise himself like that bird! "

The sergeant had copied particulars of Sam Hackitt's brief into a book, and now handed the ticket of leave back to the man.

"We may be asking to see you one of these days, Hackitt, if the Ringer turns up, " said Wembury.

Sam shook his head.

"He'll never turn up: he's drowned. I believe the newspapers. "

The Ringer

Dr. Lomond watched the stocky figure disappear through the doorway and shook his head.

"There goes a super—optimist, " he said, "and what a heid! Did you notice, Wembury, the flattening of the skull? Man, I'd like to measure him! "

CHAPTER 19

THE days that intervened before Wednesday were very long days and each seemed to consist of much more than twenty—four hours. Alan had a note from the girl in the morning, asking him to meet her at a little teashop in the West End, and he was at the rendezvous a quarter of an hour before she was due to arrive. She came at last, a trim, neat figure in blue serge, with just a little more colour in her cheeks than was ordinary.

"I'm being a dutiful servant, " she said. "I would have met you at Blackheath, only I was afraid that some of Mr. Meister's clients might have seen you and thought I was in secret communication with the police over their grisly pasts! "

He laughed at this. He had never seen her so light—hearted since the old Lenley Court days.

The teashop was only sparsely patronised. It was an hour before the rush of shoppers filled each seat and occupied every table, and he found a quiet corner where they could talk. She was full of hopeful plans for the future. Maurice (he hated to hear her call Meister by his Christian name) was going to start Johnny on a poultry farm: she had worked out to a day the end of Johnny's period of imprisonment.

"He has three months remitted for every year if he is on his best behaviour, " she said. "And Johnny is being very sensible. When he wrote the other day he told me he was going to earn his full marks. That will be wonderful, won't it, Alan? "

He hesitated to ask the question that was in his mind, but presently he put it to her, and she nodded.

"Yes, he writes about you, and he has no resentment at all. I think you could be a very good friend to him when he comes out. "

Her own days were so filled, she told him, that the time was passing rapidly, more rapidly than she had dared hope. Maurice was most kind. (How often she repeated that very sentence!) And life at Malpas Mansions was moving smoothly. She had been able to employ a little maid-of-all-work.

"A queer little thing who insists upon telling me all the horrors of Deptford." She smiled quietly. "As though I hadn't enough horrors of my own! Her favourite hero is The Ringer—do you know about him?"

Alan nodded.

"He's the hero of all the funny—minded people of Deptford," he said. "They love the thought of anybody outwitting the police."

"He is not in England, is he?" Alan shook his head. "Are you terribly interested in The Ringer?" she went on. "Because, if you are, I can tell you something—I have met his wife."

He opened his eyes wide at this.

"Cora Ann Milton?" he said incredulously, and she laughed at the impression her words had made on him.

She told him of Cora Ann's visit, and yet for some reason, which she did not understand herself, she did not give a faithful account of that interview, or even hint that Cora Ann had warned her against Meister. It was when she came to the code letter that he was more interested.

"I've only just remembered it!" she said penitently; "it is in my bureau and ought to be sent to her."

"A code card—that is very important," said Alan. "Do you think you could bring it to me tomorrow?"

She nodded.

"But why on earth did she come—the night Johnny was arrested, you say?" said Alan. "Have you seen her since?"

Mary shook her head. "Don't let's talk about The Ringer. It's shop to you, isn't it? It's shop to us both—ugh!" She shivered.

They strolled through Green Park together and dined at a little restaurant in Soho. He told her of his new bete noir—the black-bearded Inspector Bliss, and was so vehement on the subject that she dissolved into laughter. It was the day of days in Alan Wembury's

The Ringer

life, and when he left her, after seeing her on a tramcar bound southward, something of the colour of life went with her.

Meister had asked the girl to call at his house on her way home, but mentally Mary had laid down a formula which was subsequently to serve her well. She had fixed nine o'clock as the utmost limit she could work in the house, and as it was past that hour when she reached New Cross, she went straight to Malpas Mansions. One little luxury had been introduced into the flat: Maurice had insisted that she should be connected with the telephone system, and this was a great comfort to her.

The bell was ringing as she unlocked the door, and, lighting the gas, hurried to the little table where the instrument stood. As she expected, it was Meister.

"My dear girl, where have you been? " he asked testily. "I have been waiting for you since eight o'clock. "

She glanced at the watch on her wrist: it was a quarter to ten.

"I'm sorry, Maurice, " she said, "but I didn't definitely promise I'd call. "

"Have you been to a theatre or something? " he asked suspiciously. "You didn't tell me anything about it? "

"No, I've been to see a friend. "

"A man? "

Mary Lenley possessed an almost inexhaustible fund of patience, but the persistence of this cross—examination irritated her, and he must have guessed this, for, before she could reply, he went on: "Forgive my curiosity, my dear, but I am acting in loco parentis to you whilst poor Johnny is away, and I'd like to know—"

"I went to dinner with a friend, " she interrupted shortly. "I'm sorry I have put you to any inconvenience, but I did not exactly promise, did I? "

A pause.

The Ringer

"Can't you come round now?"

Her "No" was very decisive.

"It is much too late, Maurice. What is it you want doing?"

If he had answered right away she might have believed him, but the pause was just a little too long.

"Affidavits!" she scoffed. "How absurd, at this time of night! I'll come down earlier in the morning."

"Your friend was not by any chance Alan Wembury?" asked Meister's voice.

Mary considered that a very opportune moment to hang up the receiver.

She went into her little bedroom to change whilst the kettle was boiling, and the draught from the open window slammed the door behind her. She lit the gas, and closed the window with a thoughtful frown. She had given her servant a holiday, and the girl had left before her. Because of a threatening rainstorm, Mary had gone round the flat closing every window. Who had opened it? She looked round the room and a chill crept down her spine. Somebody had been in the room: one of the drawers in her chest had been forced open. As far as she could see, nothing had been stolen. Then with a gasp she remembered the code letter—it was gone! The wardrobe had been opened also; her dresses had been moved, and the long drawer beneath had been searched. By whom? Not by any ordinary burglar, for nothing except the letter had been taken.

She went back to the window and, pulling it open, looked down. There was a sheer drop into the yard of fifty feet. To the right was the tiny balcony jutting out from her kitchenette, and by its side a balance lift by which the households in Malpas Mansions could obtain their supplies from the tradesmen in the yard below. The lift was at the bottom, and she could see the long steel ropes swaying gently in the stiff breeze that was blowing. A nimble man could climb to the level of the balcony without any superhuman effort. But what man, nimble or otherwise, would risk his neck for the sake of turning over her few poor possessions and extracting Cora Ann's letter?

The Ringer

She had an electric torch in the kitchen, and she brought this to make a closer inspection. It was then she found the wet footprints on the carpet. It was a new carpet and had the disadvantage of showing every stain. Two muddy footprints were so clearly on view that she wondered she had not seen them when she came into the room.

She made another discovery: the dressing—table where she had left a number of brushes neatly arranged was all disarranged. She found one of the clothes brushes at the foot of the bed, and it had evidently been used to brush somebody who was very untidy, for it was wet and had a smear of mud at the end of the bristles. Nor had the cool intruder been satisfied with a rough toilet: he had used her hair—brushes; in the white bristles she saw a coarse black hair. She had seen its kind before: her father had a trick of straightening his beard with any brush that was handy. Somebody with a beard, a black beard, had tidied himself before the glass. She began to laugh, the idea was so absurd; but it was not long before she was serious again.

She heard the bell ring in the kitchen, and opened the front door to find the man who acted as porter to the block.

"I'm sorry to bother you, miss, but has anybody been in your flat whilst you have been out?"

"That's just what I was wondering, Jenkins," she answered, and led him into the room to show him the evidence of the visit.

"There has been a man hanging around the block all the evening," said the porter, scratching his head; "a fellow with a little black beard. One of the tenants saw him in the back courtyard just before dark, having a look at the tradesmen's lift, and the lady who lives on the opposite landing says before that he was knocking at this door for ten minutes, trying to make somebody hear. That must have been about eight o'clock Have you lost anything, miss?"

She shook her head.

"Nothing valuable." She could not explain the exact value of The Ringer's code card.

CHAPTER 20

A MAN with a beard! Where had she heard about a man with a beard? And then she suddenly remembered her talk with Alan. Inspector Bliss! That idea seemed too fantastic for words.

She took the telephone directory, and turned the pages until she found the Flanders Lane police station. A gruff voice answered her. Mr. Wembury had not returned. He had been out all day but was expected at any minute. She gave her name and telephone number, and insisted upon the private nature of the call. An hour later the telephone bell rang and Alan's voice greeted her. She told him in a few words what had happened, and she heard his gasp of astonishment.

"I don't think it could possibly have been the person you think, " he said, and she realised he was probably speaking in a room where other people were. "But if it's not too late, may I come round? "

"Do, please, " she said without hesitation.

Alan came after such a remarkably short interval that she suggested he must have flown.

"A taxi, " he explained. "One doesn't often see them in High Street, Deptford, but I was fortunate. "

It was the first time he had been in the flat since Johnny's arrest. The very arrangement of the furniture aroused ugly memories. She must have divined this, for she led him straight to her room, and showed him the evidence of the visitor's presence.

"Bliss? " he frowned. "Why on earth should Bliss come here? What on earth did he expect to find? "

"That is what I should like to know. " She could smile now. It was rather wonderful how comforting was the presence of Alan Wembury. "If it were the letter, he could have come and asked for it. "

But he shook his head. "Have you anything here of Meister's—any papers? " he asked suddenly.

The Ringer

She shook her head.

"Keys?" he suggested.

"Why, yes, of course!" she remembered. "I've the keys of the house. His old cook is rather deaf, and Maurice is seldom up when I arrive, so he has given me a key of the outer gate and the door."

"Where do you keep them?" asked Alan.

She opened her bag.

"I carry them about with me. Besides, Alan, why on earth should Mr. Bliss want the keys? I suppose he can see Mr. Meister whenever he wishes."

But Alan's mind was on another trail. Did Bliss know of the visit of Cora Ann Milton to this girl? Supposing he had set himself the task of hunting down The Ringer—and Alan Wembury had not been notified that the Central Office were playing a lone hand—would he make this difficult entry in order to test his suspicions? And suppose he were after the letter, how would he have heard of it?

"Only one man would have come after that letter—and that man is The Ringer," he said with conviction.

He had left the front door open when he came in, and now, as they returned to the dining—room, the porter appeared in the hall.

"Here you are, miss," he called eagerly. "The fellow's outside. What about calling a policeman?"

"Which fellow?" asked Wembury quickly. "Do you mean the bearded man?"

Evidently the porter did not know Alan for a police officer.

"Yes, sir. Don't you think we ought to call a policeman? There's one on point duty at the end of the road."

Wembury brushed past him and ran down the stairs. Emerging into the night, he saw a man standing on the opposite side of the road. He made no attempt to conceal himself: indeed, he was standing in the full light of the street lamp, but drew aside as Wembury crossed the road, and long before he reached the stranger he knew that Mary's surmise had been correct. It was Bliss.

"Good evening. Inspector Wembury, " was the cool greeting.

Without preliminary, Alan made his accusation.

"Somebody has broken into Miss Lenley's flat to—night, and I have reason to believe it is you, Bliss. "

"Broken into Miss Lenley's flat, eh? " The central inspector was rather amused. "Do I look like a burglar? "

"I don't know what you look like, but you were seen in the courtyard just before dark, examining the food lift. There's no doubt that the man who entered Miss Lenley's room gained admission by that means. "

"In that case, " said Bliss, "you had better take me down to your funny little police station and charge me. But before you do so, I will make your job a little easier by confessing that I did climb that infernal rope, that I did force the window of Miss Lenley's bedroom, that I did inspect the flat. But I did not find what I expected to find. The man who was there before me got that. "

"Is that your explanation? " asked Wembury, when the other had finished, "that there was another man in the flat? "

"Exactly—a perfect explanation, though it may not satisfy you. I did not climb the rope until I had seen somebody else go up that way, and open the window. It was just before dusk. Your friends will doubtless tell you that I immediately went up the stairs and knocked at Miss Lenley's door, and, receiving no answer, decided to make my entrance the same way as the unknown intruder. Does that satisfy you, Mr. Wembury, or do you think that as a police officer I exceeded my duty in chasing a burglar? "

Alan was in a quandary. If the story the man told was true, he had perfect justification for his action. But was it true?

"Did you turn out the contents of the drawers by any chance? "

The Ringer

Bliss shook his head.

"No, I'm afraid our friend forestalled me there. I opened one drawer and gathered from its confusion that my predecessor had made a search. I don't think he found what he wanted, and that he will very likely come again tonight. That is why I am here. Have you any further questions, inspector?"

"No," said Alan shortly.

"And you're not thinking of inviting me to meet your superintendent? Good! Then I think my presence for the moment is a little superfluous." And, with a jerk of his shoulder, he turned and strolled at a leisurely pace along the sidewalk.

Going back to the girl, Alan told her of his interview, and loyalty to his cloth prevented his giving his own private views on the matter.

"He may be speaking the truth," he said. "Of course it was his duty to follow a burglar. If he is lying, we shall hear no more of it, but if he is telling the truth he will have to report the matter."

He left her half an hour later, and as he went out of the flat he looked round for Bliss, but there was no sign of him. When he returned to the police station, he was taken aback to learn that Bliss had indeed reported the burglary, given times and full particulars, and had added a note to his report to the effect that Divisional Inspector Wembury had charge of the case.

Alan was baffled. If Bliss's account was true, who could have been the first man to climb up the rope? And what other object had he in burgling Mary Lenley's flat than a search for the code? It brought The Ringer too near for comfort. Here was a mystery, which was never solved until that night of horror when The Ringer came to Meister's house.

Two little problems were recurring to Mary Lenley from day to day. Not the least important of these was contained in the formula, "Shall I tell Maurice?" Should she tell Maurice that she had been to tea with Alan Wembury... should she tell him of the burglary that had been committed the night before? On the whole she felt the least unpleasant confession, the one which would probably absorb him to the exclusion, was the second of her adventures.

The Ringer

Maurice was not down when she arrived, and Mr. Samuel Hackitt, newly installed in the Meister household, was polishing wearily the window that looked out on to the leads. He had made his appearance a few days before, and in spite of his unpleasant past Mary liked the little man.

"Good morning, miss." He touched an invisible cap. "The old man's still up in bed, bless his old heart!"

"Mr. Meister had a heavy night," she said primly.

"'Thick' is the word I'd use," said Sam, wringing out a leather cloth at his leisure.

Very wisely Mary did not encourage any further revelations.

"Funny old house, this, miss." Sam knocked with his knuckle at one of the panels. "Holler. It's more like a rabbit warren than a house."

Mr. Meister's residence had been built in the days when Peter the Great was still living in Deptford, She passed this news of historical interest on to the wholly unimpressed man.

"I never knew Peter... King, was he? That sounds like one of Meister's lies."

"It's history, Sam," she said severely, as she dusted her typewriter.

"I don't take any notice of history—that's lies, too," said Hackitt, calmly. "Lor' miss, you don't know all the his'try books I've read—'Ume, Macaulay, Gibbons, the feller that wrote all about Rome."

She was astounded.

"You've read them?"

He nodded. "Studied 'em," he said solemnly, so solemnly that she laughed.

"You're quite a student: I didn't realise that you were such a well read man."

The Ringer

"You have to do something in 'stir', " said Sam, and she realised that this reading of his had whiled away some period of his incarceration.

He had an extraordinary stock of knowledge on unlikely subjects. Possibly this was gained under similar circumstances. Once or twice he strayed to the piano, although this had been dusted and polished, as she could see in her face reflected in the black top; but the piano fascinated him, and probably he had a higher respect for Mr. Meister because of his musical qualities than for his knowledge of the law. He depressed a key that tinkled sharply and apologised.

"I'm going up to Scotland Yard tomorrow, miss, " he said, and she thought it had something to do with his recent imprisonment, and expressed only a polite interest. "Never been there before, " said Sam complacently, "but I suppose it's like every other busy's office—one chair, one table, one pair of handcuffs, a sergeant and forty—five thousand perjuring liars! "

The entrance of Meister at that moment cut short his speculations. Maurice looked shaky and ill, she thought. After he had gruffly dismissed his new servitor, he told her he had slept badly.

"Where did you go—, " he began.

She thought it was an excellent moment to tell him of her burglar. And because she did not wish to talk of Cora Ann she made no reference to the stolen letter. He listened in amazement, until she came to the interview which Alan had had with Inspector Bliss.

"Bliss! That's queer! "

He stood up, his eyes tightened, as though he were facing a bright light.

"Bliss... I haven't seen him for years. He's been in America. A clever fellow... Bliss... humph! "

"But don't you think it was extraordinary, Maurice, that he should climb up into my flat, or that there should have been anybody there before him—what profit can they find in burgling my poor little apartment? "

Maurice shook his head.

The Ringer

"I don't believe it. Bliss wanted to find something in your room. The yarn about another man having gone up is all bunk."

"But what could he find?" she insisted, and Maurice Meister was not prepared to offer a convincing reason.

Bliss! He had no right in Deptford, unless—Maurice was both puzzled and apprehensive. The advent of a Central man to Deptford could only indicate some extraordinary happening, and in his mind he went over the various events which might be calculated to interest that exalted policeman. Strangely enough, Deptford at this moment was unusually well behaved. There had been no serious charges in the division for three months, and Meister, who had his finger in more lawless pies than his worst enemy gave him credit for, knew that there had been no steal of such importance that Scotland Yard would send one who was reputedly its most promising officer to conduct an independent examination.

By some extraordinary process, peculiarly his own, he decided that there was nothing sinister in this attention. Probably Headquarters were trying out the new divisional inspector, and had sent this wise and experienced officer to discover the extent of his acquaintance with the Lenleys.

Meister's breakfast was not an elaborate meal, and was usually served in his little bureau. This morning it consisted, as usual, of a cup of coffee, a small plate of fruit and a biscuit. He unfolded the newspaper by the side of his table and glanced at it idly. His life was so full that he had little time for, or interest in, the great events of the world; but a news item at the top of the columns caught his eye.

PRISON RIOT CONVICT SAVES THE LIFE OF DEPUTY GOVERNOR

He glanced through the description, expecting to find a name with which he was familiar, but, as is usual in these cases, a strict anonymity was preserved as to the identity of the prisoner concerned. There had been a riot in a county jail; the ringleaders had struck down a warder and taken possession of his keys, and would have killed the deputy governor, who happened to be in the prison hall at the time, but for the bravery of a convict who, with the aid of a broom handle, defended the official till armed warders came on the scene. Maurice pursed his lips and smiled. His regard for the

The Ringer

criminal was a very low one. They were hardly human beings; he speculated idly on what reward the heroic convict would receive. Something more than he deserved.

Opening the box of cigars that was on the table, he bit off the end and lit a long, black cheroot, and as he smoked his mind vacillated between Mary and her peculiar experience. What was Bliss doing in Deptford, he wondered; he tried to recall the man as he had known him years before, but he was unsuccessful.

Hackitt came in to clear away the breakfast things, and, glancing familiarly over Meister's shoulder, read the account.

"That deputy's a pretty nice fellow, " he volunteered. "I wonder what made the boys get up against him. But the screws are bad. "

Meister raised his cold eyes.

"If you want to keep this job, you'll not speak unless you're spoken to, Hackitt. "

"No offence, " said Hackitt, quite unperturbed. "I'm naturally chatty. "

"Then try your chattiness on somebody else! " snapped Maurice.

The man went out of the room with the tray, and had gone a few minutes before he returned, bearing a long yellow envelope. Meister, snatching it from his hand, glanced at the superscription. It was marked "Very Urgent and Confidential" and bore the stamp of Scotland Yard.

"Who brought this? " he asked.

"A copper, " said Sam.

Maurice pointed to the door.

"You can go. "

He waited till the door had closed upon his servant before he tore open the flap, and his hand shook as he drew out the folded typewritten paper.

The Ringer

SIR, I have the honour to inform you that the Deputy Commissioner, Colonel Walford, C.B., wishes to see you at his office at Scotland Yard at 11.30 in the forenoon tomorrow. The matter is of the greatest importance, and the Deputy Commissioner wishes me to say that he trusts you will make every effort to keep this appointment, and notify him by telegram if you cannot be at Scotland Yard at the hour named.

I have the honour to be, sir, etc.

A summons to Scotland Yard! The first that Meister had ever received. What did it portend?

He rose to his feet, opened a little cupboard and took out a long bottle of brandy, and splashed a generous portion into a glass, and he was furious with himself to find that his hand was shaking. What did Scotland Yard know? What did they wish to know? His future, his very liberty, depended on the answer to those questions. The morrow! The very day he had chosen to put into execution certain plans he had formulated. Unconsciously Scotland Yard had given Mary Lenley a day of respite!

CHAPTER 21

AT the lawyer's request, Mary came early to work the following morning, and she was surprised to find Maurice up and dressed. He was one of those men who usually was meticulously careful as to his dress, and indeed was almost a dandy in this respect. But he was usually a slow dresser and liked to lounge about the house in his pale green dressing—gown until the arrival of clients or the necessity for a consultation with counsel, made him shed that garment.

When she came in, he was walking up and down the room with his hands clasped behind him. He looked as if he had not slept very well, and she remarked upon this.

"Yes, I slept all right. " He spoke jerkily, nervously, and he was obviously labouring under some very strong emotion. It never occurred to Mary Lenley that that emotion might be fear. "I have to go to Scotland Yard, my dear, " said Meister, "and I was wondering"—he forced a smile— "whether you would like to come up with me—not into the Yard, " he added hastily, when he saw the look of repugnance on her face. "Perhaps you would like to stay at a—at a tearoom or somewhere until I came out? "

"But why, Maurice? " The request was most unexpected.

He was not patient to answer questions.

"If you don't wish to come, don't, my dear—" he said sharply, but altered his tone. "There are one or two things I would like to talk to you about—business matters in which I may need a little—clerical assistance. "

He walked to her desk and took up a paper.

"Here are the names and addresses of a number of people: I wish you to keep this paper in your bag. The gentlemen named should be notified if anything—I mean, if it is necessary. "

He could not tell her that he had passed that night in a cold sweat of fear, alternating snatches of bad dreams with an endless cogitation on the unpleasant possibilities which the morrow held. Nor could he explain that the names which he had written down and chosen with

The Ringer

such care, were men of substance who might vouch for him in certain eventualities. He might have confessed with truth that he wanted her company that morning for the distraction he needed during the hours that preceded his interview with the Commissioner; and if the worst happened, for somebody to be at hand whom he could notify and trust to work in his interests.

"I don't know what they want me for at Scotland Yard, " he said, with an attempt at lightness. "Probably some little matter connected with one of my clients. "

"Do they often send for you? " she asked innocently.

He looked at her quickly. "No, I have never been before. In fact, it is a most unusual procedure. I have never heard of a solicitor being sent for. "

She nodded at this. "I thought so, " she said. "Alan told me that they ask you to come to Scotland Yard either to 'pump' you or catch you! "

He glowered at this. "I beg of you not to give me at second hand the vulgarities of your police officer friend. 'To pump you'—what an expression! Obviously they have asked me to go because I've defended some rascal about whom they want information. Possibly the man is planning to rob me. "

The point was such a sore one that Mary very wisely refrained from carrying it any further.

Maurice possessed no car of his own, and it was characteristic of him that the local garage could supply no machine of sufficient magnificence to support his state. The Rolls which came to him from a West End hirer was the newest and shiniest that could be procured, and to the admiration and envy of the Flanders Laners, who stood in their doorways to watch the departure, Mary drove off with her employer. His nervousness seemed to increase rather than diminish as Deptford was left behind. He asked her half a dozen times if she had the paper with the names of his influential friends. Once, after an interregnum of gloomy silence on his part, she had tried to make conversation by asking him if he had seen an item in the newspaper.

The Ringer

"Riot in a prison? " he answered abstractedly. "No—yes, I did. What about it? "

"It is the prison Johnny is in, " she said, "and I was rather worried—he is such an impetuous boy, and probably he has done something foolish. Is there any way of finding out? "

Meister was interested.

"Was Johnny in that jail? I didn't realise that. Yes, my dear, we'll find out if you wish. "

He evidently brooded upon this aspect of the prison riot, for as the car was crossing Westminster Bridge he said: "I hope Johnny is not involved: it would mean the loss of his marks. "

She had hardly digested this ominous remark before the car turned on to the Thames Embankment and pulled up just short of the entrance to Scotland Yard.

"Perhaps you would like to sit in the car and wait? "

"How long will you be gone? " she asked.

Mr. Meister would have given a lot of money to have been able to answer that question with any accuracy.

"I don't know. These official people are very dilatory. Anyway, you can amuse yourself as you wish. "

As he was talking he saw a man drop nimbly from a tram—car and slouch across the road towards the arched entrance of police headquarters.

"Hackitt? " he said incredulously. "He didn't tell me he was coming. He served me my breakfast half an hour before you arrived at the house. "

His face was twitching. She was amazed that so small a thing could have so devastating an effect.

"All right, " he nodded and scarcely looking at her, strode away.

The Ringer

He stopped at the entrance to the Yard as some creature of the wild might halt at the entrance of a trap. What did Hackitt know about him? What could Hackitt say? When he had taken the man into his employ, he had not been actuated by any sense of charity—on the contrary, he felt he was securing a bargain. But was Hackitt in the pay of the police—a "nose," sent into his house to pry amongst his papers, unearth his secrets, reveal the mysteries of locked cellars and boarded—up attics?

Setting his teeth, he walked down the gentle slope and turned into Scotland Yard.

CHAPTER 22

MARY elected to spend the first part of her time of waiting in the car with a newspaper, but the printed page was a poor rival to the pageant of life that was moving past. The clanging trams crowded with passengers, the endless procession of vehicles crossing the beautiful bridge, the panorama of London which was visible through the front windows of the car. She wondered if business would call Alan Wembury to headquarters, and had dismissed this possibility when he made a very commonplace appearance. Somebody walked past the car with long strides: she only saw the back of him, but in an instant she was out on the sidewalk. He heard her voice and spun round.

"Why, Mary! " he said, his face lighting up. "What on earth are you doing this side of the world? You haven't come with Meister? "

"Did you know they've sent for him? "

Alan nodded.

"Is it anything very important? He is a little worried, I think. "

Wembury might have told her that Meister's worry before he went to Scotland Yard was as nothing to what it would be after.

"You didn't bring Mr. Hackitt by any chance? " he smiled, and she shook her head.

"No, Maurice didn't know that Hackitt was coming—I think that rather distressed him. What is the mystery, Alan? "

He laughed. "The mystery is the one you're making, my dear. " And then, as he saw the colour come to her face, he went on penitently: "I'm awfully sorry. That's terribly familiar. "

"I don't mind really, " she laughed. "I'm pretending that you're a very old gentleman. Do you often have these important conferences? And who is that, Alan? "

A beautiful little coupe had drawn noiselessly to the kerb just ahead of their own car. The chauffeur jumped down, opened the lacquered

The Ringer

door, and a girl got out, looked up at the facade of Scotland Yard and passed leisurely under the arch. Though it was early in the morning, and the place was crowded, a cigarette burnt between her gloved fingers and she left behind her the elusive fragrance of some eastern perfume.

"She's a swell, isn't she? And an old acquaintance of yours."

"Not Mrs. Milton!" said the girl in amazement.

"Mrs. Milton it is. I must run after her and shepherd her into a nice airy room."

She dismissed him with a nod. He took her hand in his for a moment and looked down into her eyes.

"You know where to find me, Mary?" he said in a low voice, and before she could answer this cryptic question, he was gone.

At the request of a policeman, the driver of her car moved the car beyond the gateway and came to a halt at a place where she had a more comprehensive view of the building. It did not look like a police headquarters: it might have been the head office of some prosperous insurance company, or a Government building on which a usually staid architect had been allowed to give full play to his Gothic tendencies. What was happening behind those windows? What drama or tragedy was being played out in those rooms which look upon the Embankment? She thought of Johnny and shivered a little. His record was somewhere in that building, tabulated in long cabinets, his finger—prints, body—marks, colouring. It was dreadfully odd to think of Johnny as a number in a card index. Did they have numbers in jail also? She seemed to remember reading about such things.

She was suddenly conscious that somebody was staring in at the car, and, turning her head, she met a pair of humorous blue eyes that twinkled under shaggy grey eyebrows. A tall, bent figure in a homespun suit, with an impossible brown felt hat on the back of his white head, and he was obviously wishing to speak to her. She opened the door of the car and came out.

"Ye'll be Miss Lenley, I think? My name's Lomond."

The Ringer

"Oh, yes, you're Dr. Lomond, " she smiled. "I thought I recognised you."

"But, my dear leddy, you've never seen me! "

"Alan—Mr. Wembury says you look like every doctor he has ever known."

This seemed to please him, for his shoulders shook with silent laughter.

"Ye're no' curious, or you'd ask me how I knew you, " he said. And then he looked up at Scotland Yard. "A sad and gloomy—faced place, young leddy. " He shook his head dolefully. "You've no' been called here professionally? "

As he spoke, he fumbled in his pockets, produced a silver tobacco—box and rolled a cigarette.

"They've dragged me from my studies to examine a poor wee body, " he said, and at first she took him literally, and thought he had been brought to identify some drowned or murdered man, and the look of antipathy in her face was not lost on the doctor.

"She's alive, " he gurgled, "and no' so unattractive! " He held out his long hand. "I'd like to be meeting you more often, Miss Lenley. Mebbe I'll come along and see you one day, and we'll have a bit chat. "

"I should love it, doctor, " she said truthfully.

She liked the old man: there was a geniality and a youthfulness in that smile of his that went straight to her heart. She watched him shuffling laboriously, the cigarette still twisting and rolling in his hand, until the grey pillars of the gateway hid him for view. Who was the poor wee body? She knew that he referred to a forthcoming cross—examination, for Alan had told her of his exploit with the poisoner Ann Prideaux. And then it flashed upon her—Cora Milton! She felt rather sorry for Dr. Lomond: he was such a nice, gentle soul; he would find Cora Ann Milton a particularly difficult lady.

CHAPTER 23

MARY did not see Central Detective Inspector Bliss walk quickly through the stone doorway of Scotland Yard. He scarcely acknowledged the salute of the constable on duty, and passed along the vaulted corridor to the Chief Constable's room. A slight, bearded man, pale of face, brusque of manner, he might hold the respect of his subordinates, but he had no place in their affections.

"That's Mr. Bliss, " said the officer to a younger constable. "Keep out of his way. He was bad enough before he went to America—he's a pig now! "

Mr. Maurice Meister, sitting on a hard form in one waiting—room, saw him pass the open door and frowned. The walk of the man was oddly familiar.

Sam Hackitt, ex—convict, lounging in the corridor in charge of a plain clothes police officer, scratched his nose thoughtfully and wondered where he had seen the face before. Mr. Bliss opened the door of the Chief Constable's room, walked in and slammed the door. Wembury, gazing abstractedly through the double windows which gave a view of the Embankment, turned his head and nodded. Every time he had met Central Inspector Bliss he had liked him less.

The bearded man made for the desk in the centre of the room, picked up a sheet of paper, read it and grunted. A trim messenger came in and handed him a letter, he read the address and dropped the envelope on the table. Turning his head with an impatient growl, he asked: "Why is the Assistant Commissioner holding this inquiry, anyway? It's not an administration job. Things have changed pretty considerably since I was here. "

Alan withdrew his attention from the new County Council building. "The Chief Constable had the case in hand, " he said, "but he's away ill, so Colonel Walford is taking it for him. "

"But why Walford? " snarled Bliss. "He has about as much knowledge of the job as my foot! "

Alan was very patient. He knew that he would be meeting Bliss that morning and had it in his mind to ask him about that mysterious

The Ringer

visit he had paid to Malpas Mansions, but Bliss seemed hardly in a communicative mood.

"This is a pretty big thing. If The Ringer is really back—and headquarters is pretty certain that he is—"

Bliss smiled contemptuously. "The Ringer! " And then, remembering: "Who is this man who wrote from Maidstone Prison? "

"Hackitt—a fellow who knew him. "

Bliss laughed harshly. "Hackitt! Do you think that Hackitt knows anything about him? You're getting pretty credulous at Scotland Yard in these days! "

The whole attitude of the man was offensive. It was as though he wished deliberately to antagonise the other.

"He says he'd recognise him. "

"Bosh! " said Bliss scornfully. "It's an old lag's trick. He'd say anything to make a sensation. "

"Dr. Lomond says—" began Alan, and was stopped by an explosive snort from the bearded detective.

"I don't want to know what any police surgeon says! That fellow's got a hell of a nerve. He wanted to teach me my business. "

It was news to Wembury that the pawky old police surgeon had ever crossed swords with this querulous man.

"Lomond's a clever fellow! " he protested.

Bliss was turning the leaves of a book he had taken from the table.

"So he admits in this book of his. I suppose this sort of thing impresses you, eh? I've been two years in America, the home of all this anthropology sort of muck. I've met madmen who could give points to Lomond. Suppose Hackitt says he knows The Ringer, who else is going to identify him? " he asked, throwing down the volume.

The Ringer

"You, for one. I understand you tried to arrest him after the Attaman case."

Bliss looked at him sharply. "I? I never saw the swine. He had his back to me the day I went to pinch him. I just laid my hands on him when— bingo! I was on the ground with four inches of good knife in me. Who's seen him?"

"Meister?" suggested Alan.

The other man frowned. "Meister! Will he ever have a chance of talking? That is what I want to know!"

It was the second surprise of the morning for Wembury. "Why shouldn't he?"

But Inspector Bliss avoided the question. "I'll bet Meister never saw him plainly in his life. Too full of dope, for one thing. The Ringer's clever. I hand it to him. I wish to God I'd never left Washington—I had a soft job there."

"You don't seem very happy," smiled the younger man.

"If you'd been there they'd have kept you there," snapped the other. "They wanted me back at the Yard."

In spite of his annoyance Wembury laughed. "I like your manners, but I hate your modesty," he said. "And yet we seem to have been catching 'em all right. I haven't noticed very much depression amongst the criminal classes since you returned."

But Bliss was not to be drawn. He was studying the title page of the book in his hand, and was on the point of making some sarcastic reference to Dr. Lomond and his anthropological studies when Colonel Walford came in and the two men stiffened to attention.

"Sorry, gentlemen, to keep you waiting," he said cheerfully. "Good morning, Bliss."

"Good morning, sir."

"There's a letter for you, sir," said Wembury.

The Ringer

"Yes, " growled Bliss impatiently. "The Assistant Commissioner can see that for himself. "

"The man who wrote to you from Maidstone is here, sir, " reported Alan.

"Oh, Hackitt? "

"You don't think he knows The Ringer, do you, sir? " asked Bliss with a contemptuous smile.

"Honestly, I don't. But he comes from Deptford. There's just a remote chance that he's speaking the truth. Have him up, Wembury—I'll go along and tell the Chief Commissioner I am taking the inquiry. "

When he had gone: "Hackitt! " said Bliss. "Huh! I remember him. Five—six years ago I got him eighteen months at the London Sessions for housebreaking. A born liar! "

Two minutes later, in response to Alan's telephoned instructions, the "born liar" was ushered into the room.

Mr. Samuel Cuthbert Hackitt had the pert manner of the irrepressible Cockney. He stood now, in no wise abashed by the surroundings or awed by the imponderable menace of Scotland Yard.

Alan Wembury smiled a greeting.

"Hallo, Mr. Wembury! " said Sam cheerfully. "You're looking bright an' 'ealthy. "

He was looking hard at Alan's companion.

"You remember Mr. Bliss? "

"Bliss? " Sam frowned. "You've changed a bit, ain't yer? Where did yer get your whiskers from? "

"You shut your ugly mouth, " snapped Bliss, and Sam grinned.

"That's more like yer. "

The Ringer

"Remember where you are, Hackitt, " warned Wembury.

The ex—convict showed his white teeth again. "I know where I am, sir. Scotland Yard. You don't arf do yourselves well, don't you? Where's the grand planner? Meister's got one! Look at the flowers—love a duck, everything the 'eart can desire. "

If looks could kill, the scowl on the face of Bliss would have removed one law breaker from the world. What he might have said is a matter for conjecture as the Commissioner came back at that moment.

"Good mornin', sir, " said Sam affably. "Nice pitch you've got here. All made out of thieving and murder! "

Colonel Walford concealed a smile. "We have a letter from you when you were in prison, Hackitt. " He opened a folder and, taking out a sheet of blue note—paper, read: '"Dear Sir: This comes hoping to find you well, and all kind friends at Scotland Yard—'"

"I didn't know Bliss was back, " interjected Sam.

"'There's a lot of talk about The Ringer, '" continued the Colonel, "'down here—him that was drowned in Australia. Dear sir, I can tell you a lot about him now that he's departed this life, as I once see him though only for a second and I knew where he lodged. ' Is that true? "

"Yes, sir, " nodded Sam. "I lodged in the same 'ouse. "

"Oh, then, you know what he looks like? "

"What he looked like, " corrected Sam. "He's dead. "

Colonel Walford shook his head, and the man's jaw dropped. Looking at him, Alan saw his face change colour.

"Not dead? The Ringer alive? Good morning, thank you very much! " He turned to go.

"What do you know about him? "

"Nothing! " said Hackitt emphatically. "I'll tell you the truth, sir, without any madam whatsoever. [Madam = telling the tale. EW]

The Ringer

Nosing on a dead man's one thing," said Sam earnestly; "nosing on a live Ringer is another, I give you my word! I know a bit about The Ringer— not much, but a bit. And I'm not goin' to tell that bit. And why? Because I just come out of 'stir' and Meister's give me a job. I want to live peaceable without any trouble from anybody."

"Now don't be foolish, Hackitt," said the Commissioner "If you can help us we may be able to help you."

Sam's long lip curled in a sardonic smile.

"If I'm dead, can you help me to get alive?" he asked sarcastically. "I don't nose on The Ringer. He's a bit too hot for me."

"I don't believe you know anything," sneered Bliss.

"What you believe don't interest me," growled the convict.

"Come on—if you know anything, tell the Commissioner, What are you afraid of?"

"What you're afraid of," snapped Hackitt. "He nearly got you once! Ah! That don't make you laugh! I'm very sorry; I come up here under what is termed a misapprehension. Good—bye, everybody."

He turned to go.

"Here, wait," said Bliss.

"Let him go—let him go!" The Commissioner waved Sam Hackitt out of existence.

"He never saw The Ringer," said Bliss when the man had gone.

Walford shook his head. "I don't agree. His whole attitude shows that he has. Is Meister here?"

"Yes, sir—he's in the waiting—room," replied Alan.

CHAPTER 24

A FEW seconds later came Maurice Meister, his debonair self, yet not wholly at his ease. He strode into the room, examined his wrist—watch ostentatiously, and looked from one to the other.

"I think there must be some mistake, " he said. "I thought I was going to see the Chief Constable. "

Walford nodded. "Yes, but unfortunately he's ill; I'm taking his place. "

"I was asked to call at eleven—thirty; it is now"—he consulted his watch—"twelve—forty—nine. I have a case to defend at the Greenwich Police Court. God knows what will happen to the poor devil if I'm not there. "

"I am sorry to have kept you waiting, " said Colonel Walford coldly. "Take a seat. "

As he went to sit, putting his stick and hat on the desk, he looked at Bliss. "Your face is vaguely familiar, " he said.

"My name is Bliss, " replied the detective. The eyes of the two men met.

So this was Bliss: Maurice averted his eyes from that defiant stare. "I'm sorry—I thought I knew you. "

He seated himself carefully near the desk, placed his hat on the table and drew off his gloves.

"It is a little unusual, is it not, to summon an officer of the Royal Courts of Justice to Scotland Yard? " he asked.

The Assistant Commissioner settled himself back in his chair: he had dealt with men far cleverer than Maurice Meister.

"Now, Mr. Meister, I am going to speak very frankly—that is why I brought you here. "

Meister's brows met. "'Brought' is not a word I like, Mr. Walford. "

The Ringer

"Colonel Walford," prompted Alan. The Colonel took up a minute paper and read a line or two.

"Mr. Meister," he began, "you are a lawyer with a large clientele in Deptford?" Meister nodded. "There isn't a thief in South London who doesn't know Mr. Meister of Flanders Lane. You are famous both as a defender of hopeless cases—and—er—as a philanthropist." Again Meister inclined his head as though at a compliment. "A man commits a burglary and gets away with it. Later he is arrested; none of the stolen property is found—he is apparently penniless. Yet you not only defend him personally in the police court, and through eminent counsel at the Old Bailey, but during the time the man is in prison you support his relatives."

"Mere humanity! Am I—am I to be suspect, as it were, because I—I help these unfortunate people? I will not see the wives and the wretched children suffer through the faults of their parents," said Maurice Meister virtuously.

Bliss had stepped out of the room. Why, he wondered, in some apprehension.

"Oh, yes; I'm sure of that," answered the Colonel dryly. "Now, Mr. Meister, I haven't brought you here to ask you about the money that you distribute from week to week, or where it comes from. I'm not even going to suggest that somebody who has access to the prisoner in a professional capacity has learnt where the proceeds of the robbery are hidden, and has acted as his agent."

"I am glad you do not say that, Colonel." Meister had recovered his nerve by now; was his old urbane self. There was danger here, deadly, devastating danger. He had need for a cool head. "If you had said that, I should have been extremely—"

"I'm not insisting on it, I tell you. The money comes from somewhere, Meister. I am not curious. Sometimes you do not support your clients with money—you take their relatives into your employment?"

"I help them in one way or another," admitted Meister.

The Colonel was eyeing him closely.

The Ringer

"When a convict has a pretty sister, for example, you find it convenient to employ her. You have a girl secretary now, a Miss Lenley?"

"Yes."

"Her brother Went to prison for three years on information supplied to the police—by you!"

Meister shrugged his shoulders. "It was my duty. In whatever other respect I fail, my duty as a citizen is paramount."

"Two years ago," said Walford slowly, "she had a predecessor, a girl who was subsequently found drowned." He paused, as though waiting for a response. "You heard me?"

Maurice sighed and nodded. "Yes, I heard you. It was a tragedy. I've never been so shocked in my life—never. I don't like even to think about it."

"The girl's name was Gwenda Milton." Walford spoke deliberately. "The sister of Henry Arthur Milton—otherwise known as—The Ringer!"

There was something in his tone which was significant. Meister looked at the Colonel strangely.

"The most brilliant criminal we have in our records—and the most dangerous."

Two spots of dull red came into the sallow face of the lawyer.

"And never caught. Colonel—never caught!" he almost shouted. "Although the police knew that he was passing through Paris—knew the time to a minute—he slipped through their fingers. All the clever policemen in England and all the clever policemen in Australia have never caught him."

He gained control of his voice; was his old urbane self in an instant.

"I'm not saying anything against the police. As a ratepayer, I am proud of them—but it wasn't clever to let him slip. I don't mind saying this to you because you're new to the business."

The Ringer

The Commissioner overlooked the implied insolence of this reference to his recent appointment.

"He should have been taken, I admit, " he said quietly. "But that is beside the point. The Ringer left his sister in your care. Whether he trusted you with his money I don't know—he trusted you with his sister. "

"I treated her well, " protested Meister. "Was it my fault that she died? Did I throw her into the river? Be reasonable. Colonel! "

"Why did she end her life? " asked Walford sternly.

"How should I know? I never dreamt that she was in any kind of trouble. As God is my judge! "

The Colonel checked him with a gesture. "And yet you made all the arrangements for her at the nursing home, " he said significantly.

Meister's face paled. "That's a lie! "

"It didn't come out at the inquest. Nobody knows but Scotland Yard and— Henry Arthur Milton! "

Maurice Meister smiled. "How can he know—he's dead. He died in Australia. "

There was a pause, and then Walford spoke.

"The Ringer is alive—he's here, " he said, and Meister came to his feet, white to the lips.

CHAPTER 25

MAURICE MEISTER faced the Assistant Commissioner with horror in his eyes.

"The Ringer here! Are you serious?"

The Commissioner nodded.

"I repeat—he's alive—he's here."

"That can't be true! He wouldn't dare come here with a death sentence hanging over him. The Ringer! You're trying to scare me—ha! ha!" He forced a laugh. "Your little joke, Colonel."

"He's here—I've sent for you to warn you."

"Why warn me?" demanded Meister. "I never saw him in my life, I don't even know what he looks like. I knew the girl he used to run around with an American girl. She was crazy about him. Where is she? Where she is, he is."

"She's in London. In this very building at this very moment!"

Meister's eyes opened wide.

"Here? The Ringer wouldn't dare do it!" And then, with sudden violence: "If you know he's in London, why don't you take him? The man's a madman. What are you for? To protect people—to protect me! Can't you get in touch with him? Can't you tell him that I knew nothing about his sister, that I looked after her and was like a father to her? Wembury, you know that I had nothing to do with this girl's death?"

He turned to Alan.

"I know nothing about it," said the detective coldly. "The only thing I know is that if anything happens to Mary Lenley, I'll—"

"Don't you threaten me!" stormed Meister.

The Ringer

"I don't know what women see in you, Meister! Your reputation is foul!"

Meister's lips were trembling. "Lies, more lies! They tear a man's character to rags, these scum! There have been women—naturally. We're men of the world. One isn't an anchorite. The Ringer!"—he forced a smile. "Pshaw! Somebody has been fooling you! Don't you think I should have heard? Not a bird moves in Deptford but I know it. Who has seen him?"

"Meister, I've warned you," said Walford seriously as he rang a bell. "From now on your house will be under our observation. Have bars put on your windows; don't admit anybody after dark and never leave the house by night except with a police escort."

Inspector Bliss came in at that moment.

"Oh, Bliss—I think Mr. Meister may need a little care taken of him—I put him in your charge. Watch over him like a father." The dark eyes of the detective fell upon the lawyer as he rose. "The day you take him I'll give a thousand pounds to the Police Orphanage," said Meister.

"We don't want money so badly as that. I think that is all. It is not my business to pass judgment on any man. It is a dangerous game that you are playing. Your profession gives you an advantage over other receivers—"

It was the one word above all others that Meister hated.

"Receiver! You hardly realise what you are saying."

"Indeed I do. Good morning."

Meister polished his hat on his sleeve as he walked to the door. "You will be sorry for that statement, Colonel. For my own part, I am unmoved by your hasty judgment." He looked at his watch. "Five minutes to one—"

He had left behind his walking stick. Bliss picked it up. The handle was loose, and with a twist he drew out a long steel blade. "Your swordstick, Mr. Meister—you seem to be looking after yourself pretty well," he said with an unholy grin.

The Ringer

Meister shot one baleful look at him as he went out of the room.

He scarcely remembered leaving the Chief Constable's office, but walked down the corridor and into the yard like a man in a dream. It was not possible. The Ringer back in London! All these stories at which he had scoffed were true. A terrible miracle had happened. Henry Arthur Milton was here, in this great city, might be this man or that... he found himself peering into the faces he met between the Yard and the sidewalk where his car was parked.

"Is anything wrong, Maurice?" asked Mary anxiously, as she came to meet him.

"Wrong?" His voice was thick, unnatural; the eyes had a queer, glazed expression. "Wrong? No, nothing is wrong—why? What can be wrong?"

All the time he was speaking, his head turned nervously left and right. Who was that man walking towards him, swinging a cane so light-heartedly? Might he not be The Ringer? And that pedlar, shuffling along with a tray of matches and studs before him, an unkempt, grimy, dirty-looking old man—it was such a disguise as The Ringer would love to adopt. Bliss? Where had he seen Bliss before? Somewhere... his voice, too, had a familiar sound. He racked his brains to recall. Even the chauffeur came under his terrified scrutiny: a burly man with a long upper lip and a snub nose. That could not be The Ringer...

"What is the matter, Maurice?"

He looked at her vacantly. "Oh, Mary!" he said. "Yes, of course, my dear, we ought to be getting home."

He stumbled past her into the car, dropped on to the padded seat with a little groan.

"Do you want to go back to Deptford, Maurice?"

"Yes—back to Deptford."

She gave instructions to the chauffeur and, entering the car after him, closed the door. "Was it something awful, Maurice?"

The Ringer

"No, my dear." He roused himself with a start. "Awful?... No, a lie, that's all! Tried to scare me... tried to scare Maurice Meister!" His laugh was thin and cracked and wholly unnatural. "They thought it would rattle me. You know what these police commissioners are... jumped up army officers who have been jobbed into a soft billet, and have to pretend they understand police work to keep it!" His face changed.

"That man Bliss was there—the fellow you told me about. I can't quite place him, Mary. Did your—did Wembury tell you anything about him?" She shook her head.

"No, Maurice, I only know what I told you."

"Bliss!" he muttered. "I've never seen a detective with a beard before. They used to wear them years ago: it was quite the ordinary thing, but nowadays they're clean—shaven... he comes from America, too. Did you see Hackitt?"

She nodded. "He came out about ten minutes before you and got on a tram."

He heaved a deep and troubled sigh. "I wish I'd seen him. I'd like to know what they asked him about. Of course I know now: they brought him there for an altogether different reason. They're sly, these fellows; you never know what they're after. The truth isn't in them!"

He was feeling in his pocket for the little cushion—shaped gold box, and Mary pretended not to see. She had guessed the nature of the stimulant which Maurice took at frequent intervals, and of late he had made no disguise of his weakness. He snuffled at a pinch of white, glittering powder, dusted his face with a handkerchief, and a few seconds later was laughing at himself—another man. She had often wondered at the efficacy of the drug, not realising that every week he had to increase the dose to produce the desired effect, and that one day he would be a cringing, crawling slave to the glittering white powder which he now regarded as his servant.

"Wembury threatened me, by gad!" His tone had changed: he was now his pompous self. "A wretched hireling police officer threatened me, an officer of the High Court of Justice!"

The Ringer

"Surely not, Maurice? Alan threatened you?" He nodded solemnly, and was about to tell her the nature of the threat when he thought better of it. Even in his present mood of exaltation he had no desire to raise the subject of Gwenda Milton.

"I took no notice, of course. One is used to dealing with that kind of creature. By the way, Mary, I have made inquiries and I've discovered that Johnny was not involved in the prison riot."

She was so grateful for this news, that she did not for one moment question its authenticity. Mary did not know that Scotland Yard was as ignorant of what happened in the prison as the Agricultural and Fisheries Board. But when he was under the influence of the drug, Maurice lied for the pleasure of lying: it was symptomatic of the disease.

"No, he was not in any way connected with the trouble. It was a man named—I forget the name, but it doesn't matter—who was the ringleader. And, my dear, I've been thinking over that burglary at your house." He half-turned to face her, the drug had transformed him: he was the old loquacious, debonair and carefree Meister she knew. "You can't stay any longer at Malpas Mansions. I will not allow it. Johnny would never forgive me if anything happened to you."

"But where can I go, Maurice?"

He smiled.

"You're coming to my house. I'll have that room put in order and the lights seen to. You can have a maid to look after you..."

She was shaking her head already. "That is impossible," she said quietly. "I am not at all nervous about the burglary, and I am quite sure that nobody intended harming me. I shall stay at Malpas Mansions, and if I get too nervous I shall go into lodgings."

"My dear Mary!" he expostulated.

"I'm determined on that, Maurice," she said, and he was a picture of resignation.

The Ringer

"As you wish. Naturally, I would not suggest that you should come to a bachelor's establishment without rearranging my household to the new conditions; but if you're set against honouring my little hovel, by all means do as you wish."

As they approached New Cross he woke from the reverie into which he had fallen and asked: "I wonder who is on the rack at this moment?"

She could not understand what he meant for a moment.

"You mean at Scotland Yard?"

He nodded. "I'd give a lot of money," he said slowly, "to know just what is happening in Room C 2 at this very second, and who is the unfortunate soul facing the inquisitors."

The Ringer

CHAPTER 26

DR. LOMOND could neither be described as an unfortunate soul, nor the genial Assistant Commissioner as an inquisitor. Colonel Walford for the moment was being very informative, and the old doctor listened, rolling one of his interminable cigarettes, and apparently not particularly interested in the recital.

Lomond was possessed of many agreeable qualities, and he had the dour humour of his race. Alert and quick—witted, he displayed the confidence and assurance of one who was so much master of his own particular subject that he could afford to mock himself and his science. His attitude towards the Commissioner was respectful only so far as it implied the deference due to an older man, but an equal.

He paused at the door.

"I'll not be in the way, will I? "

"Come along in, doctor, " smiled the Commissioner.

"Poor old Prideaux! " he shook his head sadly. "Man, it's on my conscience sending a man to be hanged in the suburbs! There was a dignity about Newgate and an historical value to being hanged at Tyburn. I wish I didn't know so much about criminology. Have ye ever noticed Wembury's ears, sir? He exhibited these appendages of the embarrassed Wembury in the manner of a showman. A tee—pical criminal ear! In conjunction with the prognathic process of the jaw suggests a rabid homicide! Have ye ever committed a murder? "

"Not yet, " growled Alan.

Lomond finished rolling his cigarette, and the Commissioner, who had been waiting patiently for this operation to be concluded, spoke: "I wanted to have a little chat with you, doctor. "

"About a woman, " said Lomond, without looking up.

"How the devil did you guess that? " asked the surprised Walford.

The Ringer

"I didn't guess; I knew. You see, you're a broadcaster—most people are. And I'm terribly receptive. Telepathic. It's one of the animal things left in me."

Bliss was watching, his lips lifted in derision.

"Animal?" he growled. "I always thought telepathy was one of the signs of intellect. That's what they say in America."

"They say so many things in America that they don't mean. Telepathy is just animal instinct which has been smothered under reason. What would you have me do for the lady?"

"I want you to find out something about her husband," said Walford, and the doctor's eyes twinkled.

"Would she know? Do wives know anything about their husbands?"

"I'm not so sure that he is her husband," said Bliss.

The old man chuckled.

"Ah! Then she would! She'd know fine if he was somebody else's husband. Who is she?"

The Commissioner turned to Wembury.

"What is her real name?"

"Cora Ann Milton—she was born Cora Ann Barford."

Lomond looked up suddenly.

"Barford—Cora Ann? Cora Ann! That's a coincidence!"

"Why?"

"I was hearing a lot about a Cora Ann, a few months ago," said the doctor, lighting his limp cigarette.

The Ringer

"You don't want me, sir?" said Bliss. "I've got some real work to do!" He walked to the door. "Doctor, here's a job after your own heart. A man with your wisdom ought to catch him in a week."

"I ignore that," said the doctor, smoking placidly, and the sound of his chuckle pursued Bliss down the corridor.

And now Lomond was to hear the police story of The Ringer. The Commissioner opened a dossier.

"The history of this man is a most peculiar one, and will interest you as an anthropologist. In the first place, he has never been in our hands. The man is an assassin. So far as we know, he has never gained a penny by any of the murders of which we suspect him. We know almost for certain that during the war he was an officer in the Flying Corps—a solitary man with only one friend, a lad who was afterwards shot on an ill-founded charge of cowardice made by his colonel—Chafferis—Wisman. Three months after the war ended Chafferis—Wisman was killed. We suspect, indeed we are certain, the murderer was The Ringer, who had disappeared immediately after the Armistice was signed—didn't even wait to draw his gratuity."

"He was no Scotsman," interjected Lomond.

"He had refused the D. S.O.—every decoration that was offered to him," Walford went on. "He was never photographed in any of the regimental groups. We have only one drawing of him, made by a steward on a boat plying between Seattle and Vancouver. It was on this boat that Milton was married."

"Married?"

Walford explained.

"There was a girl on the ship, a fugitive from American justice; she had shot a man who had insulted her in some low—down dance hall in Seattle. She must have confided in Milton that she would be arrested on her arrival in Vancouver, for he persuaded a parson on board to marry them. She became a British subject and defeated the extradition law," he continued. "It was a foolish, quixotic thing to do."

The Ringer

Lomond's eyes twinkled.

"Ah, then, he must be a Scotsman. He's really a terror, eh? "

"If people knew this man was in England, there would be trouble, " said the Colonel. "He certainly killed old Oberzhon, who ran a South American agency of a very unpleasant character. He killed Attaman, the moneylender. Meister, by the way, was in the house when the murder was committed. There has been method in every killing. He left his sister in Meister's charge when he had to fly the country over the Attaman affair. He did not know that Meister was giving us information about his movements. And, of course, Meister being the brute he is... " He shrugged.

"The Ringer knows? " Lomond moved his chair nearer to the desk. "Come that's interesting. "

"We know he was in Australia eight months ago. Our information is that he is now in England—and if he is, he has come back with only one object: to settle with Meister in his own peculiar way. Meister was his solicitor—he was always running around with Gwenda Milton. "

"You say you have a picture of him? "

The Commissioner handed a pencil sketch to Lomond, and the doctor gasped.

"You're joking—why—I know this man! "

"What! " incredulously.

"I know his funny little beard, emaciated face, rather nice eyes— good Lord! "

"You know him—surely not? " said Wembury.

"I don't say I know him, but I have met him. "

"Where—in London? "

Lomond shook his head.

The Ringer

"No. I met this fellow in Port Said about eight months ago. I stepped off there on my way back from Bombay. I was staying at one of the hotels, when I heard that there was a poor European who was very sick in some filthy caravanserai in the native quarter. Naturally I went over and saw him—the type of creature who pigs with natives interests me. And there I found a very sick man; in fact, I thought he was going to peg out. " He tapped the picture. "And it was this gentleman! "

"Are you certain? " asked Walford.

"No man with a scientific mind can be certain of anything. He had come ashore from an Australian ship—"

"That's our man, sir! " exclaimed Wembury.

"Did he recover? "

"I don't know. " Lomond was dubious. "He was delirious when I saw him. That is where I heard the names 'Cora Ann'. I saw him twice. The third time I called, the old lady who ran the show told me that he had wandered out in the night—the Lord knows what happened to him; probably he fell into the Suez Canal and was poisoned. Would he be The Ringer? No, it's not possible! "

The Commissioner looked at the sketch again.

"It almost seems like it. I've an idea that he is not dead. Now you may be useful, doctor. If there is one person who knows where The Ringer is to be found, it is Mrs. Milton. "

"Cora Ann. Yes? "

"Doctor, I was more than impressed by your examination of Prideaux. I want you to try your hand on this woman. Bring her up, inspector. "

When the door closed on Wembury he drew another paper from the folder. "Here are the ascertainable facts about her movements. She returned to this country on a British passport three weeks ago. She is staying at the Marlton. "

The Ringer

Lomond adjusted his glasses and read. "She came overland from Genoa— British passport, you say. Is she—er—married?"

"Oh, there's no doubt about that; he married her on the boat, but they were only a week together."

"A week? Ah, then she may still be in love with him," said the cynical Lomond. "If my Egyptian friend is The Ringer, I know quite a lot about this woman. He was rather talkative in his delirium, and I'm beginning to remember some of the things he told me. Now, let me think! Cora Ann... " He turned suddenly. "Orchids!... I've got it!"

CHAPTER 27

IT was at that moment that Cora Ann was ushered in. She was brightly and expensively dressed, and for a moment she stood looking from one to the other, poising the cigarette she held between her gloved fingers.

"Good morning, Mrs. Milton. " The Commissioner rose. "I asked you to come because I rather wanted my friend here to have a little talk with you. "

Cora scarcely looked at the shabby doctor: her attention was for the moment concentrated on the military—looking Commissioner.

"Why, isn't that nice! " she drawled. "I'm just crazy to talk to somebody. " She smiled round at Wembury. "What's the best show in London, anyway? I've seen most of 'em in New York, but it was such a long time ago—"

"The best show in London, Mrs. Milton, " said Lomond, "is Scotland Yard! Melodrama without music, and you are the leading lady. "

She looked at him for the first time.

"Isn't that cute! What am I leading? " she asked.

"Me, for the moment, " said the cheerful Scot. "You haven't seen much of London lately, Mrs. Milton—it is Mrs. Milton, isn't it? "

She nodded.

"You've been abroad, haven't you? "

"I certainly have—all abroad! " she replied slowly.

Lomond's voice was very bland. "And how did you leave your husband? " he asked.

She was not smiling now. "Say, Wembury, who is this fellow? " she demanded.

"Doctor Lomond, police surgeon, 'R' division. "

The Ringer

The news was reassuring. There was a note of amusement in her voice when she replied. "You don't say? Why, you know, doctor, that I haven't seen my husband in years, and I'll never see him again. I thought everybody had read that in the newspapers. Poor Arthur was drowned in Sydney Harbour."

Dr. Lomond's lips twitched and he nodded at the gaily attired girl. "Really? I noticed that you were in mourning."

She was baffled: something of her self—confidence left her. "Why, that's not the line of talk I like," she said.

"It's the only line of talk I have." He was smiling now. "Mrs. Milton, to revert to a very painful subject—"

"If it hurts you, don't talk about it."

"Your husband left this country hurriedly three"—he turned to Wembury— "or was it four years ago. When did you see him last?"

Cora Ann was coolness itself. She did not answer the question. Here was a man not to be despised. A crafty, shrewd man of affairs, knowledge in the deeps of his grey—blue twinkling eyes.

"You were in Sydney three months after he reached there," Lomond continued, consulting the paper which Walford had given him. "You called yourself Mrs. Jackson, and you registered at the Harbour Hotel. You had suite No. 36, and whilst you were there you were in communication with your husband."

The corners of her mouth twisted in a smile. Cora's sarcasm was a tantalising thing.

"Isn't that clever! Suite No. 36 and everything! Just like a real little sleuth!" Then, deliberately: "I never saw him, I tell you."

But Lomond was not to be put off.

"You never saw him, I guess that. He telephoned. You asked him to meet you—or didn't you? I'm not quite sure." He paused, but Cora Ann did not answer. "You don't want to tell me, eh? He was scared that there was somebody trailing you—scared that you might lead the police to him."

The Ringer

"Scared!" she repeated scornfully. "Where did you get that word? Nothing would scare Arthur Milton—anyway, he's dead!"

"And now has nothing to be scared about—if he was a Presbyterian," said Lomond—it was Lomond at his pawkiest. "Let's bring him to life, shall we?" He snapped his fingers. "Come up, Henry Arthur Milton, who left Melbourne on the steamship Themistocles on the anniversary of his wedding—and left with another woman."

Up to this moment Cora Ann had remained cool, but at the mention of the name of the ship she stiffened, and at his last words she came to her feet in a fury.

"That's a lie! There never was another woman." Recovering herself, she laughed. "Aw, listen! You put a raw one over there! I'm a fool to get sore with you! I don't know anything, that's all. You've got nothing on me—I needn't answer a single question. I know the law; there's no third degree in England, don't forget it. I'm going."

She moved towards the door, Wembury waiting to open it, his hand upon the knob.

"Open the door for Mrs. Milton," said Lomond, and added innocently: "It is Mrs. Milton, isn't it?"

She flung round at this. "What do you mean?"

"I thought it might be one of those artistic marriages that are so popular with the leisured classes," suggested Lomond, and she walked slowly back to him.

"You may be a hell of a big doctor," she said, a little breathlessly, "but your diagnosis is all wrong!"

"Really—married and everything?" Scepticism was in his voice.

She nodded. "First on the ship by a parson, and that's legal, and then at St. Paul's Church, Deptford, to make sure. Deptford is a kind of home town to me. Next to an ash—pit I don't know any place I'd hate worse to be found dead in. Folks over home talk about Limehouse and Whitechapel— they're garden cities compared with that hell—shoot! But I was married there by a real reverend

The Ringer

gentleman. There was nothing artistic about it— except my trousseau! "

"Married, eh? " The old Scot's voice spoke his doubts. "Liars and married men have very short memories—he forgot to send you your favourite orchids. "

She turned suddenly in a cold fury—a fury which had grown out of her increasing fear of this old man.

"What do you mean? " she asked again.

"He always sent you orchids on the anniversary of your wedding, " said Lomond carefully, and never once did his eyes leave hers. "Even when he was hiding in Australia, he in one town, you in another—when he was being watched for, and you were shadowed, he sent you flowers. But this year he didn't. I suppose he forgot, or possibly he had other use for orchids? "

She came nearer to him, almost incoherent in her rage.

"You think so! " She almost spat the words. "That's the kind of thought a man like you would have! Can't get that bug out of your head, can you? Another woman! Arthur thought of nobody but me—the only thing that hurt him was that I couldn't be with him. That's what! He risked everything just to see me—just to see me. I must have met him on Collins Street but didn't know him—he took the chance of the gallows just to stand there and see me pass. "

"And well worth the risk. So he was in Melbourne when you were there— but he did not send you your orchids? "

She flung out her hand impatiently.

"Orchids! What do I want with orchids? I knew when they didn't come—" She stopped suddenly.

"That he had left Australia, " accused Lomond. "That is why you came away in such a hurry. I'm beginning to believe that you are in love with him! "

"Was I? " she laughed. "I kind of like him, " Cora took up her bag. "Well, that is about all, I guess. " She nodded to the Colonel and walked a step nearer the door. "You're not going to arrest me or anything?"

"You are at liberty to go out, when you wish, Mrs. Milton," said Walford.

"Fine!" said Cora Ann, and made a little curtsy. "Good morning, everybody."

"Love is blind." The hateful voice of the inquisitor arrested her. "You met him and didn't recognise him! You want us to believe that he was so well disguised that he could venture abroad in Collins Street in daylight—oh no, Cora Ann, that won't do!"

She was very near the end of her control. Rage shook her as she turned back to her tormentor.

"On Collins Street? He'd walk on Regent Street—in daylight or moonlight. Dare? If he felt that way, he'd come right here to Scotland Yard—into the lions' den, and never turn a hair. That's the fool thing he would do. You could guard every entrance and he'd get in and get out! You laugh—laugh, go on, laugh, but he'd do it—he'd do it—"

Bliss had come into the room.

Looking past the doctor, she might see him. Alan Wembury did not follow the direction of her eyes—only he saw her face go white, saw her sway and caught her in his arms as she fell.

The Ringer

CHAPTER 28

No woman is wholly saint, or, in this enlightened age, innocent of the evil which rubs elbows with men and women alike in everyday life. Mary Lenley had passed through all the stages of understanding where Maurice Meister was concerned, beginning with the absolute trust which was a legacy of her childhood, and progressing by a series of minor shocks to a clearer appreciation of the man as he really was, and not as she, in her childish enthusiasm, had pictured him. And with this understanding ran a nice balance of judgment. She was neither horrified nor distressed when there dawned upon her mind the true significance of Gwenda Milton's fate. Nobody spoke to her plainly of that unhappy girl. She had perforce to piece together from extrinsic evidence, the scraps of information so grudgingly given, and fill in the gaps from her imagination.

It was a curious fact that she did not regard herself as being in any danger from Maurice. They had been such good friends; their earlier relationships had been so peculiarly intimate that never once did she suspect that the pulse of Maurice Meister quickened at the sight of her. His offer to place the suite upstairs at her disposal, she had regarded merely as an act of kindness on his part, which, had it been considered, he would have made, and her own refusal was largely based upon her love of independence and a distaste for accepting a hospitality which might prove irksome, and in the end, unworkable. Behind it all, was the instinctive dislike of the woman to place herself under too deep an obligation to a man. Two days after the interview at Scotland Yard, she came one morning to find the house filled with workmen who were fitting a new sash to the large window overlooking the leads.

"Putting some bars up at the window, miss, " said one of the workmen. "I hope we're not going to make too much noise for you. "

Mary smiled. "If you do I'll take my work into another room, " she said.

Why bars at the window? The neighbourhood was an unsavoury one, but never once had Mr. Meister been subjected to the indignity of harbouring an uninvited guest in the shape of a burglar. There was precious little to lose, so far as she could see, though Mr.

Meister's silver was of the finest. Hackitt was never tired of talking about the silver; it fascinated him.

"Every time I polish that milk jug, miss, I get nine months, " her told her, and the mention of imprisonment brought her mind back to Scotland Yard.

"Yes, miss, " said Sam, "I saw the Chief Commissioner—it's funny how these coppers can never find anything out, without applying to us lags! "

"What did he want to see you about, Hackitt? "

"Well, miss"—Sam hesitated—"it was about a friend of mine, a gentleman I used to know. "

He would tell her nothing but this. She was intrigued. She asked Meister at the first opportunity what the ex—convict had meant, and he also evaded the question.

"It would be wise, my dear, if you did not discuss anything with Hackitt, " he said. "The man is a liar and wholly unscrupulous. There's nothing he wouldn't say to make a little bit of a scare. Have you heard from Johnny? "

She shook her head. A letter had been due that morning but it had not arrived, and she was unaccountably disappointed. "Why are you putting these bars up, Maurice? "

"To keep out bad characters, " he said flippantly. "I prefer that they should come through the door. "

The little jest amused him. His general manner suggested that he had had recourse to his old system of stimulation.

"It's terribly lonely here at night, " he went on. "I wonder if you realise how lonely a man I am, Mary? "

"Why don't you go out more? " she suggested.

He shook his head.

The Ringer

"That is the one thing I don't want to do—just now, " he answered. "I wouldn't mind so much if I could get somebody to stay later. In fact, my dear Mary, I won't beat about the bush, but I should be very greatly obliged to you if you would spend a few of your evenings here. "

He probably anticipated the answer he received.

"I'm sorry, Maurice, but I don't wish to, " she said. "That sounds very ungrateful, I know, after all you have done for me, but can't you see how impossible it is? "

He was looking at her steadily from under his lowered lids, and apparently did not accept her refusal in the light of a rebuff.

"Won't you come to supper one night and try me? I will play you the most gorgeous sonata that composer ever dreamt! It bores me to play to myself, " he went on, forestalling her reply. "Don't you think you could be very sociable and come up one evening? "

There was really no reason why she should not, and she hesitated.

"I'll think about it, " she said.

That afternoon an unusual case came to Mr. Meister, the case of a drunken motorist who was arrested whilst he was driving a car, and she was preparing to go home that night when Mr. Meister came hurrying in from a visit to the unfortunate.

"Don't go yet, Mary, " he said. "I have a letter I want to write to Dr. Lomond about this wretched prisoner. Lomond has certified him as being drunk, but I am getting his own doctor down, and I want this old Scotsman to be present at the examination. "

He dictated the letter, which she typed and brought to him for his signature.

"How can I get this to Lomond's house? " he asked, and looked up at her. "I wonder if you would mind taking it? It is on your way—he has lodgings in Shardeloes Road. "

The Ringer

"I'll take it with pleasure," said Mary with a smile. "I am anxious to meet the doctor again."

"Again? When did you see him last?" he asked quickly.

She told him of the little conversation they had had outside Scotland Yard. Meister pinched his lip.

"He's a shrewd old devil," he said thoughtfully. "I'm not so sure that he hasn't more brains than the whole of Scotland Yard together. Give him your brightest smile, Mary: I particularly want to get this man off a very serious charge. He is a very rich stockbroker who lives at Blackheath."

Mary wondered, as she left the house, what effect her bright smile might have in altering the diagnosis the doctor had made; she very rightly surmised that the police surgeon was not the type of man who was susceptible to outside influence.

Dr. Lomond's rooms were in a dull little house in a rather dull little road, and the landlady who answered her knock seemed to have taken complete control of the doctor's well—being.

"He's only just come in, miss, and I don't think he'll see you."

But Mary insisted, giving her name, and the woman went away, to return immediately to usher her into a very Victorian parlour, where, on the most uncomfortable of horsehair chairs, sat the doctor, an open book on his knees and a pair of steel—rimmed pince—nez gripped to the end of his nose.

"Well, well, my dear," he said, as he closed the book and came cautiously to his feet. "What is your trouble?"

She handed him the letter and he opened it and read, keeping up a long string of comment in an undertone, which she supposed was not intended to reach her.

"Ah... from Meister... the slimy scoundrel... About the drunk... I thought so! Drunk he was and drunk he is, and all the great doctors of Harley Street will no' make him sober... Verra well, verra well!"

The Ringer

He folded the letter, put it in his pocket and beamed over his glasses at the girl.

"He's made a messenger of ye, has he? Will ye no' sit down. Miss Lenley? "

"Thank you, doctor, " she said, "I am due at my flat in a few minutes. "

"Are ye now? And ye'd be a wise young leddy if ye remained in your flat. "

What made her tell the doctor, she did not know: before she realised what she was saying, she was halfway through the story of her burglary.

"Inspector Bliss? " he mused. "He was the man—yes, I heard of it. Alan Wembury told me. That's a nice boy, Miss Lenley, " he added, looking at her shrewdly. "I'll tell you something. You wonder why Bliss went into your flat? I don't know, I can't tell you with any accuracy, but I'm a psychologist, and I balance sane probabilities against eccentric impulses. That's Greek to you and almost Greek to me too, Miss Lenley. Bliss went into your room because he thought you had something that he wanted very much, and when a police officer wants something very much, he takes unusual risks. You missed nothing? "

She shook her head.

"Nothing except a letter which didn't belong to me. It was left in my place by Mrs. Milton. I found it and put it in the drawer. That was the only thing taken. "

He rubbed his stubbly chin.

"Would Inspector Bliss know it was there? And if he knew it was there, would he think it worth while risking his neck to get it? And if he got it, what would he discover? "

Lomond shook his head.

"It's a queer little mystery which you've got all to yourself, young leddy. "

The Ringer

He walked out into the passage with her and stood in his carpeted feet on the top step, waving her farewell, a limp cigarette drooping from under the white moustache.

The Ringer

CHAPTER 29

ONE unpleasant change had come over Maurice Meister since his visit to Scotland Yard: he was drinking heavily, the brandy bottle was never far away from his table. He looked old and ill in the mornings; did what he had never done before—wandered into his big room soon after breakfast, and, sitting down at the piano, played for hours on end, to her great distraction. Yet he played beautifully, with the touch of a master and the interpretation of one inspired. Sometimes she thought that the more dazed he was, the better he played. He used to sit at the piano, his eyes staring into vacancy, apparently seeing and hearing nothing. Hackitt used to come into the room and watch him with a contemptuous grin, speaking to him sometimes, well assured that the mind of Meister was a million years away. Even Mary had to wait by him patiently for long periods before she could obtain any intelligible answer to her questions.

He was afraid of things, jumped at the slightest sound, was reduced to a quivering panic by an unexpected knock on his door. Hackitt, who was sleeping in the house, had dark stories to hint at as to what happened in the night. Once he came and found Maurice's table littered with brandy bottles, all empty save one. Two days after the workmen had left the house, Alan Wembury, dozing in the charge room at Flanders Lane, waiting for the arrival of a prisoner whom he had sent his men to "pull in", heard the telephone bell ring and the exchange between the desk sergeant and somebody at the other end of the line.

"For you, Mr. Wembury, " said the sergeant, and Alan, shaking himself awake, took the instrument from his subordinate's hand.

It was Hackitt at the other end, and his voice was shrill with apprehension.

"... I don't know what's the matter with him. He's been raisin' hell since three o'clock this morning. Can't you bring a doctor along to see him, Mr. Wembury? "

"What is the matter with him? " asked Alan.

The scared man at the other end would not vouchsafe an opinion.

"I don't know—he's locked up in his bedroom and he's been shoutin' an' screamin' like a lunatic."

"I'll come along," said Alan, and hung up the 'phone, as Dr. Lomond appeared from the cells.

This was the second time he had been called that night to deal with a case of delirium, and his presence at the police station at that hour of the morning was very providential. In a few words Alan retailed Hackitt's report.

"Drink it may be, dope it certainly is," said Dr. Lomond, pulling on his cotton gloves deliberately. "I'll go along with ye. Maybe I'll save an inquest!"

But Alan was half—way out of the station—house by now, and Dr. Lomond had to run to overtake him.

In a quarter of an hour Wembury was pressing the bell in the black door. It was opened immediately by Hackitt, dressed in shirt and trousers, his teeth chattering, a look of genuine concern on his face.

"This is a new stunt, isn't it, Sam?" asked Wembury sternly. "Ringing up the police station for the divisional surgeon? Why didn't you send for Meister's own doctor?"

Hackitt thought that this was a foolish question but did not say so.

"I didn't know who his doctor was, and he's been shouting blue murder—I didn't know what to do with him."

"I'll step up and see him," said Lomond. "Where is his room?"

Going to a door, Sam opened it.

"Up here, sir."

Lomond looked up and presently the sound of his footsteps treading the stairs grew fainter. "You were afraid you'd be suspected if he died, eh?" asked Wembury. "That's the worst of having a bad record, Hackitt."

The Ringer

He picked up a silver salver from the table—Meister had surprisingly good silver. Sam was an interested spectator.

"That's heavy, ain't it?" said Sam with professional interest. "That'd sell well. What would I get for that?"

"About three years," said Alan coldly, and Mr. Hackitt closed his eyes.

Presently he remembered that he had a communication to make. "'Ere, Mr. Wembury, what's Bliss doin' on your manor?" [Manor = district. E.W.]

"Bliss? Are you sure, Sam?"

"I couldn't make any mistake about a mug like that," said Sam. "He's been hanging about since I've been here."

"Why?"

"I don't know," confessed the ex—convict. "I found him hiding upstairs yesterday."

"Mr. Bliss?" To say that Wembury was surprised is to describe his emotions mildly.

"I said to him 'What are you doin' up here?'" said Sam impressively.

Wembury shook his head. "You're lying," he said.

"All right," retorted the disgusted Sam. "All you fellers hang together."

The feet of Lomond sounded on the stairs, and presently he came in.

"Is he all right, doctor?" asked Wembury.

"Meister? O, Lord, yes. What a lad! Meister? Good old English family that. Nearly came over with the Conqueror—only the Conqueror lost the war."

Lomond smelt at the decanter that was on the table, and Wembury nodded. "That's the poison that is killing him."

The Ringer

Lomond sniffed again. "It's no' poison, it's Scotch! It's the best way of poisoning yourself I know. No! "—he took a pinch of snuff from an imaginary box. "Cocaine, Wembury—that's the stuff that's settling Meister."

He looked round the room. "This is a queer kind of office, Wembury."

"Yes, " said Alan soberly, "and some queer things have happened in this room, I should imagine. Have they put the window bars in? " he asked, addressing Sam, and the man nodded.

"Yes, sir. What are they for? "

"To keep The Ringer out! "

Sam Hackitt's face was a study. "The Ringer! " he gasped. "That's what they're for? Here! I'm through with this job! I wondered why he had the bars put in and why he wanted me to sleep on the premises."

"Oh—you're afraid of The Ringer, are you? " Lomond asked, interested, and Wembury intervened.

"Don't be a fool, Hackitt. They're all scared of The Ringer."

"I wouldn't stay here at nights for a hundred thousand rounds, " said Sam fervently, and the doctor sniffed.

"It seems a fearful lot of money for a very doubtful service, " was his dry comment. "I'd like you to go away for a while, Mr. Hackitt."

He himself closed the door on the perturbed Sam.

"Come up and look at Meister, " he said, and Alan followed the slow-moving doctor up the stairs.

"He's alive all right, " said Lomond, standing in the doorway.

Meister lay on his tumbled bed, breathing stertorously, his face purple, his hands clutching at the silken coverlet.

The Ringer

A commonplace sordid ending to what promised to be high tragedy, thought Alan.

And at that moment something gripped his heart, as though an instinctive voice whispered tremendously that in this end to his first scare was the beginning of the drama which would involve not only Maurice Meister, but the girl who was to him something more than the little carriage child who passed and who swung on the gate of his father's cottage, something more than the sister of the man he had arrested, something more than he dared confess to himself.

CHAPTER 30

ONCE or twice during the hour of strenuous work which followed, he heard Sam Hackitt's stealthy feet on the stairs, and once caught a glimpse of him as he disappeared in a hurry. When he came down it was nearly seven o'clock. Sam, very businesslike in his green baize apron, with a pail of water and a wash—leather in his hand, was industriously cleaning the windows, somewhat hampered by the bars.

"How is he, sir? " he asked.

Alan did not reply. He was at the mysterious door, the bolted door that was never opened and led to nowhere.

"Where does this door lead? "

Sam Hackitt shook his head. It was a question that had puzzled him, and he had promised himself the pleasure of an Inspection the first time he was left alone in the house.

"I don't know, I've never seen it open. Maybe it's where he keeps his money. That fellow must be worth millions, Wembury. "

Alan pulled up the bolts, and tried the door again. It was locked, and he looked round. "Is there a key to this? "

Sam hesitated. He had the thief's natural desire to appear in the light of a fool.

"Yes, there is a key, " he said at last, his anxiety for information overcoming his inclination towards a reputation for innocence. "It's hanging up over the mantelpiece. I happen to know because—"

"Because you've tried it, " said Alan, and Sam protested so violently that he guessed that whatever plan he may have formed had not yet been put into execution.

Alan walked to the door leading to the room above and listened: he thought he heard Meister talking. By the time Lomond returned, Alan Wembury was growing a little weary of a vigil which he knew

The Ringer

was unnecessary. If he had admitted the truth to himself, he was waiting to see Mary Lenley.

Lomond worried him a little. This enthusiastic amateur in crime detection seemed to have come under the fascinating influence of Cora Ann. He had seen them together twice and had remonstrated.

"She's a dangerous woman, doctor."

"And I'm a fearfully dangerous man," said Lomond. "I like her—I'm sorry for the poor wee thing. That is my pet vice—being sorry for women."

"Mind that you aren't sorry for yourself some day!" said Wembury quietly, and the doctor chuckled.

"Eh? What is that? A warning to young lads?" he asked, and changed the subject.

Wembury was standing outside the house when the police surgeon returned.

"I'll go up and see this poor laddie," he said sardonically. "Are ye waiting for somebody?"

"Yes—no. I'm waiting for one of my men," said Alan, and the doctor grinned to himself—he had at last succeeded in making a police officer blush.

Meister was dozing when he looked in at him, and he came downstairs to inspect again the room which was both office and drawing-room of Meister's establishment.

Sam came in and watched the doctor's inspection with interest.

"I saw Wembury outside," he said, with the easy familiarity of his class. "I suppose he's waiting to see Miss Lenley."

The doctor looked round.

"Who is Miss Lenley?"

The Ringer

"Oh, she's the typewriter, " said Sam, and the doctor's eyebrows rose.

"Typewriter? They have a sex, have they? What a pretty idea! " He lifted the cover of the machine. "What's that one—male or female? "

"I'm talking about the young lady, sir—the lady who works it, " said the patient Sam.

"Oh, the typist? Who is she? " Lomond was interested. "Oh, yes! She's the sister of the man in prison, isn't she? "

"Yes, sir—Johnny Lenley. Got three for pinchin' a pearl necklace. "

"A thief, eh? " He walked over to the piano and opened it.

"A gentleman thief, " explained Sam.

"Does she play this? " The doctor struck a key softly.

"No, sir—him. "

"Meister? " Lomond frowned. "Oh, so I've heard! "

"When he's all dopy, " explained Sam. "Can't hear nothing! Can't see nothing. He gives me the creeps sometimes. "

"Musical. That's bad. "

"He plays all right, " said Sam with fine contempt for the classics. "I like a bit of music myself, but the things he plays—" He gave a horrible imitation of Chopin's Nocturne—"Lummy, gives you the fair hump! "

The front door bell called the ex—convict from the room, and Dr. Lomond, sitting on the piano stool, his hands thrust into his pockets, continued his survey of the room. And as he looked, a curious thing happened. Above the door, concealed in the architrave, the red light suddenly glowed. It was a signal—from whom? What was its significance? Even as he stared, the light went out. Lomond went on tiptoes to the door and listened. He could hear nothing.

Just then Hackitt returned with half—a—dozen letters in his hand.

The Ringer

"The post—" he began, and then suddenly saw Lomond's face.

"Hackitt," asked the doctor softly, "who else is in this house beside you and Meister?"

He looked at him suspiciously. "Nobody. The old cook's ill."

"Who gets Meister's breakfast?"

"I do," nodded Sam; "a biscuit and a corkscrew!"

Lomond looked up at the ceiling. "What's above here?"

"The lumber—room." Hackitt's uneasiness was increasing. "What's up, doctor?"

Lomond shook his head. "I thought—no, nothing."

"Here! You ain't half putting the wind up me! Do you want to see the lumber room, doctor?"

Lomond nodded and followed the man up the stairs, past Meister's room to a dingy apartment stacked with old furniture. He was hardly out of the room when Wembury came in with Mary Lenley.

"You're getting me a bad name, Alan," she smiled. "I suppose I shouldn't call you Alan when you are on duty? I ought to call you Inspector Wembury."

"I'd be sorry if you didn't call me Alan. Now it does require an effort to call you Mary. Never forget that I was brought up to call you Miss Mary and take off my cap to your father!"

Mary sighed.

"Isn't it odd—everything?"

"Yes—it's queer." He watched her as she took off coat and hat. "People wouldn't believe it if you put it in a book. The Lenleys of Lenley Court, and the Wemburys of the gardener's cottage!"

She laughed aloud at this.

The Ringer

"Don't be stupid. Heavens, what a lot of letters!"

There was only one which interested her: it was addressed in pencil in Maurice Meister's neat hand. Evidently its contents were of such engrossing interest that she forgot Alan Wembury's presence. He saw the colour surge to her pale cheek and a new light come to her eyes, and his heart sank. He could not know that Meister had repeated his invitation to supper and that the flush on Mary's cheek was one of anger.

"Mary," he said for the second time, "are you listening?"

She looked up from the letter she was reading.

"Yes."

How should he warn her? All that morning he had been turning over in his mind this most vital of problems.

"Are you all right here?" he asked awkwardly.

"What do you mean?" she asked.

"I mean—well, Meister hasn't the best of reputations. Does your brother know you're working here?"

She shook her head and a shadow came to her face. "No—I didn't want to worry him. Johnny is so funny sometimes, even in his letters."

Alan drew a long breath. "Mary, you know where I am to be found?"

"Yes, Alan, you told me that before." She was surprised.

"Well—er—well, you never know what little problems and difficulties you may have. I want you—I'd like you to—well, I'd rather like to feel that if anything unpleasant occurred—" He floundered on, almost incoherently.

"Unpleasant?" Did he guess, she wondered? She was panic stricken at the thought.

The Ringer

"And you were—well, distressed, " he went on desperately, "you know what I mean? Well, if anybody—how shall I put it?... If anybody annoyed you, I'd like you to come to me. Will you? "

Her lips twitched. "Alan! You're being sentimental! "

"I'm sorry. "

As he reached the door she called him by name. "You're rather a dear, aren't you? " she said gently.

"No, I think I'm a damned fool! " said Alan gruffly, and slammed the door behind him.

She stood by the table thinking; she had a vague uneasiness that all was not well; that behind the habitual niceness of Maurice Meister was something sinister, something evil. If Johnny was only free— Johnny, who would have sacrificed his life for her.

CHAPTER 31

THERE was a way into Meister's house which was known to three people, and one of these, Maurice hoped, was dead. The second was undoubtedly in prison, for John Lenley had surprised the lawyer's secret. Meister's grounds had at one time extended to the bank of a muddy creek, and even now, there was a small ramshackle warehouse standing in a patch of weed-grown grass that was part of Meister's demesne, although it was separated from the house in Flanders Road by a huddle of slum dwellings and crooked passage—ways.

That morning there walked along the canal bank a young man, who stopped opposite the factory, and, looking round to see if he was observed, inserted a key in the weather—beaten door and passed into the rank ground. In one corner was a tiny brick dwelling which looked like a magazine, and the same key that had opened the outer gate opened the door of this, and the stranger slipped inside and locked the door after him before he began to go down a winding staircase that had a been put there in recent years.

At the bottom of the stairs was a brick—vaulted passage, high enough for a short man to walk without discomfort, but not sufficiently elevated to admit the stranger's progress without his stooping. The floor was unlittered, and although there were no lights the newcomer searched a little niche half a dozen steps up the passage and found there the four electric torches which Meister kept there for his own use. The passage had recently been swept by the lawyer's own hands.

He expected that very soon a delicious visitor would pass that way, escaping the observation of the men who guarded the house, and he himself had conducted Mary Lenley through the passage which held none of the terrors that are usually associated with such subterranean ways.

The stranger walked on, flashing his light ahead of him. After three minutes' walk the passage turned abruptly to the left, and finally it terminated in what had the appearance of a cellar, from which there led upward a flight of carpeted steps. The stranger went cautiously and noiselessly up these stairs. Half—way up he felt the tread give and grinned. It was, he knew, a pneumatic arrangement by which a

The Ringer

warning lamp was lit in Meister's room. He wondered who was with him now, and whether his forgetfulness of the signal embarrassed the lawyer.

He came to a long panel and listened. He could hear voices: Meister's and—Mary Lenley's. He frowned. Mary here? He thought she had given up the work. Bending his ear close to the panel, he listened.

"... my dear, " Meister was saying, "you're exquisite—adorable. To see your fingers move over that shabby old typewriter's keys is like watching a butterfly flit from flower to flower. "

"How absurd you are, Maurice! " said Mary. Then came the slow sound of music as Meister sat at the piano. Mary's voice again, and the sound of a little struggle.

Meister caught her by the shoulders and was drawing her to him when, staring past her, he saw a hand come round the corner of the door.

He only saw this and in another second, with a scream of terror, Meister had flown from the room, leaving the girl alone.

She stood rooted to the spot terror—stricken. Farther and farther along the wall crept the hand and then the panel swung open and a young man stepped into the room.

"Johnny! "

In another instant, Mary Lenley was sobbing in the arms of her brother.

CHAPTER 32

It was Johnny Lenley!

"Darling—why didn't you tell me you were coming back?... This is a wonderful surprise! Why, I only wrote to you this morning!"

He put her away at arm's length and looked into her face.

"Mary, what are you doing in Meister's office?" he asked quietly, and something in his tone chilled her.

"I'm working for him," she said. "You knew I was, Johnny, before—before you went away." And then her hand went up to his face. "It's wonderful to see you—wonderful! Let me look at you. You poor boy, have you had a bad time?"

To the watchful and interested Mr. Hackitt, who had made an unobtrusive entrance and with whom sentiment was a weak point, this seemed an unnecessary question.

"Not so bad as it might have been," said Johnny carelessly. Then: "Why did you go to work at all? I left money with Maurice and told him I didn't want you to work any more. It was the last thing I told him at the Old Bailey."

Hackitt clicked his lips impatiently. "Left money with Meister? You're mad!"

But Lenley did not hear. "Did he stop the allowance?" he asked, his anger rising at the thought.

"No, Johnny, he didn't... I didn't know there was an allowance even."

The brother nodded. "I see," he said.

"You're not angry with me, are you, Johnny?" She raised her tearful eyes to his. "I can't believe it is you. Why, I didn't expect you home for an awful long time."

The Ringer

"My sentence was remitted," said Lenley. "A half—lunatic convict attacked the deputy governor, and I saved him from a mauling. I had no idea that the authorities would do more than strike off a few days from my sentence. Yesterday at dinner—time the governor sent for me and told me that I was to be released on licence."

Again Mr. Hackitt registered despair. Johnny Lenley's notions had never been as professional as he could have desired them, and here he was admitting without shame that he had saved the life of one of his natural enemies! The girl's hands were on her brother's shoulders, her grave eyes searching his face.

"You're finished with that dreadful life, haven't you?" she asked in a low voice. "We're going somewhere out of London to live. I spoke to Maurice about it. He said he'd help you to go straight. Johnny, you wouldn't have had that terrible sentence if you had only followed his advice."

John Lenley bit his lip. "Meister told you that, did he?" he asked slowly. "Mary, are you in love with Maurice?" She stiffened, and he mistook her indignation for embarrassment. "Do you love him?"

"He has been kind," she said coldly. She struggled hard to think of some favourable quality of Meister.

"I realise that, dear," he nodded, "but how has he been kind?" And then, seeing her distress, he gripped her shoulders and shook her gently, and the hard face softened, and into the grey, deep—set eyes came the old mother look she had loved in him. "Anyway, you'll work no more."

"Then I must work at once." She laughed, but there was a catch in her throat. "And you must be very patient... if you want to see Maurice he'll be down soon now—I think you scared him."

He watched her as she went back to her table, and then caught Hackitt's eye and jerked his head. "Sam, what's the idea?" Mr. Hackitt shrugged.

"I've only been here a few days. You're a man of the world, Johnny. Ever seen a tiger being kind to a skinned rabbit? I don't know anything more than that."

The Ringer

Lenley nodded. "Is that so?" he said.

He had come straight to the lawyer's to liquidate old debts and make an end of an unprofitable association. And then London and the stink and grime of Flanders Lane would know him no more: he would find fields where he could work without the supervision of over—armed guards, and with the knowledge that peace and comfort lay at his day's end. He stood by the door, talking to Sam, questioning him, never doubting where Meister's "kindness" would ultimately end. And then the lawyer came into the room. His eyes were all for the girl: her nimble fingers flashing amongst the keys. He went round to her and dropped his hands on her shoulders.

"My dear, forgive me! I'm just as jumpy as I can be, and I'm imagining all sorts of queer things."

"Maurice!"

The lawyer spun round, his colour coming and going. "You!" he croaked. "Out!... I thought..."

Johnny Lenley smiled contemptuously. "About two years too soon, eh? I'm sorry to disappoint you, but miracles happen, even in prison—and I'm one."

With a tremendous effort the lawyer recovered his balance and was his old genial self.

"My dear fellow"—he offered a wavering hand, but Lenley apparently did not see it—"sit down, won't you? What an amazing thing to happen! So it was you at the panel.... Hackitt, give Mr. Lenley a drink... you'll find one in the cupboard... well, this is a sight for sore eyes!"

Hackitt offered the drink, but the other shook his head. "I want to see you, Maurice." He looked significantly at Mary, and rising, she left the room.

"How did you get your ticket?" asked Meister, helping himself to the ever handy bottle.

"The remainder of my sentence was wiped out," said Lenley curtly. "I thought you'd have read that."

The Ringer

The lawyer frowned. "Oh! Were you the lag who saved the life of the governor? I remember reading about it—brave boy! "

He was trying to get command of the situation. Other men had come blustering into that office, and had poured a torrent of threats over the table, leaving him unmoved.

"Why did you allow Mary to go on working for you? "

Meister shrugged. "Because, my dear fellow, I can't afford to be charitable, " he said blandly.

"I left you the greater part of four hundred pounds, " Lenley's voice was stern and uncompromising, "the money I got from my first thefts. "

"You were well defended, weren't you? "

"I know the fee, " said Lenley quietly. "When you had had that, there was still the greater part of four hundred left. Why did you stop the allowance? "

The lawyer sat down again in the chair he had vacated, lit cigar, and did not speak until he saw the match almost burning his fingertips.

"Well, I'll tell you. I got worried about her. I like you, Johnny, I've always been interested in you and your family. And it struck me that a young girl living alone, with no work to do, wasn't exactly having a fair chance. I thought it would be kinder to you and better for her to give her some sort of employment—keep her mind occupied, you understand, old man? I take a fatherly interest in the kid. "

He met the challenging eyes and his own fell before them.

"Keep your fatherly paws to yourself when you're talking to her, will you, Maurice? " The words rang like steel on steel.

"My dear fellow! " protested the other.

"And listen! " Lenley went on. "I know you pretty well; I've known you for a long time, both by reputation and through personal acquaintance. I know just how much there is in that fatherly interest

The Ringer

stuff. If there has been any monkey business as there was with Gwenda Milton, I'll take that nine o'clock walk for you! "

Meister jerked up his head.

"Eh? " he rasped.

"From the cell to the gallows, " Lenley went on. "And I'll toe the trap with a good heart. You don't misunderstand me? "

The Ringer

CHAPTER 33

THE lawyer got up slowly. Whatever else he was, Maurice Meister was no coward when he had to deal with tangible dangers.

"You'll take the nine o'clock walk, will you? " he repeated with a sneer. "What a very picturesque way of putting things! But you won't walk for me. I shall read the account in bed. "

He strolled across to the piano and sat down, his fingers running swiftly over the keys. Softly came the dirge—like notes of "Mort d'un Cosaque"—a dreary, heart-stirring thing that Maurice Meister loved.

"I always read those accounts in bed, " he went on, talking through the music; "they soothe me. Ever go to the cinema, Johnny? " 'The condemned man spent a restless night and scarcely touched his breakfast. He walked with a firm step to the scaffold and made no statement. A vulgar end to a life that began with so much promise. ' Hanged men look very ugly. "

"I've told you, Maurice—any monkey business, and I'll get you even before The Ringer. " Johnny's voice shook with suppressed passion.

"Ringer! " he laughed. "You have that illusion, too? How amusing! "

The tune changed to "Ich liebe dich. "

"The Ringer! Here am I, alive and free, and The Ringer—where is he? That sounds almost poetical! Dead at the bottom of Sydney Harbour... or hiding in some unpleasantly hot little town, or in the bush with the sundowners—a hunted dog. "

A man was standing at the barred window behind him, glaring into the room—a bearded face was pressed to the pane.

"The Ringer is in London, and you know it, " said Lenley. "How near he is to you all the time. God knows! "

As though the eavesdropper heard, he suddenly withdrew. But for the moment Maurice Meister had no mind for The Ringer. The music intoxicated, enthralled him. "Isn't that lovely? " he breathed. "Is

The Ringer

there a woman in the world who can exalt the heart and soul of a man as this—is there a woman worth one divine harmony of the master? "

"Was Gwenda Milton? " snarled Lenley. The music stopped with a crash and Meister, rising, turned to Lenley in a cold fury.

"To hell with Gwenda Milton and Gwenda Milton's brother, alive or dead! " he roared. "Don't mouth her name to me! " He snatched the glass of whisky he had put on the top if the piano and drained it at a draught. "Do you think she is on my conscience—she's not! Any more than you or any other weak whining fool, soaked to the soul with self—pity. That's what's the matter with you, my dear boy—you're sorry for yourself! Weeping over your own miseries. The cream of your vanity's gone sour! " Suddenly his tone changed.

"Ach! Why do you annoy me? Why are you so inexpressibly common? I won't quarrel with you, my dear Johnny. Now what is it you want? "

For answer the caller took from his pocket a small package and opened it on the desk. Inside, wrapped in cotton wool, was a little jewelled bangle. "I don't know how much is due to me; this will make it more. "

Meister took the bangle and carried the glittering thing to the light. "Oh, this is the bracelet—I wondered what you had done with it. "

"I collected it on my way here: it was left with a friend of mine. That is all I had for my three years, " he said bitterly. "Three robberies and I've only touched a profit on one! "

Maurice stroked his upper lip thoughtfully.

"You are thinking of your second exploit: the little affair at Camden Crescent? "

"I don't want to discuss it, " said Johnny impatiently. "I'm finished with the game. Prison has cured me. Anyhow, in the Camden Crescent job, the man who you sent to help me got away with the stuff. You told me that yourself. "

The Ringer

In that second a plan was born in Meister's mind. "I told you a lie," he said slowly. And then, in a more confidential tone: "Our friend never got away with it."

"What!"

"He hid it. He told me before I got him off to South Africa. There was an empty house in Camden Crescent—where the burglary was committed—there is still. I didn't tell you before, because I didn't want to be mixed up in the business after the Darnleigh affair. I could have got half a dozen men to lift it—but I didn't trust them."

Irresolution showed in Lenley's face; the weak mouth drooped a little. "Let it stay where it is," he said, but he did not speak with any great earnestness.

Meister laughed. It was the first genuine laugh of his that the day had brought forth. "You're a fool," he said in disdain. "You've done your time, and what have you got for it? This!" He held up the trinket. "If I give you twenty pounds for it I'm robbing myself. There's eight thousand pounds' worth of good stuff behind that tank—yours for the taking. After all, Johnny," he said, adopting a tone of persuasion, "you've paid for it!"

"By God, I have!" said the other between his teeth. "I've paid for it all right!"

Meister was thinking quickly, planning, cross—planning, organising, in that few seconds of time.

"Knock it off to—night," he suggested, and again Lenley hesitated.

"I'll think about it. If you're trying to shop me—"

Again Meister laughed. "My dear fellow, I'm trying to do you a good turn and, through you, your sister."

"What is the number of the house? I've forgotten."

Meister knew the number well enough: he forgot nothing. "Fifty—seven. I'll give you the twenty pounds for this bracelet now."

The Ringer

He opened his desk, took out his cash—box and unlocked it. "That will do to go on with."

Lenley was still undecided; nobody knew better than the lawyer. "I want full value for the rest if I go after it—or I'll find another 'fence'."

It was the one word that aroused the lawyer to fury. "'Fence'? That's not the word to use to me, Johnny."

"You're too sensitive," said his dour client.

"Just because I help you fellows, when I ought to be shopping you...." The lawyer's voice trembled. "Get another 'fence', will you? Here's your twenty." He threw the money on the table, and Lenley, counting it, slipped it into his pocket. "Going into the country, eh? Taking your little sister away? Afraid of my peculiar fascinations?"

"I'd hate to hang for you," said John Lenley, rising.

"Rather have The Ringer hang, eh? You think he'll come back with all that time over his head, with the gallows waiting for him? Is he a lunatic? Anyway—I'm not scared of anything on God's Almighty earth."

He looked round quickly. The door that led to his room was opening.

It was Dr. Lomond: Hackitt had left him in the lumber room and had forgotten that he was in the house. The doctor was coming into the room but stopped at the sight of the young man.

"Hallo—I'm awfu' sorry. Am I butting in on a consultation?"

"Come in, doctor—come in. This—is—a friend of mine. Mr. Lenley."

To Meister's surprise the doctor nodded.

"Aye. I've just been having a wee chat with your sister. You've just come back from the—country, haven't you?"

"I've just come out of prison, if that's what you mean," said the other bluntly, as he turned to go. His hand was on the knob when

The Ringer

the door was flung open violently and a white—faced Hackitt appeared.

"Guv'nor! " He crossed fearfully to Meister and lowered his voice. "There's a party to see you. "

"Me? Who is it? "

"They told me not to give any name, " gasped Sam. "This party said: 'Just say I'm from The Ringer'. "

Meister shrank back.

"The Ringer! " said Lomond energetically. "Show him up! "

"Doctor! "

But Lomond waved him to silence. "I know what I am doing, " he said.

"Doctor! Are you mad? Suppose—suppose—"

"It's all right, " said Lomond, his eyes on the door.

The Ringer

CHAPTER 34

PRESENTLY it opened, and there came into view of the white-faced Maurice a slim, perfectly dressed girl, malicious laughter in her eyes.

"Cora Ann!" croaked Meister.

"You've said it! Gave you all one mean fright, eh?" She nodded contemptuously. "Hallo, doc!"

"Hallo, little bunch of trouble. You gave me heart disease!"

"Scared you, too, eh?" she scoffed. "I want to see you, Meister."

His face was still pallid, but he had mastered the panic that the name of The Ringer had evoked.

"All right, my dear, Johnny!" He looked hard at Lenley. "If you want anything, my dear boy, you know where you can get it," he said, and Johnny understood, and went out of the room with one backward glance of curiosity at the unexpected loveliness of the intruder.

"Get out, you!" Maurice spoke to Hackitt as though he were a dog, but the little Cockney was unabashed.

"Don't you talk to me like that, Meister—I'm leaving you today."

"You can go to hell," snarled Maurice.

"And the next time I'm pinched I'm going to get another lawyer," said Sam loudly.

"The next time you're pinched you'll get seven years," was the retort.

"That's why I'm goin' to change me lawyer."

Maurice turned on him with a face of fury. "I know a man like you who thought he was clever. He's asked me to defend him at the Sessions."

The Ringer

"I don't call that clever."

"Defend him! I'd see him dead first."

"And he'd be better off!" snapped Sam.

Lomond and the girl made an interested audience.

"That's what you get for helping the scum!" said Meister, when his truculent servant had gone.

Obviously he wanted to be alone with the girl, and Dr. Lomond, who had good reason for returning, said that he had left his bag upstairs in Meister's room, and made that the excuse for leaving them. Maurice waited until the door closed on the old man before he spoke.

"Why—my dear Cora. Ann. You're prettier than ever. And where is your dear husband?" asked Meister blandly.

"I suppose you think that because you're alive, he's dead?"

He laughed. "How clever of you! Did it take you long to think that out?"

She was staring round the room. "So this is the abode of love!" She turned fiercely upon the lawyer. "I never knew Gwenda—I wish to God I had! If Arthur had only trusted me as he trusted you! I heard about her suicide, poor kid, when I was on my way to Australia and flew back from Naples by airplane."

"Why didn't you wire me? If I had only known—"

"Meister—you're a paltry liar!" She went to the door through which the doctor had passed, opened it and listened. Then she came back to where Meister sat lighting a cigar. "Now listen—that Scotch sleuth will be coming back in a minute." She lowered her voice to an intense whisper. "Why don't you go away—out of the country—go somewhere you can't be found—take another name? You're a rich man—you can afford to give up—this hole!"

Maurice smiled again.

The Ringer

"Trying to frighten me out of England, eh?"

"Trying to frighten you!" The contempt in her voice would have hurt another man. "Why, it's like trying to make a nigger black! He'll get you, Meister! That's what I'm afraid of. That is what I lie in bed and think about—it's awful... awful...!"

"My dear little girl"—he tried to lay his hand on her cheek, but she drew back—"don't worry about me."

"You! Say, if I could lift my finger to save you from hell I wouldn't! Get out of the country—it's Arthur I want to save, not you! Get away— don't give him the chance that he wants to kill you."

Maurice beamed at her.

"Ah! How ingenious! He dare not come back himself, But he has sent you to England to get me on the run!"

Cora's fine eyes narrowed. "If you're killed—you'll be killed here! Here in this room where you broke the heart of his sister! You fool!"

He shook his head. "Not such a fool, my dear, that I'd walk into a trap. Suppose this man is alive: in London I'm safe—in the Argentine he'd be waiting for me. And if I went to Australia he'd be waiting for me, and if I stepped ashore at Cape Town... No, no, little Cora Ann, you can't catch me."

She was about to say something when she heard the door open. It was the "Scotch sleuth"; whatever warning she had to deliver must remain unspoken.

"Had your little talk, Cora Ann?" asked Lomond, and in spite of her anxiety the girl laughed.

"Now listen, doctor, only my best friends call me Cora Ann," she protested.

"And I'm the best friend you ever had," said the doctor.

Meister was in eager agreement. "She doesn't know who her best friends are. I wish you'd persuade her."

The Ringer

Neither gave him encouragement to continue. He had the uncomfortable feeling that he was an intruder in his own house, and the arrival of Mary Lenley gave him an excuse to wander to the little office alcove where he was out of sight but not out of hearing.

"I like meeting you, Cora Ann," said the doctor.

She laughed. "You're funny."

"I've brought the smile to the widow's eye," said Lomond unsmilingly.

She shot a swift sidelong glance at the man. "Say, Scottie! That widow stuff—forget it! There are times when I almost wish I was—no, not that—but that Arthur and I had never met."

He was instantly sympathetic. "Arthur was a bad lad, eh?"

She sighed. "The best in the world—but not the kind of man who ought to have married."

"There isn't any other kind," said Lomond, and then, with a cautious look round at Meister: "Were you very much in love with him?"

She shrugged. "Well—I don't know."

"Don't know? My dear young person, you're old enough to know where your heart is."

"It's in my mouth most times," she said, and he shook his head.

"Ye poor wee devil! Still, you followed him to Australia, my dear?"

"Sure I did. But that kind of honeymoon takes a whole lot of romance out of marriage. You don't have to be a doctor to know that."

He bent over her. "Why don't you drop him, Cora Ann? That heart of yours is going to wear away from being in your mouth all the time."

The Ringer

"Forget him? " Lomond nodded. "Do you think he wants me to forget him? "

"I don't know, " said Lomond. "Is any man worth what you are suffering? Sooner or later he will be caught. The long arm of the law will stretch out and take him, and the long leg of the law will boot him into prison! "

"You don't say! " She looked round to where Meister was sitting by Mary Lenley, and her tone grew very earnest. "See here. Dr. Lomond, if you want to know—my Ringer man is in danger, but I'm not scared of the police. Shall I tell you something? "

"Is it fit for me to hear? " he asked.

"That'll worry me! " she answered sarcastically. "I'm going to be frank with you, doctor. I've a kind of hunch there is only one man in God's wide world that will ever catch Arthur Milton—and that man is you! "

The Ringer

CHAPTER 35

Lomond met her eyes.

"You're just daft! " he said.

"And why? "

"A pretty girl like you—hooking on to a shadow—the best part of your life wasted. "

"You don't say! "

"Now, you know it's so, don't you? It's a dog's life. How do you sleep? "

"Sleep! " She threw out her arms in a gesture of despair. "Sleep! "

"Exactly. You'll be a nervous wreck in a year. Is it worth it? "

"What are you trying out? " she asked breathlessly. "What's your game? "

"I'll tell you—shall I? I wonder if you'll be shocked? " She was looking at him intently. "Wouldn't it be a good idea for you to go away and forget all about The Ringer? Cut him out of your mind. Find another— interest. " He laughed. "You think I'm being unpleasant, don't you? But I'm only thinking of you. I'm thinking of all the hours you're waiting for something to happen—with your heart in your mouth. "

Suddenly she sprang to her feet. "Listen! You've got some reason behind all this! " she breathed.

"I swear to you—"

"You have—you have! " She was in a fury. "You're a man—I know what men are. See here—I've put myself in hell and I'm staying put! "

She picked up her bag from the table.

The Ringer

"I've given you your chance," said Lomond, a little sadly.

"My chance. Dr. Lomond! When Arthur Milton says 'I'm tired of you—I'm sick of you—you're out,' then I'll go. My way—not your way. You've given me my chance—Gwenda Milton's chance! That's a hell of a chance, and I'm not taking it!"

Before he could speak she had flung from the room.

Meister had been watching, and now he came slowly to where the doctor was standing. "You've upset Cora Ann."

"Aye," nodded Lomond, as he took up his hat and bag thoughtfully. "Aye."

"Women are very strange," mused Meister. "I rather think she likes you, doctor."

"You think so?" Lomond's manner and voice were absent. "I wonder if she'd come out and have a bit of dinner with me?"

"How marvellous it would be if she liked you well enough to tell you a little more about The Ringer," suggested Maurice slyly.

"That's just what I was thinking. Do you think she would?"

Maurice was amused. Evidently there was no age limit to men's vanity. "You never know what women will do when they're in love—eh, doctor?"

Dr. Lomond did not reply; he went out of the room, counting the silver in his hand.

Meister's head was clear now. Johnny was a real menace... he had threatened, and a young fool like that would fulfil his threat, unless... Would he be mad enough to go to Camden Crescent that night? From Johnny his mind went to Mary. His love for the girl had been a tropical growth. Now, when it seemed that she was to be taken from him, she had become the most desirable of women. He sat down at the piano, and at the first notes of the "Liebestraum," the girl entered.

The Ringer

He was for the moment oblivious of her presence, and it was through a cloud of dreams that her voice brought him to realities.

"Maurice...." He looked at her with unseeing eyes. "Maurice." The music stopped. "You realise that I can't stay here now that Johnny's back?" she was saying.

"Oh, nonsense, my dear!" His tone had that fatherly quality which he could assume with such effect.

"He is terribly suspicious," she said, and he laughed.

"Suspicious! I wish he had something to be suspicious about!"

She waited, a picture of indecision. "You know I can't stay," she said desperately.

He got up from the piano, and coming across to her, laid his hands on her shoulder. "Don't be silly. Anyone would think I was a leper or something. What nonsense!"

"Johnny would never forgive me."

"Johnny, Johnny!" he snapped. "You can't have your life governed and directed by Johnny, who looks like being in prison half his life."

She gasped. "Let us see things as they are," he went on. "There's no sense in deceiving oneself. Johnny is really a naughty boy. You don't know, my dear, you don't know. I've tried to keep things from you and it has been awfully difficult."

"Keep things from me—what things?" Her face had gone pale.

"Well—" his hesitation was well feigned—"what do you think the young fool did—just before he was caught? I've been his best friend, as you know, and yet—well, he put my name to a cheque for four hundred pounds."

She stared at him in horror.

"Forgery!"

"What is the use of calling it names? " He took a pocket—book from his dressing—gown and extracted a cheque. "I've got the cheque here. I don't know why I keep it, or what I'm going to do about Johnny. "

She tried to see the name on the oblong slip, but he was careful to keep it hidden. It was, in fact, a cheque he had received by the morning post, and the story of the forgery had been invented on the spur of the minute. Inspirations such as this had been very profitable to Maurice Meister.

"Can't you destroy it? " she asked tremulously.

"Yes—I suppose I could. " His hesitation was artistic. "But Johnny is so vindictive. In self—defence I've got to keep this thing. " He put the cheque back in his pocket. "I shall never use it, of course, " he said airily. And then, in that tender tone of his: "I want to talk to you about Johnny and everything. I can't now, with people walking in and out all the time and these policemen hanging round. Come up to supper—the way I told you. "

She shook her head. "You know I can't. Maurice, you don't wish people to talk about me as they are talking about—Gwenda Milton. "

The lawyer spun round at the words, his face distorted with fury. "God Almighty! Am I always to have that slimy ghost hanging round my neck? Gwenda Milton, a half—wit who hadn't the brains to live! All right—if you don't want to come, don't. Why the hell should I worry my head about Johnny? Why should I? "

She was terrified by this sudden violence of his.

"Oh, Maurice, you're so unreasonable. If you really want—"

"I don't care whether you do or whether you don't, " he growled. "If you think you can get along without me, try it. I'm not going on my knees to you or to any other woman. Go into the country—but Johnny won't go with you, believe me! "

She caught his arm, frantic with the fear his half—threat had roused. "Maurice—I'll do anything you wish—you know I will. "

The Ringer

He looked at her oddly. "Come at eleven, " he said, and: "If you want a chaperon, bring The Ringer! "

The words were hardly spoken when there came three deliberate raps at the door, and Maurice Meister shrank back, his shaking hand at his mouth. "Who's there? " he asked hoarsely.

The deep tone of a man answered him. "I want to see you, Meister. "

Meister went to the door and flung it open. The sinister face of Inspector Bliss stared into his.

"What... what are you doing here? " croaked the lawyer.

Bliss showed his white teeth in a mirthless smile. "Protecting you from The Ringer—watching over you like a father, " he said harshly. His eyes strayed to the pale girl. "Don't you think, Miss Lenley—that you want a little watching over, too? "

She shook her head. "I am not afraid of The Ringer, " she said; "he would not hurt me. "

Bliss smiled crookedly.

"I'm not thinking of The Ringer! " he said, and his menacing eyes wandered to Maurice Meister.

CHAPTER 36

THE return of John Lenley was the most supremely embarrassing thing that had ever happened within Maurice Meister's recollection. If he had resented the attitude of the young man before, he hated him now. The menace in his words, the covert threat behind his reference to Gwenda Milton, were maddening enough, but now there was another factor operating at a moment when it seemed that all his dreams were to be realised, and Mary Lenley, like a ripe plum, was ready to fall into his hands; when even the fear of The Ringer had evaporated in some degree, there must enter upon the scene this young man whom he thought he would not see again for years.

Prison had soured and aged him. He had gone away a weakling, come back a brooding, vicious man, who would stop at nothing—if he knew. There was nothing to know yet. Meister showed his teeth in a smile. Not yet...

Maurice Meister was no coward in his dealings with other men: he had all the qualities of his class. Known dangers he could face, however deadly they might be. He could have met John Lenley and without wincing could have told him of his evil plan—if he were sure of Mary. Yet the sight of a door opening slowly and apparently through no visible agency brought him to the verge of hysteria.

The Ringer was alive: the worst of Meister's fear died with the sure knowledge. He was something human, tangible; something against which he could match his brains.

That afternoon, when they were alone, he came in to Mary and, standing behind her, dropped his hands upon her shoulders. He felt her stiffen, and was amused.

"You haven't forgotten what you promised this morning? " he asked. She twisted from his clasp and came round to meet his eyes.

"Maurice, was it true about the cheque? You were not lying? " He nodded slowly. "We're alone now, " she said desperately. "Can't we talk... is it necessary that I should come tonight? "

"Very necessary, " said Meister coolly. "I suppose you are aware that there are three people in the house besides ourselves? Do, for

The Ringer

Heaven's sake, take a sane view of things, Mary; see them as they are, not as you would like them to be. I have to protect myself against Johnny—an irresponsible and arrogant young man—and I am very much afraid of—" he nearly said "fools" but thought better of it—"young men of his peculiar temperament. " He saw the quick rise and fall of her bosom: it pleased him that he could stir her even to fear. How simple women were, even clever women! He had long ceased to be amazed at their immense capacity for believing. Credulity was one of the weaknesses of human-kind that he could never understand.

"But, Maurice, isn't this as good an opportunity as we can get? Nobody will interrupt you... why, you are here with your clients for hours on end! Tell me about the cheque and how he came to forge it. I want to get things right. "

He spread out his hands in a gesture of mock helplessness.

"What a child you are, Mary! How can you imagine that I would be in the mood to talk of Johnny, or plan for you? Keep your promise, my dear! "

She faced him squarely. "Maurice, I'm going to be awfully plain-spoken. " What was coming? he wondered. There was a new resolution in her voice, a new courage in her eyes. She was so unlike the wilting, terrified being of the morning that he was for a moment staggered. "Do you really wish me to come tonight... just to talk about the cheque that Johnny has forged? "

He was so taken aback by the directness of the question that he could not for the moment answer. "Why, of course, " he said at length. "Not only about the forgery, but there are so many other matters which we ought to talk over, Mary. If you're really going into the country, we must devise ways and means. You can't go flying off into Devonshire, or wherever it is you intend settling, at a minute's notice. I am getting some catalogues from one of my—from a house agent I represent. We can look over these together—"

"Maurice, is that true? I want to know. I'm not a child any longer. You must tell me. "

She had never looked more lovely to him than in that moment of challenge.

The Ringer

"Mary," he began, "I am very fond of you—"

"What does that mean—that you love me?" The cold—bloodedness of the question took his breath away. "Does it mean, you love me so much that you want to marry me?" she asked.

"Why, of course," he stammered. "I am awfully fond of you. But marriage is one of the follies that I have so far avoided. Does it mean anything, my dear? A few words mumbled by a paid servant of the Church..."

"Then you don't want to marry me, Maurice?" she said quietly. "I am right there, aren't I?"

"Of course, if you wish me—" he began hastily.

She shook her head. "I don't love you and I don't wish to marry you, if that is what you mean," she said. "What do you really want of me?' She was standing close to him when she asked the question, and in another instant she was struggling in his arms.

"I want you—you!" he breathed. "Mary, there is no woman in the world like you... I adore you..."

Summoning all her strength, she broke free from his grasp and held him breathlessly at arm's length. "I see!" She could hardly articulate the words. "I guessed that. Maurice, I shall not come to this house tonight."

Meister did not speak. The wild rush of passion which had overcome him had left him curiously weak. He could only look at her; his eyes burnt. Once he put up his trembling hand as though to control his lips. "I want you here tonight." The voice was scarcely audible. "You have been frank with me; I will be as frank with you. I want you: I want to make you happy. I want to take away all the dread and fear that clouds your life. I want to move you from that squalid home of yours. You know what has happened to your brother, don't you? He's been released on ticket-of-leave. He has two years and five months to serve. If I prefer a charge of forgery against him, he will get seven years and the extra time he has not served. Nine and a half years... you realise what that means? You'll be over thirty before you see him again."

The Ringer

He saw her reel, thinking she was going to faint, caught her by the arm, but she shook off his hand. "That puts the matter in a different light, doesn't it?"

He read agreement in a face which was as white as death.

"Is there no other way, Maurice?" she asked in a low voice. "No service I can render you? I would work for you as a housekeeper, as a servant—I would be your best friend, whatever happened to you, your loyalist helper."

Meister smiled.

"You're getting melodramatic, my dear, and that is stupid. What a fuss over a little supper party, a little flirtation."

Her steady eyes were of his. "If I told Johnny—" she began slowly.

"If you told Johnny, he'd come here, and be even more melodramatic. I should telephone for the police and that would be the end of Johnny. You understand?"

She nodded dumbly.

CHAPTER 37

AT five o'clock Meister told her she could go home for the evening. Her head was aching; she had done practically no work that afternoon, for the letters were blurred and illegible specks of black that swam before her eyes. No further reference was made to the visit of the evening, and she hurried from the house into the dark street. A thin fog lay on Deptford as she threaded a way along the crowded side—walk of High Street.

Suppose she went to Alan? The thought only occurred to be rejected. She must work out her own salvation. Had Johnny been at home when she arrived, she might have told him, even if he had not guessed from her evident distress that something unusual had occurred.

But he was out; had left a note on the table saying that he had gone to town to see a man he knew. She remembered the name after a while; it was a gentleman farmer who had been a neighbour of theirs in the old days at Lenley. It was a dismal thought that all these preparations of Johnny's would come to naught if—She shuddered. Either prospect she did not dare think about.

She went to her room and presently came her little maid—of—all—work with the announcement that a gentleman had called to see her.

"I can't see anybody. Who is it?"

"I don't know, miss. He's a fellow with a beard."

She walked quickly past the girl across the dining—room into the tiny hall.

"You don't know me, I think," said the man at the door. "My name is Bliss."

Her heart sank. Why had this man come from Scotland Yard? Had Maurice, in one of those paroxysms of unreasonable temper, sent him?

"Come in, please."

The Ringer

He walked into the room, a cigarette drooping from his bearded mouth, and slowly took off his hat, as though he were reluctant to pay even this tribute of respect to her.

"I understand your brother's been released from prison today—or was it yesterday?"

"Yesterday," she said. "He came home this morning."

To her surprise, he made no further reference to Johnny, but took from his pocket a morning newspaper and folded it to show a column on the front page. She read the advertisement his finger indicated.

X2Z. LBa4T. QQ57g. LL4i8TS. A79Bf.

"What does it mean?" she asked.

"That is what I want to know," said Bliss, fixing his dark eyes on her. "It is a message either from The Ringer to his wife, or from his wife to The Ringer, and it is in a code which was left at this flat last week. I want you to show me that code."

"I'm sorry, Mr. Bliss"—she shook her head—"but the code was stolen— I thought by—"

"You thought by me?" His lips twisted in a grim smile. "So you didn't believe that cock—and—bull story I told about my having seen a man climbing into the flat and going up after him? Miss Lenley, I have reason to believe that the code was not taken from your house, but that it is still here, and that you know where it is."

She had a feeling that, insulting as he was, he was merely testing her. His attitude was that of a man who wished to be convinced.

"The code is not here," she said quietly. "I missed it the night I came back and found the flat had been burgled."

She wondered if the peculiar look she saw indicated relief or scepticism.

The Ringer

"I'll have to take your word," he said, and folded up the paper. "If what you say is true, no other person than The Ringer and his wife has this code."

Mary was a trifle bewildered. "Of course," she said, "unless the person whom you saw climb into my room—"

"My theory is that that was The Ringer himself," said Bliss. He had not taken his eyes off her all the time he had been speaking. "Are you scared of The Ringer, Miss Lenley?"

In spite of her trouble she smiled. "Of course not. I told you today. Why should I be scared of him? I have done him no harm, and from what I know of him he is not the kind of man who would hurt any woman."

Again that fleeting smile. "I'm glad you have such a high opinion of the scoundrel," he said, in a more genial tone. "I am afraid it is one that I do not share. How do you like Meister?"

Everybody asked her that question; it was beginning to get on her nerves; and he must have seen this, for, without waiting for her answer, he went on quickly: "You've got to look after that brother of yours. Miss Lenley. He's a pretty foolish young man."

"So Maurice Meister thinks," she was stung into replying.

"Does he?" The answer seemed to amuse him. "That is about all. I'm sorry to have disturbed you."

He walked to the door and turned round.

"Rather a nice fellow, Wembury, eh? A bit of an impetuous young fool, but rather nice?" Again he did not wait for an answer, but pulled the door close behind him, and she opened it in time to see him shut the front door. She herself had to go out again; the shops did not close till seven, and the evening was the only time she had for marketing. She made a list of all the things that Johnny liked; steadfastly kept out of her mind the pitiful possibilities which might disturb this housekeeping of hers.

The Ringer

With a basket on her arm she went out into the Lewisham High Road and shopped for an hour, and she was hurrying back to Malpas Mansions when she saw a tall man walking ahead of her. He wore a grey overcoat, but she could not mistake that shuffling gait and bent shoulders. She intended passing him without speaking, but almost before she came abreast, Dr. Lomond, without turning his head, hailed her. "It's fine to see a lassie with a basket, but the eggs ye bought were no' so good."

She gasped at this and laughed. It was the first time that day she had been genuinely amused.

"I didn't know I was under police observation," she said.

"It's a verra peculiar thing, that few people do," he said drily. "But I was watching ye in the egg shop—lassie, you've a trusting disposition. Those new—laid eggs you bought are contemporaneous with the eggs of the great roc." And then, seeing her rueful face in the light of a shop window, he chuckled. "I tell ye this, Miss Lenley; I'm a verra good obsairver. I obsairve eggs and skulls, jaws, noses, eyes and detectives! Was Mr. Bluss very offensive?" (He always referred to the ill—favoured inspector as "Bluss".) "Or was it merely a social call?"

"Did you know Mr. Bliss had been to see me?" she asked in astonishment.

The old man nodded "He's been around here a' the afternoon. When he came to Malpas Mansions I happened to be passing and gave him good night, but he's a sorry fellow wi'oot any milk of human kindness in his dour system."

"Are you watching somebody now?" she asked mischievously, and was staggered when he pointed ahead. "Yon's the fellow," he said.

"Mr. Bliss?" She peered into the night, and at that moment saw in the light of a street standard the dapper figure of the Central Inspector.

"He interests me, that body," admitted Lomond. "He's mysteerious, and mysteerious things are very attractive to a plain, matter—of—fact old man like me."

The Ringer

She left him to his chase and got back to the Mansions just as Johnny returned. He was in excellent spirits; joked with her on her marketing, and uttered gloomy forebodings as to the effect upon his digestion. She could not remember when she had last seen him in that mood. And then he said something which gladdened her heart.

"That fellow Wembury isn't such a bad chap, after all. Which reminds me that I ought to call at Flanders Lane and register myself."

She heard this with a little pang.

"You are on ticket of leave, aren't you, Johnny. If anything happened… I mean, if you were silly again, would you have to serve the full sentence?"

"If I'm silly again?" he asked sharply. "What do you mean?" And then with an air of unconcern: "You're being silly now, Mary. I'm going to lead a highly respectable life."

"But if you were—"

"Of course I should have to serve the unfinished portion of my sentence in addition to any other I might get; but as I'm most unlikely to be what you call silly, we needn't consider that. I suppose, Meister's finished with you for the day? I hope in a week or two you'll be finished with him for good. I don't like you working there, Mary."

"I know, Johnny, but—"

"Yes, yes, I quite understand. You never work there at night, do you, dear?"

She could say "No" to this truthfully.

"I'm glad. You'll be wise to see Maurice only in business hours."

He lit a cigarette, blew a cloud of smoke into the air. Johnny was trying to frame the lie he must tell her.

The Ringer

"I may be late tonight, " he said eventually. "A man I know has asked me to go to supper in the West End. You don't mind, do you? "

She shook her head. "No. What time will you be back? "

He considered this before he answered. "Not before midnight—probably a little later, " he said.

Mary found her breath coming more quickly. "I—I may be late myself, Johnny. I've promised to go to a party... some people I've met. "

Would he be deceived? she wondered. Apparently he was, for he accepted her story of this mythical engagement without question.

"Get as much fun out of life as you can, old girl, " he said, us he stripped his coat and walked into his bedroom. "I suppose it'll be a ghastly party after the wonderful shows we had at Lenley Court in the old days. But wait till we get on to our farm; we're going to do a bit of hunting—keep a horse or two... "

He was in his bedroom now and she did not hear the remainder of his highly coloured plans.

He left the house by eight o'clock, and she sat down to wait for the hours to pass. How would this day end? And what would Alan think about it all? Alan, to whom she was something sacred and apart. She closed her eyes tightly us if to shut out some horrible vision. The world would never again be the same as it was. She had thought that, the day Johnny went away, when she had walked down the broad steps of the Old Bailey, her heart broken, her future wrecked. But now she watched the minute hand of the little American clock move all too quickly towards the hour of fate, she realised that her supreme hour of trial had yet to come.

The Ringer

CHAPTER 38

THE fog which lay over Deptford extended to a wider area. An hour after Mary had had her little talk with Johnny, a powerful two—seater car came whizzing through the mist which shrouded the countryside between Hatfield and Welwyn, turned from the main road into a bumpy cart track and continued till, ahead of the driver, loomed the great arch of an abandoned hangar. The place had been an aerodrome in the days of the war, but it had been sold and re—sold so often that the list of its owners was of considerable length.

Stopping the car, he dimmed the lights and stepped briskly from the machine, walking towards the hangar. He heard a dog bark and the challenge of a man's voice. "Is that you, Colonel? "

The motorist answered.

"I've got your machine ready and it's all tuned up, but you won't be able to take your trip to Paris tonight. The fog's thick, and I've just been on the 'phone to the Cambridge aerodrome. They say that one of their pilots went up and found the fog was two thousand feet deep and extending over the channel. "

"What could be nicer? " said the man called "Colonel Dane" cheerfully. "Fog driving is my speciality! "

The keeper of the hangar grunted something about every man to his taste, and walked ahead, swinging a dim lantern. Using all his strength, he rolled back the soft squeaking door of the hangar, and a long propeller and a portion of the fuselage of a Scout machine were revealed in the nickering light of the lantern.

"She's a beauty, Colonel, " said the man admiringly. "When do you expect to come back? "

"In a week, " said the other.

The collar of his overcoat was turned up and it was impossible to see anything save a pair of keen eyes, and these were only visible at intervals, for his soft felt hat was pulled down over his forehead and afforded a perfect shade.

The Ringer

"Yes, she's a beauty, " said the man. "I've been tuning her up all the afternoon. "

He was an ex—Air Force mechanic, and was for the moment the tenant of the garage, and the small cottage where he lived. Incidentally, he was the best paid aeroplane mechanic in England at the moment.

"The police were here today, sir, " he said. "They came nosing around, wanting to know who was the owner of the 'bus—I told them you were an ex—officer of the Flying Corps who was thinking of running a light aircraft club. I've often wondered what you really are, sir? "

The man whom he called "Colonel" laughed softly.

"I shouldn't do too much wondering, Green, " he said. "You're paid to think of nothing but struts and stays, carburettors and petrol supply! "

"I've had all sorts of theories, " the imperturbable Green went on. "I thought maybe you were running dope to the Continent. If you are, it's no business of mine. " Then he went off at a tangent. "Have you heard about The Ringer, sir? There's a bit in tonight's paper. "

"The Ringer? Who on earth is The Ringer? "

"He's a fellow who disguises himself. The police have been after him for years. "

Green was the kind of man who had the police news at his finger—tips and could give the dates of the conviction and execution of every murderer for the past twenty years. "He used to be in the Air Force, from what they say. "

"I've never heard of him, " said the Colonel. "Just stand outside, will you. Green? "

He walked into the hangar and, producing a powerful electric lamp from his pocket, made a minute examination of the aeroplane, testing wires, and eventually climbing into the fuselage to inspect the controls.

185

The Ringer

"Yes, she's all right, " he said as he dropped lightly down. "I don't know what time I shall be going, but probably some hour of the night. Have her taken out behind the garage facing the long field. You've been over the ground—I don't want to get her scratched before I start to rise. "

"I've combed the ground, sir, " said Green complacently.

"Good! "

"Colonel Dane" took from his pocket a flat wad of notes, counted a dozen and placed them in the hand of his assistant.

"Since you are so infernally curious, I will tell you, my friend. I am hoping tonight to be running away with a lady—that sounds a little romantic, doesn't it? "

"She's somebody's wife, eh? " said Green, scenting a scandal.

"She's somebody's wife, " agreed the Colonel gravely. "With any kind of luck I shall be here either at two o'clock tomorrow morning or two o'clock the following morning. The thicker the fog, the better I shall like it. I shall be accompanied by a lady, as I have told you. There will be no baggage, I want to carry as much juice as I can. "

"Where are you making for, Colonel? "

The Ringer laughed again. He was easily amused tonight.

"It may be France or Belgium or Norway or the North Coast of Africa or the South Coast of Ireland—who knows? I can't tell you when I shall return, but before I go I shall leave you enough money to live in comfort for at least a year. If I'm not back in ten days, I advise you to let the garage, keep your mouth shut, and with any kind of luck we shall be meeting again. "

He picked his way back to the car, and Green, with all the curiosity of his kind, sought vainly to catch a glimpse of his face. Never once had he seen this strange employer of his, who had engaged him by night, and by night had visited him, choosing always those conditions which made it necessary to wear either a long mackintosh or a heavy ulster.

The Ringer

Green was always under the impression that his employer wore a beard, and in subsequent evidence that he gave adhered to this statement. Bearded or clean—shaven, he could not have penetrated beyond the muffling collar even now, as he escorted the "Colonel" back to his car.

"Talking about this Ringer—" began Green.

"I wasn't, " said the other shortly, as he stepped into the car and jammed his foot on the self—starter. "And I advise you to follow my example. Green. I know nothing about the fellow, except that he's a dangerous man—dangerous to spy upon, more dangerous to talk about. Keep your mind fixed on aeroplanes. Green; they are less deadly! "

In another few seconds the rear light of his car was out of sight.

CHAPTER 39

SAM HACKITT had other trials than were represented by a vigilant constabulary. There was, for example, a lady whom in a misguided moment he had led to the altar—an act he had spent the rest of his life regretting. She was a loud, aggressive woman, who hated her husband, not for his offences against society but for certain weaknesses of his which led him to neglect his home—a collection of frowsy furniture in a dingy little room off Church Street.

Sam was as easy—going as most criminals, a fairly kind man, but he lived in terror of his wife. Since his release from prison he had very carefully avoided her, but the news of his return had spread, and there had been two scenes, one on Meister's doorstep and one in High Street, Deptford, when a raucous virago had followed him along the street explaining to the world at large the habits, character and delinquencies of Mr. Samuel Hackitt.

One day, Sam in an off moment had strolled up west, and in a large window in Cockspur Street he had seen many glowing booklets describing the wonder of the life on the western prairies of Canada; and though agriculture was a pursuit which had never wholly attracted him, he became from that instant an enthusiastic pioneer. But to reach Canada, money was needed, and to acquire property required more money. Sam Hackitt sat down cold—bloodedly to consider the problem of transportation and sustenance. He had sufficient money saved to buy his ticket, but this he did surreptitiously, passing the emigration doctor with flying colours. Sam decided that, all being fair in love and war, and his relationships with Mr. Meister being permanently strained, it would be no hurt to his conscience to help himself to a few portable and saleable souvenirs.

That which he most strenuously coveted was a small black metal cash-box, which Meister usually kept in the second drawer of his desk. The lawyer, by reason of the peculiar calls made upon him, generally had a large sum of money in his cash—box, and it was this which Sam most earnestly desired.

There had been no opportunity in the past two days even to look at the box, and now, with the return of Johnny and his own summary

The Ringer

ejection— Meister, as an act of grace, had told him he could stay on for the remainder of the week—a moment of crisis had arisen.

He had no grudge against Mary Lenley, but he had found a sense of bitter resentment growing towards the girl that day when, after the sixth attempt to walk into the room and make a quick extraction, he found her covering her typewriter before going home.

"You are leaving us, Hackitt?" she said on this occasion.

Sam thought that he could leave with greater rapidity if she would be kind enough to give him an opportunity of opening the second drawer of Mr. Meister's desk.

"Yes, Miss. I can't stand Meister any longer. I suppose you're glad about your brother coming back, Miss?"

"Very glad. We're going into the country."

"Taking up farming, Miss?" asked Sam, interested.

She sighed.

"I'm afraid we shan't be much use as farmers."

"I thought of going in for farming myself," said Sam. "I've had a bit of experience—I worked in the fields down at Dartmoor."

"Are you going to farm in England?" she asked, surprised out of her mood.

Sam coughed. "I'm not exactly sure. Miss, but I thought of going abroad. Into the great open spaces as it were."

"Sam, you've been to the pictures," she accused him, and he grinned.

"This is no country for a man who's trying to get away from the arm of the police," he said. "I want to go abroad and make a fresh start."

She looked at him oddly.

The Ringer

"Why are your eyes always on Mr. Meister's desk? Is there anything wrong with it? " she asked.

"No, no, Miss, " said Sam hastily, "only I thought of giving it a rub up tomorrow. Look here, miss, "—he walked nearer to her and lowered his voice to a confidential tone—"you've known old Meister for years, haven't you? "

She nodded.

"I don't suppose you know very much about him except that he's a snide lawyer, " said Sam outrageously. "Don't you think it'd be a good idea if you had another young lady in to help you? This may be my last word to you. "

She looked at him kindly: how well he meant. "There isn't enough work for two people, " she said.

He nodded knowingly.

"Yes, there is. Miss. You make enough work—do a little bit of miking. "

"'Miking'? "

"Slowing up, ca' canny—it's a Scottish expression. "

"But why should I do that? It wouldn't be very honest, would it? " she smiled in spite of herself.

The honesty of things never made any very great appeal to Sam Hackitt.

"It mightn't be honesty, but it'd be safe, " he said, and winked. "I hope you won't be offended, but if I had a sister I wouldn't pass her within half a mile of Meister's house. "

He saw her expression change and was instantly apologetic, and took the first opportunity of getting out of the room.

There was only one way for Sam: the steel grille which protected the window leading on to the leads was an effective barrier to the average thief, but Sam was above the average And, moreover, when

The Ringer

he cleaned the windows that morning, he had introduced a little appliance to the lock, an appliance which the maker had not foreseen. If Alan Wembury had examined the bars carefully he would have seen a piece of steel wire neatly wrapped round a bar, and had he followed the wire to its end he would have discovered that it entered the lock in such a way that a person outside the window had only to loosen the wire and pull, to force back the catch. It was an ingenious contrivance and Sum was rather proud of it.

That night, after Alan Wembury had gone, Sam crouched on the leads. He heard Alan come and go. It was an unpleasant experience crouching there, for the fog was alternated with a drizzle which soaked him through and chilled him to the bone. He heard Meister talking to himself as he paced up and down the room, heard the rattle of knife against plate, and then Sam cursed. Meister was at the piano—he might be there for hours. And Sam hated music. But apparently the man was in a fitful mood: the music ceased, and Sam heard the creak of a chair, and after a while his stertorous, regular breathing. The lawyer was asleep and Sam waited no longer. A quick pull and the grille was unfastened. He had greased the window sash and it rose noiselessly.

Meister sat at the piano, his eyes wide open, an unpleasant sight. Sam no more than glanced at the little table, near the settee, which was covered by a cloth. Tiptoeing across the room, he reached for the switch and turned out the lights.

The fire burnt low; but he was a famous night worker, and by touch located the drawer, fitted the little instrument he carried into the lock, and pulled. The drawer opened, and his hand groped in the interior. He found the cash—box instantly, but there were other treasures. A small cupboard under the disused buffet held certain priceless articles of Georgian silver. He went back to the window, lifted inside his portmanteau and packed until the case could hold no more. Lifting the suit—case, he stepped softly back towards safety, and was nearly opposite the mystery door when he heard a faint click and stood, petrified, all his senses alert.

It might have been a cooling cinder in the fire. He moved stealthily, one hand extended before him, an instinctive gesture common to all who work in the dark. He was opposite the mystery door, when suddenly a cold hand closed on his wrist!

The Ringer

He set his teeth, stifled the cry which rose, and then, with a quick jerk, wrenched free. Who was it? He could see nothing, could only hear quick breathing, and darted for the window. In a second he was on the leads and in another he was racing across the courtyard. The fear of death in his heart.

There could be only one explanation for that cold and deathly hand—The Ringer had come for Meister!

CHAPTER 40

EARLY that evening Alan Wembury made a hurried call at Meister's house. The girl was gone but Meister was visible. He came down in his inevitable dressing—gown and was so gloomy and nervous a man that Alan formed the impression that he had been sent for so urgently to soothe the lawyer's nerves.

But in this he was wrong.

"Sorry to bother you, inspector... " Meister was, for the first time in his life, at a loss as to how he should proceed. Alan waited. "The fact is... I've got a very unpleasant duty to perform—very unpleasant. To tell you the truth, I hate doing it. "

Still Alan said nothing to encourage the coming confidence and Meister hardly wanted encouragement.

"It's about Johnny. You understand my position, Wembury? You know what the Commissioner said to me? I am under suspicion—unjustly, it is true—but I am suspect by police headquarters. "

What was coming next? Alan wondered. This was so unlike the Meister he knew that he might be excused his bewilderment.

"I can't afford to take risks, " the lawyer went on. "A few weeks ago I might have taken a chance, for the sake of Mary—Miss Lenley. But now I simply dare not. If I know of a felony about to be committed or contemplated, I have only one course—to inform the police. "

Now Alan Wembury understood. But he still maintained his silence.

Maurice was walking nervously up and down the room. He sensed the antagonism, the contempt of the other man, and hated him for it. Worse than this, he was well aware that Alan knew that he was lying: knew full well that the betrayal was cold—blooded and deliberate.

"You understand? " asked Meister again.

"Well? " said Alan. He was nauseated by this preliminary. "What felony is Lenley committing? "

The Ringer

Meister drew a long breath.

"I think you should know that the Darnleigh affair was not Johnny's first job. He did the burglary at Miss Bolter's about a year ago. You remember?"

Wembury nodded. Miss Bolter was an eccentric maiden lady of great wealth. She had a house on the edge of Greenwich—a veritable storehouse of old jewellery. A robbery had been committed and the thieves had got away with £8,000 worth of jewels.

"Was Lenley in that—is that the information you are laying?"

"I am laying no information," said Maurice hastily. "I merely tell you what I believe to be true. My information, which you will be able to confirm, is that the jewels were never got away from the house—you will remember that the burglars were disturbed at their nefarious work."

Alan shook his head. "I still don't understand what you're driving at," he said.

Meister looked round and lowered his voice. "I understand from some hint he dropped that he is going to Camden Crescent tonight to get the jewels! He has borrowed the key of the house next door, which happens to be my property and is empty. My theory is that the jewels are hidden on the roof of No. 57. I suggest—I do no more than suggest, that you post a man there tonight."

"I see!" said Alan softly.

"I don't want you to think that I intend harm to Johnny—I'd rather have cut off my right hand than hurt him. But I have my duty to do—and I am already under suspicion and deeply involved, so far as John Lenley is concerned."

Alan went back to Flanders Lane police station with a heavy heart. He could do nothing. Meister would report to headquarters that he had given him the information. To warn John Lenley would mean ruin—disgrace—probably an ignominious discharge from the service.

He sent a man to take up a position on the roof of Camden Crescent.

The Ringer

Within an hour he had his report. He was standing moodily before the fire when the telephone bell rang. The sergeant pulled the instrument over to him.

"Hallo! " He looked up at the clock mechanically to time the call in his book. "What's that? " He covered the receiver with his hand. "The night watchman at Cleavers reports there's a man on the roof in Camden Crescent. "

Alan thought for a moment. "Yes, of course. Tell him not to worry; it is a police officer. "

"On the roof of Camden Crescent? " asked the sergeant incredulously.

Alan nodded, and the officer addressed himself to his unknown vis-a-vis.

"That's all right, son. He's only one of our men... eh? He's sweeping the chimney... yes, we always have policemen sweep chimneys and we usually choose the night. " He hung up the receiver. "What's he doing up there? "

"Looking round, " said Alan indifferently.

His men were searching for another criminal that night. Sam Hackitt had disappeared from Meister's house, and the slatternly woman who was known as Mrs. Hackitt had been brought in earlier in the evening charged with fighting. It was the old sordid story... a younger woman who had taken the erratic fancy of the faithless Sam. In her fury Mrs. Hackitt had "squeaked"—the story of Sam's plans was told to the station sergeant's desk—and two of Wembury's men were looking for him.

Dr. Lomond had once said that he felt the police were very hard on little criminals, that they sought crime, and grew callous to all the sufferings attendant upon its detection. Alan wondered if he had grown callous. Perhaps he had not. Perhaps no police officer should. They came to be rather like doctors, who have two personalities, in one of which they can dissociate from themselves all sentiment and human tenderness. And then the object of his thoughts appeared and Wembury's heart leapt. John Lenley came into the charge—room, nodding to the sergeant.

The Ringer

"I'm reporting here," he said.

He took some papers out of his pocket and laid them on the desk.

"My name's Lenley. I'm a convict on licence."

And then he caught Wembury's eye and came over to him and shook hands.

"I heard you were out, Lenley. I congratulate you." All the time he was speaking, there was in his mind the picture of that crouching, waiting figure of justice on the roof of Camden Crescent. He had to clench his teeth to inhibit the warning that rose to his lips.

"Yes, I came out yesterday," said Johnny.

"Your sister was glad to see you?"

"Yes," said Lenley curtly, and seemed disinclined to make any further reference to Mary.

"I'd like to find a job for you, Johnny," said Alan, in desperation. "I think I can."

John Lenley smiled crookedly.

"Prisoners' Aid Society?" he asked. "No, thank you! Or is it the Salvation Army you're thinking of? Paper sorting at twopence a hundredweight? When I get a job, it will be one that a waster can't do, Wembury. I don't want helping; I want leaving alone."

There was a silence, broken by the scratching of the sergeant's pen.

"Where are you going tonight?" asked Alan. At all costs this man must be warned. He thought of Mary Lenley waiting at home. He was almost crazy with the fear that she might in some way conceive the arrest of this man as a betrayal on his part.

John Lenley was looking at him suspiciously. "I'm going up west. Why do you want to know?"

The Ringer

Alan's indifference was ill assumed. "I don't wish to know particularly, " And then: "Sergeant, how far is it from here to Camden Crescent? "

He saw Johnny start. The man's eyes were fixed on his.

"Not ten minutes' walk, " said the sergeant.

"Not far, is it? " Alan was addressing the ticket—of—leave man. "A mere ten minutes' walk from Camden Crescent to the station house! "

Johnny did not answer.

"I thought of taking a lonely stroll up west, " Alan went on. "Would you like to come along and have a chat? There are several things I'd like to talk to you about. "

Johnny was watching him suspiciously. "No, " he said quietly. "I've got to meet a friend. "

Alan picked up a book and turned the leaves slowly. He did not raise his eyes when he said: "I wonder if you know whom you're going to meet? You used to be a bit of an athlete in your early days, Lenley—a runner, weren't you? I seem to remember that you took prizes? "

"Yes, I've got a cup or two, " he said, in a tone of surprise.

"If I were you"—still Alan did not raise his eyes from the book—"I'd run and not stop running until I reached home. And then I'd lock the door to stop myself running out again! "

The desk sergeant was intrigued.

"Why? " he asked.

Johnny had turned his back on Wembury and was apparently absorbed in the information he was giving to the sergeant. Then he walked to the door.

"Good night, Lenley, if I don't see you again, " said Wembury.

The Ringer

Johnny spun round. "Do you expect to see me again? " he asked. "Tonight? "

"Yes—I do. "

The words were deliberate. It was the nearest to a warning that he could give consistent with his duty; and when, with a shrug, Johnny Lenley went out into the night, the heart of Alan Wembury was sore.

"What fools these people are! " he said aloud.

"And a good job, too! " returned the sergeant. "If they weren't fools, you'd never catch 'em! "

Wembury would have gone out had it not been for his promise to meet Dr. Lomond here. He did not want to be round when the inevitable happened and Johnny Lenley was brought in—unless he had taken the hint. Had he? It seemed impossible of belief that he could have the situation so plainly put before him, and yet ignore the warning.

The Ringer

CHAPTER 41

LOMOND had just shuffled in and was cursing the weather when there was a heavy footfall in the corridor outside and the lawyer lurched in. His overcoat was open, his silk hat was on the back of his head, an unaccustomed cigarette drooped from his lips. The transition from the dark street to the well—lit charge—room temporarily blinded him. He leered for a long time at the doctor.

"The man of medicine and the man of law!" he said thickly and thumped himself on the chest. "My dear doctor, this is almost an historic meeting!"

He turned to Alan. "Have they brought him in? I didn't think he'd be fool enough to do the job, but he's better away, my dear Wembury, very much better."

"Did you come to find out? You might have saved yourself the trouble by telephoning," said Alan sternly.

The whole mien of Meister suddenly changed. The look that Alan had seen in his eyes before reappeared, and when lie spoke his voice was harsh but coherent.

"No, I didn't come for that." He looked round over his shoulder. The policeman had come from the door to the sergeant, and was whispering something to him. Even the doctor seemed interested. "Hackitt cleared out and left me alone—the dirty coward! Alone in the house!"

Up went the hand to his mouth.

"It got on my nerves, Wembury. Every sound I heard, the creak of a chair when I moved, a coal falling from the fire, the rattle of the windows—"

Out of the dark beyond the doorway loomed a figure. Nobody saw it. The three men talking together at the desk least of all. Inspector Bliss stared into the charge—room for a second and vanished as though he were part of some magician's trick. The policeman at the desk caught a glimpse of him and walked to the door. The sergeant and the doctor followed at a more leisurely pace.

The Ringer

"Every sound brings my heart into my mouth, Wembury. I feel as though I stood in the very presence of doom."

His voice was a husky whine.

"I feel it now—as though somewhere near me, in this very room, death were at my elbow. Oh, God, it's awful—awful!"

Suddenly he swayed, and Alan Wembury caught him just in time. Fortunately the doctor was at hand, and they sat him on a chair whilst Sergeant Carter delved into his desk for an ancient bottle of smelling—salts that had served many a fainting lady, overcome in that room by her temporary misfortunes.

"What's the matter with him?"

"Dope," answered the doctor laconically. "Take him into the inspector's room, sergeant, he'll be all right in a few minutes!"

He watched the limp figure assisted from the charge—room and shook his head. Then he strolled back to the main door and into the corridor. He was peering out into the night.

"What is it, doctor?" asked Alan.

"There he is again!" Lomond pointed to the dark street.

"Who is it?"

"He's been watching the station ever since Meister came in," said Lomond, as he came back to the charge—room and drew up a chair to the fire.

"Who is the mysterious watcher?" asked Wembury, smiling.

"I don't know. It looked like Bliss to me," said Lomond, rolling a cigarette; "he doesn't like me—I don't know why."

"Do you know anybody he likes—except Bliss?" growled Wembury.

"I heard quite a curious thing about him at the club this afternoon," said Lomond slowly. "I met a man who knew him in Washington—a

The Ringer

doctor man. He swears that he saw Bliss in the psychopathic ward of a Brooklyn hospital."

"When was this?"

"That is the absurd part of it. He said he saw him only a fortnight ago."

Wembury smiled. "He has been back months."

"Do you know Bliss very well?"

"No, not very well," admitted Wembury. "I never met him until he returned from America. I had seen him—he's u much older man than I, and my promotion was rather rapid. He was a sub—inspector when I was only a constable—hallo!"

A man strode into the charge—room and walked straight to the sergeant's desk. It was Inspector Bliss.

"I want a gun," he said shortly.

"I beg pardon?" Carter stared at him.

"I want an automatic."—louder.

Wembury chuckled maliciously.

"That's right, sergeant—Central Inspector Bliss from Scotland Yard wants an automatic. What do you want it for, Bliss? Going ratting?"

Bliss favoured him with a crooked smile.

"Yes, but you needn't be afraid, though. What's it to do with you?"

"Quite a lot," said Wembury, quietly, as the sergeant produced an automatic. "This is my division."

"Any reason why I shouldn't have it?" demanded the bearded man.

"None," said Wembury, and as the other made for the door: "I should sign for it, though. You seem to have forgotten the routine, Bliss."

The Ringer

Bliss turned with a curse. "I've been away from this damned country, you know that."

The doctor's eyes were twinkling. "Good evening, Mr. Bliss."

For the first time it seemed Bliss noticed the police surgeon's presence. "'Evening, Professor. Caught The Ringer yet?"

"Not yet," smiled Lomond.

"Huh! Better write another book and then perhaps you will!"

"We are amused," responded Lomond dryly. "No, I haven't caught The Ringer, but I dare say I could put my hand on him."

Bliss looked at the other suspiciously. "Think so? You've got a theory, eh?"

"A conviction, a very strong conviction," said Lomond mysteriously.

"Now you take a tip from me. Leave police work to policemen. Arthur Milton's a dangerous man. Seen his wife lately?"

"No—have you?"

Bliss turned. "No; I don't even know who she's living with."

The doctor's face hardened. "Would you remember you're speaking of a particular friend of mine?" he demanded.

Inspector Bliss allowed himself the rare luxury of a chuckle. "Oh, she's caught you, too, eh? She does find 'em!"

"Have you never heard of a woman having a disinterested friend?" demanded Lomond.

"Oh yes, there's one born every minute," was the harsh reply, and, seeing Wembury's disapproving eye on him: "You're a bit of a sentimental Johnny, too, aren't you, Wembury?"

"That's my weakness," said Alan coolly.

The Ringer

"That girl Lenley—she's in Meister's office, isn't she? "

Wembury smiled his contempt. "You've found that out, have you? There are the makings of a detective in you, " he said, but Bliss was not perturbed by the studied insult.

"Sweet on her, they tell me. Very romantic! The old squire's daughter and the love—sick copper! "

"If you must use thieves' slang, call me 'busy'. Were you ever in love, Bliss? "

"Me! Huh! No woman can make a fool of me! " said Inspector Bliss, one hand on the door.

"It takes a clever woman to improve on God's handiwork. What are you doing down here, anyway? " retorted Alan rudely.

"Your job! " snapped Bliss, as he went out, banging the door behind him.

CHAPTER 42

Carter was intrigued.

"It's curious that the inspector doesn't know station routine, isn't it, sir?"

"Everything about Mr. Bliss is curious," said Alan savagely. "Bliss! Where he got his name from I'd like to know!"

Lomond went to the door of the inspector's room, where Meister lay under the watchful eye of a "relief". He was rapidly recovering, the doctor said. As he returned, a policeman came in and whispered to Wembury.

"A lady to see me? Who is it?"

"It's Cora Ann Milton," said Lomond, again displaying that uncanny instinct of his. "My future bride!"

Cora Ann came in with an air in which defiance and assumed indifference were blended. "Say, is there something wrong with your date book, doctor?"

Alan regarded the old doctor suspiciously as Lomond took the woman's hand in his.

"There's something wrong with you. Why, you're all of a dither, Cora Ann."

She nodded grimly. "I never wait longer than an hour for any man."

Wembury looked up at this.

"Good Lord! I was taking ye to dinner!" gasped the doctor. "I was called down here and it slipped out of my mind."

Cora Ann looked round with every indication of distaste.

"I can't blame you. If I were called to a place like this my mind would slip a cog. So this is a police station? My idea of hell, only not

The Ringer

so bright! " She looked at Wembury. "Say, where's your fancy dress? Everybody else is in uniform. "

"I keep that for wearing at parties, " he smiled.

She shuddered.

"Ugh—doesn't it make you sick? How can you stay here? There must be something wrong with a man's mind who likes this sort of life. "

"There's something wrong with you, " said Lomond quietly. "There's a queer vacant look in your eye. "

She eyed him steadily. "The vacancy isn't in my eye—I haven't had anything to eat since lunch! "

Lomond was all remorse. "You poor hungry mite—could you not eat by yourself? "

"I prefer to take my meals under the eye of a medical man, " said Cora.

"I'm not so sure that it would be safe, " he bantered. "Do you think I'll poison you? "

"You might poison my mind. "

All the time Wembury was listening with undisguised astonishment. What was the doctor's game? Why was he making friends with this girl?

"Are you going to take pity on a poor hysterical female? " she demanded.

There was an element of desperation in her tone; it was as though she were making one last effort to… what? Alan was puzzled.

"I'd love to, Cora Ann, but—" Lomond was saying.

"But! But! " she mocked. "You're a 'butter', eh? Listen, Scottie, you won't have to pay for the dinner! "

The Ringer

He grinned at this. "That's certainly an inducement, but I've got work to do."

In a second her face had grown haggard. "Work!" She laughed bitterly, and with a shrug of her shoulders walked listlessly towards the door. "I know the work! You're trying to hang Arthur Milton. That's your idea of work! All right."

"Where are you going now, lassie?" asked the doctor, anxiously.

She looked at him, and her smile was a little hard. "It's too late for dinner. I think I'll go and have supper and a music lesson at the same time. I've a friend who plays the piano very, very well."

Lomond walked to the door and peered out into the fog after her. "That sounds like a threat to me," he said.

Alan did not answer immediately. When he spoke his voice was very grave.

"Doctor—I wish you wouldn't make love to The Ringer's wife."

"What do you mean?"

"I mean—I don't want the possibility of two tragedies on my mind."

Carter, who had been into the room where Meister was lying, came back to his desk at that moment.

"How is he now?"

"He's all right, sir," said the sergeant.

Tramp, tramp, tramp!

Alan's keen ears had caught the sound of the measured march, the peculiar tempo of a man in custody, and he drew a long breath as Johnny Lenley, his arm gripped by a plain—clothes policeman, came through the door and was arrayed before the desk. There was no preliminary.

"I am Detective—Constable Bell," said the tall man. "This evening I was on the roof of 57, Camden Crescent, and I saw this man come up

The Ringer

through a trap—door in the attic of No. 55. I saw him searching behind the cistern of 57, and took him into custody. I charged him with being on enclosed premises for the purpose of committing a felony."

Lenley stood looking down at the floor. He scarcely seemed interested in the proceedings, until he raised his head and his eyes found Wembury's, and then he nodded slowly.

"Thank you, Wembury," he said. "If I had the brain of a rabbit I shouldn't be here."

Carter at the desk dipped his pen in the ink. "What is your name?" he asked automatically.

"John Lenley." Silence and a splutter of writing.

"Your address?"

"I have no address."

"Your trade?"

"I'm a convict on licence," said Johnny quietly.

The sergeant put down his pen. "Search him," he said. Johnny spread out his arms and the tall officer ran his hands through his pockets and carried what he had found to the desk. "Who put me away, Wembury?"

Alan shook his head. "That is not a question to ask me," he said. "You know that very well." He nodded to the desk to call the prisoner's attention to the man who was, for the moment, in supreme authority.

"Have you any explanation for your presence on the roof of 57, Camden Crescent?" asked the sergeant.

Johnny Lenley cleared his throat.

"I went after some stuff that was supposed to be planted behind a cistern. And it wasn't there. That's all. Who was the snout? You needn't tell me, because I know. Look after my sister, Wembury;

207

The Ringer

she'll want some looking after, and I'd sooner trust you than any man—"

It was unfortunate for all concerned that Mr. Meister chose that moment to make his bedraggled appearance. He stared foolishly at the man in the hands of the detectives, and Johnny Lenley smiled.

"Hallo, Maurice!" he said softly.

The lawyer was staggered.

"Why—why—it's—it's Johnny!" he stammered. "You haven't been getting into trouble again, have you, Johnny?" He raised his hands in a gesture of despair. "What a misfortune! I'll be down at the court to defend you in the morning, my boy." He ambled up to the sergeant's desk. "Any food he wants, let him have it at my expense," he said loudly.

"Meister!" The word came like the clang of steel on steel. "There was no swag behind the cistern!"

Mr. Meister's face was a picture of wonder and amazement.

"No swag behind the cistern? 'Swag?' I don't know what you're talking about, my boy."

Lenley nodded and grinned mirthlessly.

"I came out too soon for you. It interfered with your little scheme, didn't it, Meister? You swine!"

Before Wembury could realise what was happening, Johnny had the lawyer by the throat. In a second four men were struggling in a heap on the ground.

As they rolled on the floor, the door of the charge room flung open, and Inspector Bliss appeared. He stood for a second, and then with one leap was in the thick of the scrum.

It was Bliss who flung the boy back. He walked to the prostrate Meister.

"Is he hurt?" he demanded.

The Ringer

White with rage, Johnny glared at the lawyer.

"I wish to God I'd killed him! " he hissed.

Bliss turned his hard eyes upon the prisoner.

"Don't be so damned selfish, Lenley! " he said coldly.

CHAPTER 43

ALAN WEMBURY had only one thought in his mind as he walked from the police station, and that a supremely wretched one. Mary had to be told. Again he was to be an unwilling messenger of woe. A fog was blowing up from the river, and lay so thick in some places that he had to grope his way feeling along the railings. In the dip of Lewisham High Road ii was clearer, for some reason. Being human, he cursed the log; cursed John Lenley for his insensate folly; but it was when he thought of Maurice Meister that he found it most difficult to control his anger. The base treachery of the man was almost inhuman.

He climbed up the stone staircase of Malpas Mansions and knocked at the door of Mary's flat. There was no answer. He knocked again, and then he heard an inner door open with the snap of a lock as it was turned back, and: "Is that you, Johnny? I thought you had the key."

"No, my dear, it is I."

"Alan!" She took a step back and her hand went to her heart. "Is anything wrong?"

Her face was twitching with anxiety. He did not answer until he had closed the door behind him and followed her into the room.

"Is there anything wrong?" she asked again…. "Is it Johnny?"

He nodded. She sank into a chair and covered her eyes with her hands.

"Is he… arrested?" she whispered.

"Yes," said Alan.

"For the forgery?" She spoke in a voice little above a whisper.

"For the forgery?" He stared down at her. "I don't know what you mean, my dear." And she turned a white, bewildered face up to his. "Isn't it for forgery?" she asked, in wonder; and then, as she realised her indiscretion: "Will you forget that I asked that, Alan?"

The Ringer

"Of course I'll forget, Mary, my dear. I know nothing about a forgery. Johnny was arrested for being on enclosed premises."

"For burglary—oh, my God!"

"I don't know what it's all about. I'm a little at sea myself," said Alan. "I wish I could tell you everything I guess: perhaps I will, even if I am fired out of the force for it."

He dropped his hand gently on her shoulder.

"You've got to stand up to this, Mary; there may be some explanation. I can't understand why Johnny should have been such a lunatic. I did my best to warn him. I still think there is a chance for him. After I leave here and have seen Meister, I'm going to knock up a lawyer friend of mine and get his advice. I wish he hadn't gone for Meister."

And then he told her of the scene at the police station, and she was horrified.

"He struck Maurice? Oh, he's mad! Why, Maurice has it in his power—" She stopped short.

Alan's keen eyes searched her face.

"Go on," he said gently. "Maurice has it in his power—?" And, when she did not speak: "Is it the forgery you are thinking of?"

She looked at him reproachfully.

"Alan, you promised—"

"I didn't promise anything," he half smiled, "but I'll tell you this, that anything you say to me is to Alan Wembury the individual, and not to Alan Wembury the police officer. Mary, my dear, you're in trouble: won't you let me help you?"

She shook her head.

"I can't, I can't! This has made things so dreadful. Maurice is so vindictive, and he will never forgive Johnny. And he was going to be so nice... he was getting us a little farm in the country."

The Ringer

It was on the tip of Alan's tongue to tell her the truth about the betrayal, but the rigid discipline of the police force was triumphant. The first law and the last law of criminal detection is never to betray the informer.

"It's a mystery to me why Johnny went to this house. He told some story about there being loot, the proceeds of an old burglary, hidden in a cistern, but of course there was nothing of the sort."

She was crouching over the table, her head on her hands, her eyes closed. He thought for a moment she was going to faint, and his arm went about her shoulder.

"Mary, can't I help you?" His voice was husky. He found a difficulty in breathing. "I don't care how you think of me, whether it is as the son of your old servant, as Inspector Wembury the police officer, or just Alan Wembury... who loves you!"

She did not move; made no attempt to withdraw from his encircling arm.

"I've said it now and I'm glad," he went on breathlessly. "I've always loved you since you were a child. Won't you tell me everything, Mary?"

And then suddenly she pushed him away and came to her feet, wild—eyed, her lips parted as at some horrible thought.

"I can't, I can't!" she said, almost incoherently. "Don't touch me, Alan.... I'm not worthy of you.... I thought I need not go, but now I know that I must... for Johnny's sake."

"Go where?" he asked sternly, but she shook her head. Then she flung her hands out impulsively and caught him in a frenzied clasp.

"Alan, I know you love me... and I'm glad... glad! You know what that means, don't you? A woman wouldn't say that unless she... she felt that way herself. But I've got to save Johnny—I must!"

"Won't you tell me what it is?"

She shook her head. "I can't. This is one of the hard places that I've got to go through without help."

The Ringer

But he was not to be silenced. "Is it Meister? " he asked. "Is it some threat that he is holding over you? "

Mary shook her head wearily.

"I don't want to talk about it, Alan—what can I do for Johnny? Is it really a bad charge—I mean, will he be sent to penal servitude again? Do you think that Maurice could save him? "

For the moment Johnny's fate did not interest the police officer. He had no mind, no thought for anybody but this lonely girl, battered and bruised and broken. His arms went round her; he held her to his breast and kissed her mid lips.

"Don't, please, Alan, " she murmured, and realising that she had no physical strength to resist, he released her gently.

He himself was shaking like an aspen when he moved to the door.

"I'm going to solve a few mysteries—about Johnny and about other things, " he said, between his teeth. "Will you stay here where I can find you? I will come back in an hour. "

Dimly divining his purpose, she called him back, but he was gone.

Meister's house was in darkness when Alan struggled through the fog into Flanders Lane. The police officer on duty at the door had nothing to report except that he had heard the sound of a piano coming faintly from one of the upper rooms.

The policeman had the key of the gate and the front door, and, leaving the man on duty outside, Alan strode into the house. As he mounted the stairs, the sounds of a Humoresque came down to him. He tried Meister's door: it was locked. He tapped on the panel.

"What do you want? " asked Meister's slurred voice. "Who is it? "

"Wembury. Open the door, " said Alan impatiently.

He heard the man growl as he crossed the room, and presently the door was opened. He walked in; the room was in darkness save for a light which came from one standard lamp near the piano.

The Ringer

"Well, what's that young blackguard got to say for himself? " demanded Maurice. He had been drinking heavily; the place reeked with the smell of spirits. There was a big bruise on his cheek where John Lenley had struck him.

Without invitation, Alan switched on the lights, and the lawyer blinked impatiently at him.

"I don't want lights. Curse you, why did you put those lights on? " he snarled.

"I want to see you, " said Wembury, "and I would like you to see me. "

Meister stared at him stupidly.

"Well, " he asked at last, "you wanted to see me? You seem to have taken charge of my house, Mr. Wembury. You walk in and you go out as you wish; you turn on my lights and put them off at your own sweet will. Now perhaps you will condescend to explain your attitude and your manner. "

"I've come to ask you something about a forgery. "

He saw Maurice start. "A forgery? What do you mean? "

"You know damned well what I mean, " said Alan savagely. "What is this forgery you've told Mary Lenley about? "

Drunk as he was, the question sobered the man. He shook his head. "I really don't understand what you're talking about. " Maurice Meister was no fool. If Mary had told the story of the forged cheque, this bullying oaf of a police officer would not ask such a question. He had heard a little, guessed much—how much, Meister was anxious to learn.

"My dear man, you come here in the middle of the night and ask me questions about forgeries, " he went on in a flippant tone. "Do you really expect me to be conversational and informative—after what I have experienced tonight? I've dealt with so many forgeries in my life that I hardly know to which one you refer. "

214

The Ringer

His eyes strayed unconsciously to a little round table that was set in the centre of the room, and covered by a fine white cloth. Alan had noticed this and wondered what the cloth concealed. It might be Meister's supper, or it might be — Only for a second did he allow his attention to be diverted, however.

"Meister, you're holding some threat over the head of Mary Lenley, and I want to know what it is. You've asked her to do something which she doesn't want to do. I don't know what that is either, but I can guess. I'm warning you—"

"As a police officer? " sneered Maurice.

"As a man, " said Alan quietly. "For the evil you are contemplating there may be no remedy in law, but I tell you this, that if one hair of Mary Lenley's head is hurt, you will be sorry. "

The lawyer's eyes narrowed.

"That is a threat of personal violence, one presumes? " he said, and in spite of the effort to appear unconcerned his voice trembled. "Threatened men live long, Inspector Wembury, mid I have been threatened all my life and nothing has come of it. The Ringer threatens me, Johnny threatens me, you threaten me—I thrive on threats! "

The eyes of Alan Wembury had the hard brightness of burnished steel. "Meister, " he said softly, "I wonder if you realise how near you are to death? "

Meister's jaw dropped and he gaped at the young man who towered over him.

"Not at my hands, perhaps; not at The Ringer's hands, nor John Lenley's hands; but if what I believe is true, and if I am right in suspecting the kind of villainy you contemplate tonight, and you carry your plans through, be sure of one thing, Maurice Meister— that if The Ringer fails, I shall get you! "

Meister looked at him for a long time and then forced a smile.

"By God, you're in love with Mary Lenley, " he chuckled harshly. "That's the best joke I've heard for years! "

The Ringer

Alan heard his raucous laugher as he went down the stairs, and the echo of it rang in his ears all the way down Flanders Lane.

He had a call to make—a lawyer friend who lived in Greenwich. His interview with that gentleman was very satisfactory.

The Ringer

CHAPTER 44

ALAN WEMBURY came into the charge—room and glanced at the clock. He had been gone two hours.

"Has Mr. Bliss been in?" he asked.

Bliss had vanished from the station almost as dramatically as he arrived.

"Yes, sir; he came in for a few minutes: he wanted to see a man in the cells," said Carter.

Instantly Alan was alert. "Who?" he asked.

"That boy Lenley. I let him have the key."

What interest had the Scotland Yard man in Johnny? Wembury was puzzled. "Oh—he didn't stay long?"

"No, sir. Above five minutes."

Alan shook his rain—soddened hat in the fireplace. "No messages?"

"No, sir: one of our drunks has been giving a lot of trouble. I had to telephone to Dr. Lomond—he's with him now. By the way, sir, did you see this amongst Lenley's papers? I only found it after you'd gone."

He took a card from the desk and gave it to Wembury, who read: "Here is the key. You can go in when you like—No. 57."

"Why, that's Meister's writing."

"Yes, sir," nodded Carter, "and No. 57 is Meister's own property. I don't know how that will affect the charge against Lenley."

As he read a great load seemed to roll from Alan Wembury's heart: everything his lawyer friend had said, came back to him. "Thank God! That lets him out! It was just as I thought! Meister must have been very drunk to have written that—it is his first slip."

The Ringer

"What is the law?"

Wembury was no lawyer, but when he had discovered that the arrest had been made on Meister's property, he had seen a loophole. Johnny Lenley went at Meister's invitation—it could not be burglary. Meister was the landlord of the house.

"Was there a key?" he asked.

"Yes, sir." Carter handed the key over. "It has Meister's name on the label."

Alan sighed his relief. "By gad! I'm glad Lenley is inside, though. If ever I saw murder in a man's eyes it was in his!"

Carter put a question that had been in his mind all the evening. "I suppose Lenley isn't The Ringer?" he asked, and Alan laughed.

"Don't be absurd! How can he be?" As he spoke he heard his name called, and Lomond ran into the charge—room from the passage leading to the cells. "Is anything wrong?" asked Alan quickly. "What cell did you put Lenley in?"

"Number eight at the far end," said Carter. "The door's wide open—it's empty!" Carter flew out of the room. Alan picked up the 'phone from the sergeant's desk.

"By God, Lomond, he'll be after Meister." Carter came into the room hurriedly.

"He's got away all right," he said. "The door is wide open, and so is the door into the yard!"

"Two of my men, Carter," said Wembury quickly, and then the number he had asked for came through.

"Scotland Yard?... Give me the night officer... Inspector Wembury speaking. Take this for all stations. Arrest and detain John Lenley, who escaped tonight from Flanders Lane police station whilst under detention. Age twenty—seven, height six feet, dark, wearing a—"

"Blue serge," prompted Sergeant Carter.

The Ringer

"He's a convict on licence, " continued Wembury. "Sort that out, will you? Thank you. "

He hung up the receiver as a detective came in.

"Get your bicycle and go round to all patrols. Lenley's got away. You can describe the man. "

To the second man who came in: "Go to Malpas Mansions—Lenley lives there with his sister. Don't alarm the young lady, do you understand? If you find him, bring him in. "

When the men had hurried out into the thick night, Alan strode up and down the charge—room. This danger to Meister was a new one. Dr. Lomond was going and collecting his impedimenta.

"How the devil did he get away? " Wembury put his thoughts into words.

"I have my own theory, " said Lomond. "If you allow Detective Inspector Bliss too near a prisoner, he'll get away easily enough. "

On which cryptic note he left.

He had to wait at the head of the steps to allow Sam Hackitt to pass in—and Hackitt did not come willingly, for he was in the hands of a detective and a uniformed policeman.

Alan heard a familiar plaint and looked over his shoulder.

"'Evening, Mr. Wembury. See what they've done to me? Why don't you stop 'em 'ounding me down? " he demanded in a quivering voice.

"What's the trouble? " asked Alan testily. He was in no mood for the recital of petty larcenies.

"I saw this man on Deptford Broadway, " said the detective, "and asked him what he had in his bag. He refused to open the bag, and tried to run away. I arrested him. "

"That's a lie, " interposed Sam. "Now speak the truth: don't perjure yourself in front of witnesses. I simply said: 'If you want the bag, take it.'"

"Shut up, Hackitt, " said Wembury. "What is in the bag? "

"Here! " said Sam, hastily breaking in. "I want to tell you about that bag. To tell you the truth, I found it. It was layin' against a wall, an' I says to meself, ' I wonder what that is? '—just like that. "

"And what did the bag say? " asked the sceptical Carter.

The bag "said" many damning things. The first thing revealed was the cash-box. Sam had not had time to throw it away. The sergeant opened it, and took out a thick wad of notes and laid them on the desk.

"Old Meister's cash—box! " Sam's tone was one of horror and amazement. "Now how did that get there? There's a mystery for you, Wembury! That ought to be in your memories when you write them for the Sunday newspapers. 'Strange and mysterious discovery of a cash—box! '"

"There's nothing mysterious about it, " said Wembury. "Anything else? "

One by one they produced certain silver articles which were very damning.

"It's a cop, " said Sam philosophically. "You've spoilt the best honeymoon I'm ever likely to have—that's what you've done, Wembury. Who shopped me? "

"Name? " asked Carter conventionally.

"Samuel Cuthbert 'Ackitt—don't forget the haitch. "

"Address? "

Sam wrinkled his nose.

"Buckingham Palace, " he said sarcastically.

The Ringer

"No address. What was your last job?"

"Chambermaid! 'Ere, Mr. Wembury, do you know what Meister gave me for four days' work? Ten bob! That's sweating! I wouldn't go into that house—'aunted, I call it—"

The 'phone rang at that moment and Carter answered it. "Haunted?"

"I was in Meister's room, and I was just coming away with the stuff when I felt—a cold hand touch me! Cold! Clammy like a dead man's hand! I jumped for the winder and got out on the leads!"

Carter covered the telephone receiver with his palm.

"It's Atkins, sir—the man at Meister's house. He says he can't make him hear—Meister's gone up to his room but the door's locked."

Alan went to the 'phone quickly.

"It's Mr. Wembury speaking. Are you in the house?... You can't get in? Can't make him hear?... You can't get any answer at all? Is there a light in any of the windows?... You're quite sure he's in the house?"

Carter saw his face change.

"What's that? The Ringer's been seen in Deptford tonight! I'll come along right away."

He hung up the receiver.

"I don't know how much of that cold hand is cold feet, Hackitt, but you're coming along to Meister's house with me. Take him along!"

Protesting noisily, Mr. Hackitt was hurried into the street.

From his hip pocket Wembury slipped an automatic, clicked back the jacket and went swiftly to the door.

"Good luck, sir!" said Carter.

Alan thought he would need all the luck that came his way.

CHAPTER 45

THE car was worse than useless—the fog was so thick that they were forced to feel their way by railing and wall. One good piece of luck they had—Alan overtook the doctor and commandeered his services. The route led through the worst part of Flanders Lane—a place where police went in couples.

Wembury's hand lamp showed a pale yellow blob that was almost useless.

"Is that you, doctor?" he asked and heard a grunt.

"What a fearful hole! Where am I?"

"In Flanders Lane," said Wembury. He had hardly spoken the words before a titter of laughter came from somewhere near at hand.

"Who is that?" asked Lomond.

"Don't move," warned Alan. "Part of the road is up. Can't you see the red light?"

He thought he saw a pinkish blur ahead.

"I've been seeing the red light all the evening," said Lomond. "Road up, eh?"

Some unseen person spoke hoarsely in the fog. "That's him that's going to get The Ringer!" They heard the soft chuckle of many voices.

"Who was that?" asked Lomond again.

"You are in Flanders Lane, I tell you," replied Alan. "Its other name is Little Hell!"

The doctor dropped his voice.

"I can see nobody."

The Ringer

"They are sitting on their doorsteps watching us," answered Alan in the same tone. "What a night for The Ringer!"

Near at hand and from some miserable house a cracked gramophone began to play. Loudly at first and then the volume of sound decreased as though a door were shut upon it.

Then from another direction a woman's voice shrieked: "Pipe the fly doctor! 'Im that's goin' to get The Ringer!"

"How the devil can they see?" asked Lomond in amazement.

Alan shivered. "They've got rats' eyes," he said. "Hark at the rustle of them—ugh! Hallo there!"

Somebody had touched him on the shoulder.

"They're having a joke with us. Is it like this all the way, I wonder?"

Ahead, a red light glowed and another. They saw a grimy man crouching over a brazier of coke: a watchman. For a second as he raised his hideous face, Lomond was startled.

"Ugh! Who are you," he demanded.

"I'm the watchman. It's a horrible place, is Flanders Lane. They're always screaming—it'd freeze your blood to hear the things I hear." His tone was deep—sepulchral.

"She's been hangin' round here all night—the lady?" he said amazingly.

"What lady?" asked Wembury.

"I thought she was a ghost—you see ghosts here—and hear 'em."

Somebody screamed in one of the houses they could not see.

"Always shoutin' murder in Flanders Lane," said the old watchman gloomily. "They're like beasts down in them cellars. —some of 'em never comes out. They're born down there and they die down there."

The Ringer

At that minute Lomond felt a hand touch his arm.

"Where are you?" he asked.

"Don't go any farther—for God's sake!" she whispered, and he was staggered.

"Cora Ann!"

"Who is that?" asked Alan turning back.

"There's death there—death"—Cora's low voice was urgent—"I want to save you. Go back, go back!"

"Trying to scare me," said Lomond reproachfully. "Cora Ann!"

In another instant she was gone and at that moment the fog lifted and they could see the street lamp outside Meister's house.

Atkins was waiting under the cover of the glass awning, and had nothing more to report.

"I didn't want to break the door until you came in. There was no sound that I could hear except the piano. I went round the back of the house, there's a light burning in his room, but I could see that, of course, from under his door."

"No sound?"

"None—only the piano."

Alan hurried into the house, followed by the manacled Hackitt and his custodian, Atkins and the doctor bringing up the rear. He went up the stairs and knocked at the door heavily. There was no answer. Hammering on the panel with his fist, he shouted the lawyer's name, but still there was no reply.

"Where is the housekeeper?" he asked. "Mrs. K.?"

"In her room, sir. At least, she was there a few hours before. But she's deaf."

The Ringer

"Stone deaf, I should say, " said Alan, and then: "Give me any kind of key—I can open it, " said Hackitt.

They stood impatiently by whilst he fiddled with the lock. His boast was justified—in a few seconds the catch snapped back and the door opened.

Only one big standard lamp burnt in the room, and this threw an eerie light upon the yellow face of Meister. He was in evening dress and sat at the piano, his arms resting on the top, his yellow face set in a look of fear.

"Phew! " said Alan, and wiped his streaming forehead. "I've heard the expression 'dead to the world', but this is certainly the first time I've seen a man in that state. "

He shook the dazed lawyer, but he might as well have shaken himself for all the effect it had upon the slumberer.

"Thank Gawd! " said a voice behind. It was Hackitt's trembling voice. "I never thought I'd be glad to see that old bird alive! "

Alan glanced up at the chandelier that hung from the ceiling. "Put on the lights, " he said. "See if you can wake him, doctor. "

"Have you tried burning his ears? " suggested the helpful Hackitt, and was sternly ordered to be quiet. "Can't a man express his emotions? " asked Mr. Hackitt wrathfully. "There's no law against that, is there? Didn't I tell you, Mr. Wembury? He's doped! I've seen him like that before—doped and dizzy! "

"Hackitt, where were you in this room when you felt the hand? " asked Alan. "Take the cuff off. "

The handcuff was unlocked, and Hackitt moved to a place almost opposite the door. Between the door and the small settee was a supper table, which Wembury had seen the moment he came into the room. So Mary had not come: that was an instant cause of relief. "I was here, " said Hackitt. "The hand came from there. "

He pointed to the mystery door, and Wembury saw that the bolts were shot, the door locked, and the key hung in its place on the wall.

The Ringer

It was impossible that anybody could have come into the room from that entrance without Meister's assistance.

He next turned his attention to the window. The chintz curtains had been pulled across; Hackitt had noticed this immediately. He had left them half—drawn and window and grille open.

"Somebody's been here, " he said emphatically. "I'm sure the old man hasn't moved. I left the bars unfastened. "

The door leading to Mary's little office room was locked. So was the second door, which gave to the private staircase to Meister's own bedroom. He looked at the bolts again, and was certain they had not been touched that night. It was a dusty room; the carpet had not been beaten for months, and every footstep must stir up a little dust cloud. He wetted his finger, touched the knob of the bolt, and although he had handled it that afternoon, there were microscopic specks to tell him that the doorway had not been used.

Atkins was working at the sleeping Meister, shaking him gently, encouraged thereto by the uncomfortable snorts he provoked, but so far his efforts were unsuccessful. Wembury, standing by the supper table, looked at it thoughtfully.

"Supper for two, " he said, picked up a bottle of champagne and examined it. "Cordon Rouge, '11. "

"He was expecting somebody, " said Dr. Lomond wisely and, when Wembury nodded: "A lady! "

"Why a lady? " asked Wembury irritably. "Men drink wine. "

The doctor stooped and picked up a small silver dish, piled high with candy.

"But they seldom eat chocolates, " he said, and Wembury laughed irritably.

"You're becoming a detective in spite of yourself. Meister has— queer tastes. "

The Ringer

There was a small square morocco case under the serviette that the doctor moved. He opened it. From the velvet bed within there came the glitter and sparkle of diamonds.

"Is he the kind of man who gives these things to his—queer friends?" he asked with a quiet smile.

"I don't know." Wembury's answer was brusque to rudeness.

"Look, governor!" whispered Hackitt.

Meister was moving, his head moved restlessly from side to side. Presently he became aware that he was not alone.

"Hallo, people!" he said thickly. "Give me a drink."

He groped out for an invisible bottle.

"I think you've had enough drink and drugs for one night, Meister. Pull yourself together. I've something unpleasant to tell you."

Meister looked at him stupidly.

"What's the time?" he asked slowly.

"Half—past twelve."

The answer partially sobered the man.

"Half—past twelve!" He staggered rockily to his feet. "Is she here?" he asked, holding on to the table.

"Is who here?" demanded Wembury with cold deliberation.

Mr. Meister shook his aching head.

"She said she'd come," he muttered. "She promised faithfully... twelve o'clock. If she tries to fool me—"

"Who is the 'she', Meister?" asked Wembury, and the lawyer smiled foolishly.

"Nobody you know," he said.

The Ringer

"She was coming to keep you company, I suppose?"

"You've got it.... Give me a drink." The man was still dazed, hardly conscious of what was going on around him. Then, in his fuddled way, he saw Hackitt.

"You've come back, eh? Well, you can go again!"

"Hear what he says?" asked the eager Hackitt. "He's withdrawn the charge!"

"Have you lost your cash—box?" asked Wembury.

"Eh? Lost...?" He stumbled towards the drawer and pulled it open. "Gone!" he cried hoarsely. "You took it!" He pointed a trembling finger to Sam. "You dirty thief...!"

"Steady, now," said Wembury, and caught him as he swayed. "We've got Hackitt; you can charge him in the morning."

"Stole my cash—box!" He was maudlin in his anger and drunkenness. "Bit the hand that fed him!"

Mr. Hackitt's lips curled.

"I like your idea about feeding!" he said scornfully. "Cottage pie and rice puddin'!"

But Meister was not listening. "Give me a drink."

Wembury gripped him by the arm. "Do you realise what this means?" he asked. "The Ringer is in Deptford."

But he might have been talking to a man of wood.

"Good job," said Meister with drunken gravity, and tried to look at his watch. "Clear out: I've got a friend coming to me."

"Your friend has a very poor chance of getting in. All the doors of this room are fastened, except where Atkins is on duly, and they will remain fastened."

The Ringer

Meister muttered something, tripped and would have fallen if Wembury had not caught him by the arm and lowered him down into the chair.

"The Ringer!... " Meister sat with his head on his hands. "He'll have to be clever to get me... I can't think tonight, but tomorrow I'll tell you where you can put your hands on him, Wembury. My boy, you're a smart detective, aren't you? " He chuckled foolishly. "Let's have another drink. "

He had hardly spoken the words when two of the three lights in the chandelier went out.

"Who did that? " asked Wembury, turning sharply. "Did anybody touch the board? "

"No, sir, " said Atkins, standing at the door and pointing to the switch. "Only I could have touched it. "

Hackitt was near the window, examining the curtains, when the light had diverted his attention.

"Come over this side of the room: you're too near that window, " said Wembury.

"I was wondering who pulled the curtains, Mr. Wembury, " said Hackitt in a troubled voice. "I'll swear it wasn't the old man. He was sleeping when I left him and you couldn't get any answer by telephone, could you? "

He took hold of the curtain and pulled it aside and stared out into a pale face pressed against the pane: a pale, bearded face, that vanished instantly in the darkness.

At Hackitt's scream of terror Alan ran to the window. "What was it? "

"I don't know, " gasped Sam. "Something! "

"I saw something, too, " said Atkins.

The Ringer

Danger was at hand. There was a creeping feeling in Alan Wembury's spine, a cold shiver that sent the muscles of his shoulders rippling involuntarily.

"Take that man," he said.

The words were hardly out of his lips when all the lights in the room went out.

"Don't move, anybody!" whispered Alan. "Stand fast! Did you touch the switch, Atkins?"

"No, sir."

"Did any of you men touch the switch?"

There was a chorus of Noes.

The red light showed above the door.

Click!

Somebody had come into the room!

"Atkins, stand by Meister—feel along the table till you find him. Keep quiet, everybody."

Whoever it was, was in the room now. Alan heard the unquiet breathing, the rustle of a soft foot on the carpet, and waited. Suddenly there was a flicker of light. Only for a second it showed a white circle on the door of the safe, and was gone.

An electric hand lamp, and they were working at the safe. Still he did not move, though he was now in a position that would enable him to cut across the intruder's line of retreat.

He moved stealthily, both hands outstretched, his ears strained for the slightest sound. And then suddenly he gripped somebody, and nearly released his hold in his horror and amazement.

A woman! She was struggling frantically.

"Who are you?" he asked hoarsely.

The Ringer

"Let me go!" Only a whispered voice, strained, unrecognisable.

"I want you," he said, and then his knee struck something sharp and hard. It was the corner of the settee, and in the exquisite pain his hold was released. In another second she had escaped... when he put out his hands he grasped nothing.

And then he heard a voice—deep, booming, menacing.

"Meister, I have come for you...."

There was the sound of a cough—a long, choking cough....

"A light, somebody!"

As Wembury shouted, he heard the thud of a closing door.

"Strike a match. Haven't any of you men torches?"

And when the lights came on they looked at one another in amazement. There was nobody in the room save those who had been there when the lights went out, and the door was locked, bolted, had not been touched; the key still hung on the wall.

Alan stared; and then his eyes, travelling along the wall, were arrested by a sight that froze his blood.

Pinned to the wall by his own swordstick drooped Maurice Meister, and he was dead!

From somewhere outside the room came a laugh: a long, continuous, raucous laugh, as at a good joke, and the men listened and shivered, and even the face of Dr. Lomond changed colour.

The Ringer

CHAPTER 46

IT was an hour after Meister's body had been removed and Dr. Lomond was making a few notes.

He was the reverse of nervous. And yet twice in the last half—hour he had heard a queer sound, that he could not but associate with human movements.

"I'm going to see Mr. Wembury, " he said to the waiting constable. "I'll leave my bag here. "

"Mr. Wembury said he was coming back, sir, if you care to wait, " Harrap told him. "The sergeant's going to make a search of the house. There ought to be some queer things found here. Personally, " he added, "I'd like to have the job of searching the pantry or the wine—cellar, or wherever he keeps the beer. "

Again Lomond heard a sound. He went to the door leading to Meister's room and, pulling it open, stared. Alan Wembury was coming down the stairs.

"There are three ways into the house. I've found two of them, " he said.

Atkins, who had been searching some of the lower rooms, came in at that moment.

"Have you finished? " asked Wembury.

"Yes, sir. Meister was a fence all right. "

Alan nodded slowly. "Yes, I know. Is your relief here? "

"Yes, sir. "

"All right. You can go. Good night, Atkins. "

Lomond was looking at Wembury narrowly. He waited until the man had gone before he drew up a chair to the supper table.

The Ringer

"Wembury, my boy, you're worried about something—is it about Miss Lenley?"

"Yes—I've been to see her."

"And, of course, it was she who came into the room at that awkward moment?"

Alan stared at him.

"Lomond, I'm going to take a risk and tell you something, and there is no reason why I shouldn't, because this business has altered all The Ringer stuff. What happened tonight may mean ruin to me as a police officer... and still I don't care. Yes, it was Mary Lenley."

The doctor nodded gravely.

"So I supposed," he said.

"She came to get a cheque that Meister told her young Lenley had forged—a pure invention on Meister's part."

"How did she get into the room?" asked Lomond.

"She wouldn't tell me that—she's heartbroken. We took her brother, and although I'm certain he will get off, she doesn't believe that."

"Poor kid! Still, my boy—happy ending and all that sort of thing," said Lomond with a yawn.

"Happy ending! You're an optimist, doctor."

"I am. I never lose hope," said Lomond complacently. "So you've got young Lenley? That laugh we heard—ugh!"

Wembury shook his head.

"That wasn't Lenley! There is no mystery about the laugh—one of the Flanders Lane people going home—normally tight. The policeman on duty outside the house saw him and heard him."

"It sounded in the house," said Lomond with a shiver. "Well, The Ringer's work is done. There's no danger to anybody else, now."

The Ringer

"There's always danger enough—" began Wembury, and lifted his head, listening. The sound this time was more distinct.

"What was that? Sounded like somebody moving about the house, " said Lomond. "I've heard it before. "

Alan rose. "There is nobody in the house except the fellow outside. Officer! "

Harrap came in. "Yes, sir? "

"None of our people upstairs? "

"Not that I know of, sir. "

Wembury went to the door, opened it and shouted: "Anybody there? " There was no answer. "Just wait here. I'll go and see. "

He was gone quite a long time. When he returned his face was pale and drawn.

"All right, officer, you can go down, " he said shortly, and when the man saluted and went out: "There was a window open upstairs—a cat must have got in. "

Lomond's eyes did not leave his face.

"You look rather scared. What's the matter? " he demanded.

"I feel rather scared, " admitted Wembury. "This place stinks of death. "

But the answer did not satisfy the shrewd Lomond.

"Wembury—you saw something or somebody upstairs, " he challenged.

"You're a thought—reader, aren't you? " Alan's voice was a little husky.

"In a way, yes, " said the other slowly. "At this moment you are thinking of Central Inspector Bliss! "

The Ringer

Wembury started, but he was relieved of the necessity for replying. There was a tap at the door and the policeman entered.

"It has just been reported to me, sir, that a man has been seen getting over the wall," he said.

Wembury did not move.

"Oh!... How long ago?"

"About five minutes, sir."

"Was that the cat?" asked Lomond satirically, but Alan did not answer.

"You didn't see him?" he asked.

"No, sir; it happened when I was up here," said Harrap. "Excuse me, sir; my relief's overdue."

Wembury snapped round impatiently. "All right, all right. You can go!"

There was a long silence after the man had gone.

"What do you make of that?" asked Lomond.

"It may have been one of the reporters; they'd sit on a grave to get a story."

Again came the sound of footsteps—stealthy footsteps moving in the room upstairs.

"That's not a cat, Wembury."

The nerves of Alan Wembury were at breaking point. "Damn the cat!" he said. "I don't know what it is, and I am not going up to see. Doctor, I am sick and tired of the case—heartily sick of it."

"So am I," nodded Lomond. "I am going home to bed." He got up with a groan. "Late hours will be the death of me."

The Ringer

"Have a drink before you go." Alan poured out a stiff whisky with a hand that shook.

Neither man saw the bearded face of Inspector Bliss at the window or heard the grille open noiselessly as the Scotland Yard man came noiselessly into the room.

"Do you know, doctor," said Alan, "I don't hate The Ringer as much as I should."

Lomond paused with his glass raised.

"There are really no bad men who are all bad—except Meister—just as there are no really good men who are all good."

"I want to tell you something, Lomond"—Alan spoke slowly—"I know The Ringer."

"You know him—really?"

"Yes; well." And then, with fierce intensity: "And I'm damned glad he killed Meister."

Bliss watched the scene from behind the curtain of the alcove, his eyes never leaving the two.

"Why? Did he get Mary Lenley?" Lomond was asking.

"No, thank God—but it was only by luck that she was saved. Lomond, I—I can tell you who is The Ringer."

Slipping from the shadow of the curtains. Bliss came towards Lomond, an automatic in his hand.

"You can tell me, eh—then who is The Ringer?"

A hand stretched out and snatched at his hat.

"You!" said the voice of Bliss. "I want you—Henry Arthur Milton!"

Lomond leapt to his feet.

"What the hell—?"

The Ringer

No longer was he the grey—haired doctor. A straight, handsome man of thirty—five stood in his place.

"Stand still!" Alan hardly recognised his own voice.

"Search him!" said Bliss, and Alan stripped off the 'doctor's' overcoat.

The Ringer chuckled.

"Bliss, eh? It doesn't fit you! You're the fellow who said I knifed you when you tried to arrest me three years ago."

"So you did," said Bliss.

"That's a lie! I never carry a knife. You know that."

Bliss showed his teeth in an exultant grin.

"I know that I've got you. Ringer—that's all I know. Come from Port Said, did you—attended a sick man there? I thought your woman knew I suspected you when she was scared that day at Scotland Yard."

Henry Arthur Milton smiled contemptuously. "You flatter yourself, my dear fellow. That woman—who happens to be my wife—was scared not because she even saw you—but because she recognised me!"

"That Port Said story was good," said Bliss. "You saw a sick man there—Dr. Lomond, a dope who'd been lost to sight for years and sunk to native level. He died and you took his name and papers."

"I also nursed him—and I paid for his funeral," added Milton.

"You tried to make people suspicious of me—you've got a cheek! It was you who let Lenley out of the cell!"

The Ringer inclined his head.

"Guilty. Best thing I ever did."

The Ringer

"Clever! " approved Bliss. "I hand it to you! Got your job as police surgeon by smoodging a Cabinet Minister you met on the boat, didn't you? "

The Ringer shuddered.

"'Smoodging' is a vulgar word! 'Flattering' is a better. Yes, I was lucky to get the post—I was four years a medical student in my youth—Edinburgh—I present you with that information. "

Bliss was beside himself with excitement.

"Well, I've got you! I charge you with the wilful murder of Maurice Meister. "

Alan could bear the gloating no longer.

"I say. Bliss—" he began.

"I'm in charge of this case, Wembury, " said Bliss sourly. "When I want your advice I'll ask you for it—who's that? "

He heard the patter of footsteps on the stairs. In another minute Cora Ann had flown into her husband's arms.

"Arthur! Arthur! "

"All right, Mrs. Milton. That'll do, that'll do, " cried Bliss.

"I told you—I told you—oh, Arthur! " she sobbed.

Bliss tried to pull her away.

"Come on. "

"One minute, " said The Ringer, and then, to the girl; "Cora Ann, you haven't forgotten? " She shook her head. "You promised me something: you remember? "

"Yes—Arthur, " she said, Instantly all the suspicions of Bliss were aroused and he dragged the woman away.

"What's the idea? You keep off and don't interfere. "

The Ringer

She turned her white face to his.

"You want to take him and shut him away, " she cried wildly—"like a wild animal behind bars; like a beast—like something that isn't human. That's what you want to do! You're going to bury him alive, blot out his life, and you think I'll let you do it! You think I'll stand right here and watch him slip into a living grave and not save him from it. "

"You can't save him from the gallows! " was the harsh reply.

"I can't, can't I? " she almost screamed. "I'll show you that I can! "

Too late Bliss saw the pistol, but before he could snatch it from her hand she had fired. The Ringer collapsed into a settee.

"You little brute—Wembury! " yelled Bliss.

Wembury went to his assistance and wrenched the revolver from her hand. As he did so, The Ringer rose swiftly from the place where he had been lying limp and apparently lifeless, and walked out of the door, locking it behind him.

"My God! He's gone! " roared Bliss, and threw open the chamber of the revolver. "Blank cartridge. After him! "

Wembury rushed to the door and pulled at it. It was locked!

Cora was laughing.

"Smash in the panel, " cried Bliss. "The key's on the other side, " And then, to the girl: "Laugh, will you—I'll give you something to laugh at! " With a crash the panel split, and in another few seconds Wembury was flying down the stairs.

"Clever—clever; aren't you clever, Mister Bliss! " Cora's voice was shrill and triumphant. "But The Ringer's got you where he wants you. "

"You think so—" said Bliss, between his teeth, and shouted for the officer on duty in the hall below.

The Ringer

"There's a car waiting for him outside, " taunted Cora, "and a new disguise which he kept in the little room downstairs. And an aeroplane ten miles out, and he's not afraid to go up in the fog. "

"I've got you, my lady! " howled Bliss. "And where you are, he'll be. I know The Ringer! Officer! " he shouted.

A policeman came through the door.

"I'm Inspector Bliss from the Yard. Don't let her out of your sight, or I'll have the coat off your back. "

He ran out, stopping only to lock the door. Cora flew after him, but he had taken the key, and she turned, to see the policeman opening the long panel by the door. Then in a flash off came helmet and cape, and she was locked in the arms of this strange man.

"This way, Cora, " he said, and pointed to the panel. "La Via Amorosa. "

He kissed her and lifted her through the panel. Presently it closed upon them. No man saw The Ringer again that night or for the many nights which followed.

THE END